THE LAST OF US

Harriet Cummings is a freelance writer with a background in history of art and gender studies. Her debut novel *We All Begin as Strangers* was shortlisted for the Books Are My Bag Readers Awards. She lives in Leamington Spa with her husband and springer spaniel.

Follow Harriet on Twitter @HarrietWriter or find out more at www.harrietcummingsauthor.com

THE
LAST
OF US

Harriet Cummings

ORION

First published in Great Britain in 2018 by Orion Books,
an imprint of The Orion Publishing Group Ltd
Carmelite House, 50 Victoria Embankment,
London EC4Y 0DZ

An Hachette UK company

1 3 5 7 9 10 8 6 4 2

A CIP catalogue record for this book
is available from the British Library.

ISBN (Hardback) 978 1 4091 6908 6
ISBN (Trade Paperback) 978 1 4091 6909 3

Typeset by Deltatype Ltd, Birkenhead, Merseyside

Printed in Great Britain by Clays Ltd, Elcograf S.p.A.

MIX
Paper from
responsible sources
FSC   FSC® C104740
www.fsc.org

www.orionbooks.co.uk

For the mums, Barbara and Lee

1

2015

1

She knows they're outside waiting. A crouched figure in the barn, knees pressed to the dirt. Another lingering by the field. They never come to the house but throw stones at the windows, trying to crack the glass into silver webs. The sound is like a dare to open the back door and shout at them to leave her alone. Instead Nettie hides in the pantry until it goes quiet, then edges out to listen. Nothing. Still gripping her apron, she sees her reflection repeated in the row of brass jugs, her back curved, her eyes pulled wide. Not so long ago she laughed at the kids who surrounded the farmhouse, but every week it happens and the parents do nothing.

Sometimes they throw stones at her bedroom window when she's still beneath the sheets and she goes down to the piano. Sat in her nightdress, she plays a sonata or something wilfully bright. Her fingers can no longer stretch an octave but she tries anyway, missing some keys and playing onwards, hearing the rest in her mind. It's only when the last note dies that she begins to shiver, to stare at her arms mottled with age spots.

But today she is determined not to cower inside. She unlocks the door. The morning light is forceful and her eyes can't adjust.

'Hello?' she calls into the haze of white.

When no shuffle or whisper answers, Nettie steps out. The chickens need feeding and already she can hear their clucking grow fevered. No movement disturbs the shadows of the barn, the kids hopefully gone, so she pushes on to reach the coop where the tub of grain is waiting. Despite herself, she can't help smiling at their squabbles, gazing at Jemima's blur of reddish brown. Her granddaughter named them after Beatrix Potter characters when she got the books one year for Christmas. Does she still like them? Difficult to say. Nettie reaches for an egg which she slips into her apron pocket. The next is warm and she dares cradle it for a moment. The chickens had full roam of the yard until last month when she found the lower rung of her gate kicked into a chaos of splintered wood, leaving a hole large enough for a bird to pass through. Really she needs to ask someone to fix the gate. To find a telephone number in those endless leaflets that are pushed through the door. The idea of someone helping makes her teeth grind, though. They never just do the job; they share their opinions or else stare straight at her. But she shouldn't be proud, not if the chickens might get hurt. Maybe next week when her pension comes.

She's retrieving another egg when there's a scuffle ahead. For a long moment she peers into the barn's darkness. No one is there and she returns to the chickens, shaking her head at her trembles.

But then the two figures are either side of her, close enough

4

to show their young faces – the boy's rampant freckles, the girl's flat forehead.

She braces herself for the stones, almost willing them to throw the damn things. Maybe if they released their sharp little furies, she could be done with all this. But she just hears their laughing and a scrape of shoes on the concrete. Then a white light flares as a mobile phone is pointed at her.

'What is it you want?' Nettie asks.

She refuses to let them hurt the chickens, although she's the one who drops the egg. It falls with a crack, yolk bleeding across the ground.

Soon they've run off and the yard is empty again. Maybe her daughter is right – she should move into a home. Away from this town, where she can be just another old biddy packed into an endless corridor of rooms. The thought makes her squirm – a schedule for every meal, never escaping the other men and women. No, if the chickens are free range, she can be too. She's almost at the door when something nudges against her leg. It's Rufus who has trotted over and is waiting for her to scratch beneath his chin. His fur is less soft these days, more bristles than hair. She touches the bristles on her own face and smiles to think of them matching.

'Hello, boy,' she says, grateful he missed the kids.

The dog slopes towards the house. He's a long-time resident, almost thirteen years, and was also named by her grand-daughter. Some days it seems her family is everywhere in the farmhouse. Everywhere and nowhere. She tries to be hopeful she'll see them soon.

Back in the kitchen she wonders at the time. Church bells aren't yet clanging so she places the remaining eggs in a box, careful not to let any slip, and finds the cloth bag she laundered yesterday. Sure enough it smells acceptably fresh. She's never been fastidious about this sort of thing – not since she started a family and realised you couldn't keep everything clean – but the other week a woman at the post office pointed out a stain on her blouse. *Spilt something, have we?* The words sit heavily in her now. She should try to make an effort. Getting old involves a battle to keep on caring, to push back the tide of complacency through a series of routines: rising at seven, making breakfast, picking up the stones or whatever glass might've been broken during the night.

In the bedroom she notices a box by the mirror. A new prescription of spectacles – when did she get these? She puts them on and details of the room arrange themselves. On the window ledge sit photographs and trinkets from the fifties, when she and her sister collected china from jumble sales around Hackney. Some are clothed in dust. She wipes them, humming to remember the old tunes by Jerry Lee Lewis and The Stargazers that her mum used to play. They were nothing like the folk songs they'd listened to at school while learning the maypole, told off for the wrong steps. No – these songs required you to move your hips. They were scandalous really, but their mum said if they were going to dance, they should do it properly. After dragging back the settee she would show them the moves in the living room. Nettie now sways from side to side, but soon catches herself in the mirror and stops. Is that really her? Wrinkles spread like the contours of a map, rendering her a landscape of craggy features. Never mind, she tells herself, and ignores her trembling hands as she reaches for her lipstick. The jade earrings clip on and catch the light. They're fake but no one would know. She used to take clothing seriously – deliberate over outfits, which shoes to pair with a yellow summer dress – but over the years she has seen how fashions change and go in circles, one generation laughing at the next. It feels silly to dress up and she shrugs if a blouse misses a button or clashes somehow, though she always wears gloves. Despite the warm day ahead, she finds her faux silk ones and pulls them on.

Her farmhouse is on the edge of town but she's glad of the walk, the rhythmic clack of her stick on the pavement. The clang of church bells has started and guides her along the main road that crosses the river and its string of ducks. She turns onto Middlebridge Street and listens for the next round, feeling the bells as if part of her own body. In the last couple of decades Romsey has grown, which must be a good thing. More traffic but also more jobs for the young. In the rest of the country local businesses are closing but here there's a busy market place of shops, a Waitrose and a train into Southampton. Even if not everyone can afford the escalating house prices, there's hope that more homes will be built. As she ambles past a cluster of thistles, seeds drift into the air, each a wish to be caught.

It's only when she reaches the cobbles of Corn Market that she hesitates. A man is standing by a Land Rover, looking at her. People always say women turn invisible as they age. That folk no longer notice them or whistle when they wear skirts. She now wishes she were invisible, like a breeze through the trees but high up, little noticed. She clutches her bag of eggs and tries to hurry past.

On entering the abbey grounds, she peers back. The man isn't following and neither is anyone else. Women linger behind her, but they are waiting for someone in their group.

Sometimes she is paranoid but then it's always been hard to tell what exists in and outside the mind.

The church is busier than usual and she sits near the back where the chairs are empty. The perfume of lilies tinges the air, making her cough. Some things are supposed to be sweet but just aren't. When she and Harold married they had bunches of daffodils and bluebells, tied with string. The signing of the register was, in fact, over in the verger's office. Is that right? Her mind spins with memories that won't settle. She places both sandals on the floor to anchor herself until the dizziness subsides and her body weights the seat again. Maybe she's thinking of someone else's wedding, when she was playing the organ. Yes, that must be it.

The Sunday service is on forgiveness. Marianne is a good speaker. Not slick or dramatic like the previous vicar who moved on last year. A short woman with a blunt fringe, she sometimes looks hesitant and tends to fidget with the pages of the Bible on the pulpit. But her words are placed one after the other like careful schoolchildren, keen to impress. It's this precision that has the churchgoers sitting up in their seats. Only the odd person slips a mobile phone from their pocket or glances around. From the stained-glass window an enthroned God watches. Nettie sometimes casts her eyes to meet his but never likes to look too long.

'Forgiving others is a gift to them but also to ourselves. That doesn't make it easy. Life can be long and we all throw stones to hurt others.'

The words make Nettie shift, her thighs numb against the seat.

'And forgiveness is never easy, no matter our age, faith or how wonderful we think we are!'

Some people chuckle and Nettie follows suit, not wanting to be rude. Marianne continues with a passage from Corinthians and, as the woman's voice softens, Nettie lets her thoughts drift. They turn, inevitably, to when Catherine might visit. She used to come most summers with the girls and they'd go for trips to the town's swimming pool or just stay at the farmhouse, chasing Rufus or the chickens, getting bored, the occasional tantrum sending crayons flying across the floor. One summer they even took the train to the coast and tossed leftover chips to the gulls.

Although they only live in London, their last trip was four years ago. The girls will be growing up, using all sorts of words and phrases they'd need to teach her. At the beginning of July Nettie had a surge of hope that left her breathless. But with every passing week the prospect of a visit becomes less likely. Schools are about to break for the holiday. Whenever the phone rings she wills the voice on the other end to be Catherine's. It isn't implausible – her daughter might announce they're coming to stay in that haphazard way of hers. But the call is yet to come and the flip of the letterbox sets her heart tripping even though Catherine never writes letters. No one does these days. It's just leaflets, the free newspaper, one time a horrible note unsigned and with no postmark, delivered straight through the door.

Something tells her if she doesn't see them this summer that'll be it, the girls too old to want to visit their granny. She'll be just another elderly woman who they pass in the street, embalmed in rose oil and spittle. Appalled at the thought, she clamps her hands on her cheeks, then knocks her knuckles against the bones harder and harder. No one notices – the sound softened by her gloves – but she stops herself. Perhaps she could ring Catherine again. But there's no point in begging. That never helped anyone.

At the end of the service a queue forms to thank Marianne, who shakes hands with everyone, even the kids. A few people ahead of Nettie there's a flash of white-blonde hair. It's the girl who was throwing stones earlier – she recognises the flat forehead. Now she wears a smart jacket, her arms rigid at her sides. She's just a child, Nettie tells herself, remembering how she was once a girl with her own personal crusades.

'Thank you, Vicar,' she says when she eventually reaches Marianne. 'That was a lovely service.'

'Thanks for coming, Annette.' The woman smiles to reveal a capped tooth that's overly white, and a silence stretches. When Marianne first arrived in this parish, Nettie thought they might be friends, the sixty-something woman unmarried and maybe wanting company. It seems Nettie's forgotten how to make friends, though, she strains to think of the necessary steps. The offer of tea, perhaps, but the woman is already looking past her to the church that needs clearing. Nettie moves along and rests her stick against the bench, to dig in her purse for change. Marianne leaves the collection plate in the shadowy entrance so no one need feel embarrassed, maybe she does it for Nettie's sake. As she drops in a fifty-pence piece, her gloves feel dirtied by the money and she wipes them on her skirt. It's only when she's outside that she remembers the eggs. They were meant as a gift for the vicar – a first step to getting to know each other. But Marianne is nowhere to be seen, so Nettie steps back into the glare of daylight.

2

She's almost home when she sees him: a young man stood by her gate. For a second she stops. The day's heat has risen and she feels damp along her collar. Her mind must've turned heady too because for a moment the man is Harold and he's forgotten his keys. They'll go inside and he'll tease her about the mess of breakfast dishes. *I don't know how they got here,* she'll claim, *the burglars must have been hungry.* It's not him though. Of course it isn't. The man is about to leave – hitching a large rucksack onto his back – when he catches her eye. There's something unnerving about how he blocks the gate.

'Is this your place?' he asks.

'Perhaps.'

He raises an eyebrow before glancing across the yard. 'One of your chickens was wandering in the road.'

Sure enough, Peter is scratching about with rumpled feathers.

'Oh.' Nettie clutches her stick. 'He must've flown over the coop. Thank you so much.'

'I was worried he'd cause an accident.' He wipes sweat from his brow and a feather clings to his finger. 'You'll want to fix your gate. What happened?'

'I'll take care of it. Not to worry.'

He smiles but doesn't move. Perhaps in his mid-thirties, he has a ruddy face with hair combed in a side parting. His denim shirt is unpressed so its collar curls upwards and his rucksack bulges in all directions, the straps straining against a metal cup. 'Do you have an outdoor tap?'

'Why do you ask?'

'It's a hot day.'

She hesitates, tempted to lie and be rid of him. 'I do. You can help yourself.'

He walks into the yard and, without asking, heads for the rear of the house. Affronted, Nettie wonders what to say before realising: he's spotted a bucket which he uses to block the hole in the gate.

'Good thinking,' she mutters, wondering why she'd not thought of it herself. As he runs the tap Peter squawks. God knows how it would've felt to find him hurt on the road. She winces as the man fills his cup. 'Would you like to come inside for a minute?' she asks, hoping he'll say no. 'I could fetch you a glass of water.'

'A tea would be nice.' He gives her a well-practised smile which pushes his cheeks out, lines creasing in great arches. It's an actor's face, full of emotion, with grey eyes that shine like marbles. 'Thank you muchly.'

Inside, he walks past the Aga and runs a finger along the length of the table. He's the first visitor to have been in the house for some weeks. Who was the last? Nettie can't recall. She puts down the box of eggs then takes off her gloves, leaving them on a pile of newspapers. Seeing the room through his eyes, she's conscious of the unopened post strewn about, the used teabags plump in the sink. The man nudges the rusted dog bowl with his boot but says nothing.

She wonders which cups to serve tea in. Her wedding china waits on the shelves but she opts for the set bought for the grandkids. They're sturdier, with a nicely painted Moroccan print. As she fills the kettle Nettie expects him to sit but he doesn't. He's not tall but wide with an odd button sewn onto his shirt. In heavy-soled boots he walks over to look at the shelf of wedding china, then the brass jugs below, smoothing his hair in a reflection.

'Where are you from?' she asks to break the silence.

'I spent most of my childhood up north, in various places.'

'And what brings you to Romsey?'

'I'm taking a career break. I've been staying in London for a while and ...'

He's distracted, eyeing the sitting room. For a second she expects him to drift inside to look around and she flushes to realise she's let a complete stranger into the house. What if he refuses to leave? She'd tell the police what exactly? That she invited him in for tea. Then helped him pack her silverware into a suitcase. Tied her own wrists together with rope. But he stays where he is and motions to the photographs on top of the fireplace. 'Is that Cate? Cate Ravenscroft?'

'Catherine, yes!' Nettie says. 'You know my daughter?'

He gives a bemused smile. 'She was the one who recommended this area to me. She said the Hampshire countryside was worth a visit.'

Nettie's head lightens. Her daughter hasn't discarded her after all, telling this man about the town. 'How do you know Catherine?'

'How do I know her?' he repeats.

'Yes.'

'Ah. Well, I'm not sure it's my place to say.'

'Why not?'

He laces his fingers. 'It's a bit delicate.'

Despite the questions itching in her, she gestures to the tea. 'Shall we drink it in the garden?'

'Sounds like a good idea,' he says, then, 'I'm James, by the way.'

'Oh.' She stutters. 'I'm Annette.'

'Can I call you Nettie?'

In the yard he takes his time peering at the barn, then over at the open stretch of field. The tray heavy in her arms, she wonders if he's oblivious to how the cups tinkle against their saucers, the milk jug threatening to topple. As she edges into his eyeline he says nothing except, 'Is that your field?' She doesn't answer, instead focusing on not tripping in the long grass of the back garden. Where once waited a design of roses and other blooms, now creeps a mass of green that rises in all directions, the pond water thick with algae and weeds. The only plant she regularly tends to is the oleander whose pink buds require plenty of water, and pruning every summer. Even at a distance she can smell their oily perfume, imagine the tingle of their leaves on her skin.

James is still behind her. What is he doing – inspecting the place? She wants to ask what he's up to but he's soon jogging in front to wipe dead leaves from the table. 'Let me help.' He takes the tray, then lifts the teapot lid to inspect its colour. Really that's her job as host and she bristles as he goes to pour.

'I'll do that,' she says.

The teapot is already raised but he puts it down again, before turning the handle to her. 'Of course – where are my manners?'

After Nettie pours the tea, they sit in silence beneath the pale blue sky. It seems he's waiting for her to begin but he's the one who should be explaining himself. A fly suckles on the milk jug and Nettie steers it away.

'It's nice that my daughter has a friend,' she says.

He thinks for a moment. 'Families are never easy, are they?'

'I suppose not.' She frowns. 'Won't you tell me how you know her?'

James sighs. 'Catherine and I both struggle with the same addiction,' he says carefully. 'In fact, I'm sleeping above a pub tonight and know that's a terrible idea.'

'You mean, you both struggle with drink?'

'Exactly. We go to meetings together in London. Supposedly anonymous ones but, well, you must know what she goes through.'

'Oh yes,' she says. In actual fact she wasn't aware her daughter was still in AA. Really she should be proud. In her forty-odd years Catherine has stuck to little else. 'How is she?'

He turns back to the garden so only insects answer with their hissing wings. They sit in silence and she's grateful when Rufus trots over.

'What a handsome chap,' he says. As he kneels down to scratch the dog she takes the chance to study him – how he's closely shaved, though with the occasional patch forgotten as if he was impatient to be finished. His fingers trail over Rufus's belly, a bare stretch of skin. 'I've heard about you too.'

'So Catherine talks about me?'

With a knee still on the ground, James peers up. 'I know things have been difficult between you. I've been trying to help her. Some people aren't good at accepting help, though.' He begins rubbing Rufus again. There's something painful about the neat lines in his thinning hair. She pictures him dragging the comb. 'Are they?'

'I suppose not.'

James sits back again and pours himself more tea. It would be sensible to phone Catherine and ask about this fellow but she doesn't want to leave him here alone and, besides, what if her daughter refuses to talk to her? She gazes at the overgrown garden, the honeysuckle that sprouts curling tendrils year after year. The sprigs of white cow parsley that sway and merge like ghosts.

3

She sits on her bed and clasps her hands together. Prays that Harold is safe in Heaven. It's been over twenty years since she last saw him and felt his warmth against her. Although the farmhouse has changed, often it feels like he's still here, in the light reflected in a window pane, or woven into the fabric of their old quilt. *When you're ill, you're ill,* Harold had said. *None of us last for ever.* Now she herself is growing tired, aches spreading, and yet there are things she still wants to do. The more she thinks of Catherine, the more determined she is to enjoy her granddaughters for a final summer.

A creak from downstairs interrupts her prayers and she wonders what Harold would think of her guest. Maybe she should be praying to keep *herself* safe.

James is still in the house despite it being almost five o'clock. Who knows how this has happened. Granted she, at first, wanted him to stay longer but he's remained tight-lipped about Catherine, so why doesn't he leave? Instead the man has been playing with Rufus, walking around the garden, seemingly lost in his thoughts although she has no clue what these are. He does look worn, his clothes grubby and she's not had the heart to turn him onto the street yet.

On making her way downstairs, she sees his rucksack has moved further into the hallway. She could nudge the thing back to where it had been. But it's hard to be irked by this rucksack, which slumps against the wall. She knows how it feels. The tin cup saddens her too – its basic design like something from the army, hanging from the strap all on its own.

Singing is coming from the kitchen, his voice higher than she'd expect – alto maybe – and the words those of 'Edelweiss', 'Small and white, clean and bright, you look happy to meet me ...' She pads through and sees his silhouette hunched over the sink. He's washing up the tea cups along with her breakfast dishes.

'You needn't do that.'

The singing stops. 'My dad always does it straight away, you see. Otherwise the dishes gather like a mobilising army.' He chuckles to himself.

'All right, well – thank you,' she says.

'My dad likes an army metaphor. Or is that a simile?'

It's her cue to ask about his family but she doesn't know where the conversation will lead. What will be its end point.

'Don't worry, Nettie.' He turns with a smile. 'I'll be on my way soon.'

She loosens her hold on the stick, realising her palm is sore. 'You'll be all right above the pub?'

'Ah, well I was going to ask you about that. I ...' He stops

18

mid-sentence and peers through the window. Someone is in the yard and Nettie moves to the door, ready to lock it at the sight of kids. But it's Marianne, holding a newspaper above her head. It's spotting with rain and the smell of wet soil wafts in as Nettie opens the door.

'Come in,' she says.

Dressed in faded jeans and a T-shirt, Marianne smiles but hovers in the doorway. 'I just popped by to see if you were all right.'

Her tone makes Nettie grimace. The woman visits every now and then but as – she supposes – part of her duties to the parish. Now she's getting wet on Nettie's account, the newspaper turning soggy.

'Please, come in for a minute.'

She edges in and begins, 'We didn't speak much after the service and—'

'Hello,' says James. He stands by the sink, still holding a teacup that drips water onto the floor. For a second, Nettie thinks Marianne will ask him to explain himself. An unknown man in her house. But she steps forwards and extends a hand to shake his.

'Hi there,' she says, smiling. She wipes hair from her forehead. The woman doesn't hide her wrinkles under make-up. She has a masculine face beneath her blunt-cut fringe, her only concession to being the fairer sex is a clip stuck in her hair. But now she seems self-conscious around James, who must be at least twenty years younger than her. 'Just here for a visit?'

'Yes, I had a stroke of luck today.'

'Oh?'

'It turns out I know Nettie's daughter.'

'That's nice.' Marianne hasn't met Catherine although

19

might've heard about her; it's hard to know exactly how much the townspeople talk. 'How is she getting on these days?'

'Fine,' says James.

'She's very well,' chimes in Nettie.

He smiles at her like they're in on something together and she ignores him. She wants to talk to Marianne alone to discuss the idea she had yesterday: a summer fete in the town park. Stalls like they had a few years back – face painting and the like, with fun, jangly music. And those machines that spin the pink fluffy stuff, the name of which she can't recall, that her granddaughters love. She can picture them running around shrieking with hair whipped across their faces.

But James is talking to Marianne about AA meetings and the woman listens, nodding along as he blathers about how much one person relies on the next.

'And Catherine is a valued member,' he says. 'She—'

'Candy floss!'

'Sorry?' says Marianne.

'I didn't mean to interrupt,' she says, flushing and pulling a chair to sit down. 'I just thought we might put on a summer fete.'

Marianne wipes her eyes. 'A fete? Well …'

'I can help organise it, of course.'

'We can talk about it another time soon.' She glances at James who smiles. 'Anyway, have a nice dinner you two,' she says, gesturing to the box of eggs on the table.

'He's not staying.'

Marianne is taken aback, which makes Nettie flush even deeper. Whatever hope she had of them being friends is shrinking with every second. 'Well, I suppose he could.'

James chuckles. 'That's very kind.' He lays the tea towel on the side and she waits for him to say no, to ask Marianne for a lift into town. But he picks up another teacup. 'I could stay for some dinner. No hurry, is there?'

After Marianne has gone – claiming too many emails to join them – Nettie puts on a saucepan of water. Although steam clouds her glasses she stays by the hob. She's not sure about this man. Why hasn't he left yet? The eggs rattle against the spoon and she takes a breath before lowering them into the water. He's sat at the table reading the newspaper. 'Awful about this drought in South Africa. All those kids suffering.'

'Truly awful, yes.'

'But there's nothing to be done.'

'We can send money to charity.'

'Have you done that?' He raises an eyebrow as she goes silent and focuses on the pan. An egg cracks and white spills out, turning into a stretched line that quivers and bubbles. She's been meaning to send money but keeps forgetting. Or maybe she hasn't been, maybe she is simply a spoilt old woman who wants the few pounds for herself.

Although light-headed, she manages to lay the eggs on toast, ignoring his offer of help.

'These are fresh?' he says as she puts down the plates. 'Oh goodie.'

She frowns. Picking up his cutlery, he looks like a young man ready to go to war, hair neatly parted and his back straight. But the world has changed around her and she's not sure what things mean any more. His grey eyes shine in the light. 'Aren't you going to sit down?' he asks after swallowing.

'Of course.'

'Don't worry, Nettie. I'll be on my way soon. Then you'll be rid of me.'

She grimaces but says nothing. It's quiet then, with just the clink of cutlery. Her taste buds have weakened in the past couple of years and she grinds salt liberally over the eggs. He has none on his and she wonders if he's being polite. He takes small mouthfuls as though he's savouring the meal, something Catherine never did. Always eating too much, especially pudding, making herself sick as a child. Nettie tried to teach her portion control but it obviously didn't work.

Without asking, James rises to fetch each of them a glass of water. She sips it gratefully, the salt stinging her mouth.

'We've been talking about my family,' she says, picking up the earlier conversation. 'What about yours?'

'Mine?'

'Yes. Are you married? With a family?'

His fork stops in the air. 'Once, yes.'

It's like he's paralysed as his face stiffens and she feels bad for saying the wrong thing. He's quiet for another moment before he pushes a piece of toast into the yolk. Her own swallows become work-like and she refuses to think of how Harold chided her for being a slow eater. Sometimes the memories feel like a rising tide she must build a wall to contain.

James finishes the toast and presses a finger into a crumb on the table. 'I confess, Catherine has been a help to me,' he says and pulls his shoulders back. 'I don't know what I would've done without her actually.'

'I'm glad to hear it.'

'Although she won't accept any credit, of course.'

'No?'

'I try to tell her but ...' He lays his hands on the table. 'She has her ways, doesn't she? Her complete inability to accept friendship when it's offered.' A daze takes him then and she doesn't dare look into his eyes. They've turned overly dark like water down a well.

In the dining room she picks up the telephone and starts to dial Catherine's number to ask about this man – but is it 776 or 667 on the end? She always knew it by heart, her daughter in the same flat for the last eight years. Now it's been scrambled, her mind letting her down.

'I've done those dishes,' James calls from the hallway.

'That's kind of you,' she manages, placing the phone in its cradle.

The tin cup rattles as he picks up his rucksack and begins to leave. She knows the pub is no place for him; Catherine would certainly struggle with the waft of ale, the taunt of clinking glasses. 'I have a spare bedroom,' she hears herself say and instantly regrets the words.

He turns, surprised. 'You do?'

'It's nothing special.'

'It'd be terrific to stay here.' He swings off his rucksack so easily she's suddenly aware of his bulk. 'How very kind.'

Upstairs she pulls on the sheets but can't reach the far corner. No one has stayed in the spare bedroom since the girls. The sheet jumps free of the mattress and she gives up.

He appears behind. 'I'm ever so grateful.'

'You'll have to finish the bed,' she says, no longer bothering to be polite.

He steps back and waits until she's in the hallway before entering the room, appraising the space. 'It must be your socialist values, eh? Letting me stay like this.'

She feels unsteady as she walks into her own room. That he knows about her past makes her wonder how much Catherine has told him of their family. The trunk is locked but she finds the key in her bedside drawer. Inside is the shotgun Harold persuaded her to buy for shooting pheasants: a bizarre pastime she could never get used to. She puts it underneath her bed, shuddering at the rattle of trigger against wood. It's just a silly precaution. Something to help her sleep. Through the wall she hears him move around, almost as though he's calculating the dimensions of the room. In the morning she'll find out exactly what he knows about Catherine.

Once she's in bed with her spectacles off, the room blurs and she tries to imagine Harold in the shadows. It's too dark in the room, though, with no streetlight this side of the house. Instead an image floods: her in the car with Catherine, the two of them arguing, hedgerows shooting past as her daughter gripped the wheel. She didn't want to talk about her dad. *I can't bear to hear his name*, she'd shouted over and over. He's now in Heaven, Nettie tells herself, isn't he? The doubt weighs on her chest as she lies beneath the cold sheet.

At some point she wakes. It's quiet in the room but something must have disrupted her sleep. She strains to hear, remembering her visitor, and gets up to check. The shotgun is heavy in her hands and makes her feel like a child play-acting or someone in a television show. No one is on the landing, the door to the spare room closed, and she almost returns to bed. But through her window she sees the barn doors are open. Did she leave them that way? Usually she checks before bed but maybe she forgot this evening. It takes her a while to get outside and she pulls her dressing gown tighter, fingers clamped on the gun, before she calls out to the thick dark of the barn. 'Hello?'

There's no response and she can't see any movement, so she closes the doors with a scrape of metal, prompting a cry from the chickens.

Inside she finds James sitting in the living room in her armchair. Only a weak moonlight comes through the window, rendering him a mass of shapes. He doesn't notice her at first. He's staring at an object on the table. As she switches on the light he blinks, the scene coming into focus for them both.

'Jesus,' he says, face flushed. It's a bottle of her gin that waits unopened on the table.

'You don't want any of that,' is all she can think to say. Then: 'What are you doing up?'

'I couldn't sleep.' He fixes his eyes on the gun which she has hooked under her arm, pointed just shy of him. 'A nice weapon there. What is it? A Purdey?'

'I'm not sure.' She's embarrassed to be holding it, aware he must be frightened. But he only stretches and yawns. 'Haven't had a proper night's sleep for months. No reason to shoot a man, is it?'

She lets her arm go limp, the shotgun dropping as he ambles past, back upstairs to bed.

1966

I

November 1966

The floor of King's Cross station was covered in marks. Tar-like smears from suitcases, the pricks of high heels and puddles streaked with reflected light from the tobacconist. Nettie tried not to get flustered. She was several minutes late to pick up her sister, but it was all right. Edith would understand and she resisted reaching into her handbag for the box of pills that nestled in the pocket.

A stream of November air carried leaves through the door and she scuttled past, eyes fixed on the floor. To look up would be to see the faces stare back – it felt in those haphazard moments people saw her for what she was, not what she presented to the world: the half smile, hair ironed of its frizz, overly tall but dressed fashionably enough. No, she was caught unaware. Glimpsed like an odd creature fleeing the daylight.

Luckily Edith was standing where they'd arranged to meet, by the florist. She was dressed in a pale blue trench coat and had her hair pinned back. From beneath her white kitten heels curled a leaf – she'd been outside already. Checking bus times, presuming that Nettie wouldn't know them despite the fact she was the one who still lived in London. There was no point in being annoyed, though. Her sister was here for a whole weekend.

'Edie!' she called, her voice overly loud. Nettie had barely spoken all afternoon in the factory, the machines chattering in the place of human conversation.

'Hello, Annette.' Her little sister gave a tight smile. She was not yet thirty but appeared older than last time she visited. Sometimes Nettie longed to buy a camera just to keep her sister's face young, a box of pictures always there to look at.

As she leant in for a hug Edith asked, 'Where's your coat? It's freezing.'

'I'm too hardy to bother with one!' Nettie joked, noticing how her cardigan had expanded with the rain, wet and bulging. In truth she'd left the factory in such a whirl she'd not remembered her mac.

They made for the exit with Nettie insisting she carry the suitcase. Her sister's job as a secretary in the military saw her travel across Europe, to places Nettie needed to look up in the library. She did try to be pleased for Edith, three years her junior but with a passport of stamps and her own leather suitcase which their mum used savings to buy.

At the bus stop a queue had formed of people wrapped in coats and scarves, stamping their feet on the pavement to keep warm.

'We'll get a taxi,' said Edith. 'Otherwise you'll freeze.'

'No, it's too far.'

'Don't be silly, I'll pay.'

Seeing her sister about to step into the road, Nettie hoped the gesture was right as she stuck out her own arm. Sure enough a black cab pulled up and she clambered inside, then grimaced at the people left out on the pavement.

Leaving the city centre, they passed the factories and scrubland of the East, the silhouettes of towers rising like fists. Darkness soon claimed the streets and Nettie looked forward to reaching her flat, where fairy lights dangled above the window. She'd put on the electric fire and cook a proper tea. The casserole recipe was one she'd practised the week before. She'd even pretended her sister was there, imagining what they'd discuss over sherry. It was good to have a list of questions ready. Usually Edith's visits were dominated by trips to see their mum or aunts, who asked about nonsense things like the weather and price of bread. Their mum was busy that night and would see them the next day for lunch. She'd sounded strange on the phone, her voice overly breathy, but Nettie needn't worry about that yet.

'How long has it been?' she asked despite knowing the answer: eleven months. It was expensive to travel from West Berlin so her sister's trips weren't as frequent as either of them would have liked. Mostly they exchanged letters, though recently Edith's were slow to come and half the length of her own.

They arrived at Nettie's building which was down a leafy side street in Bethnal Green. The exterior wasn't much to look at but inside, on the top floor, Nettie had filled her flat with prints she'd cut from magazines: catwalk models dressed by Yves Saint Laurent and Barbara Hulanicki; geometric 'op art' prints from exhibitions she'd not visited but would have if she could stomach the crowds. She had a picture of Eleanor Marx too, one she hung proudly in the middle as if this suffragette was as appealing as any film star.

'You don't have photographs of me,' said Edith, feigning surprise.

'I do.' In fact the picture of her sister and mum was reserved for her bedroom after her ex commented on Edith being 'so small and pretty like their mum'. Since then she stared at the photograph in bed before she went to sleep, wondering if she actually belonged to this family. It was an unhealthy habit and she tried to focus, instead, on getting through the texts she bought second-hand: *Das Kapital* and Trotsky's *The Revolution Betrayed*. She'd long been interested in socialism after growing up in the East End – asking her mum about the lines of workers who were so poorly dressed, the flashy car parked outside the factory – but it was only in the last couple of years that she'd started attending meetings and reading the books. They would fill her up, plug the gap, she was sure – if only she absorbed every word.

She got tea ready as Edith wandered about. By the record player waited a pile of songs she'd chosen the night before – the Lesley Gore track 'You Don't Own Me' left on top. Maybe they'd have an evening of chatting politics – she'd show how much she cared.

'I have something for you,' her sister said and went to open her suitcase. She brought out something wrapped in tissue paper. 'Sorry it's late.'

It was a belated birthday gift – a dress covered in cream bead-work that was like nothing Nettie had ever worn. Usually she went for bright colours – long-sleeved turtlenecks, corduroy dresses. Things she considered fun. She held this dress between pinched fingertips.

'I realise it's not your usual thing,' Edith said, reaching to feel the hem. 'But isn't it sophisticated?'

'It really is.'

'You could wear it tonight,' she said. 'We're going out, aren't we?'

Surprised, Nettie turned to the window. Night had fallen and it was entirely black, while inside the casserole simmered on the hob. But her sister was already at her suitcase again, pulling out an outfit of her own.

'Of course,' said Nettie. 'That's what I was thinking too.'

The place was two doors down from the building where her socialist meetings were held. Countless times she'd seen men linger outside and hurried past, glimpsing the stairs that plunged into the basement. Dance halls were where the factory girls met their friends or even a date for the following weekend; they'd never appealed to Nettie except on the odd occasion when a band she liked was playing and she'd stand at the side, leaving if it got too busy. At the doorway Nettie tugged down the dress, such an unlikely gift. Usually her sister gave her perfumed lotions or a pair of slippers. It was an image she cultivated – that of the eccentric spinster. She'd started carrying around library books and stopped denying that on a Friday all she wanted was to put music on at home, swaying around as she ate gherkins from the jar. But now she was in this dress and this dance hall, as if her sister was willing her to be different.

The man waved them past, music throbbing as they descended to the basement. A Stones record was playing, though one she wasn't familiar with. The crowd sang along – mostly men in their twenties whose foreheads glistened with sweat beneath the low ceiling, their feet shuffling about in no obvious pattern. Something white was streaked on the floor – perhaps talcum powder to help them grip.

'What is this dance?' Edith asked.

'The Mod, I think.'

Lingering on the final step Edith took off her coat. Wearing a starched blouse with a brown skirt and nylons, she looked like a woman from a magazine. Maybe not *Vogue* or a fashion one but a mail order catalogue for woman professionals. It was the way she stood, pulled up tall in her kitten heels.

They headed for the drinks stand. Apart from a few couples, the floor was dominated by men in a circle, dressed in suits that looked nothing like what you'd wear to an office. Shirt tails hung over trousers, ties overly short and black. A single woman was twisting her knees and laughing in a mini-skirt that rode up her thighs. Edith looked around her.

'What a place,' she said, clutching her coat.

Nettie hid her smile. At least she'd have something to say on Monday morning. The glove factory was less than a mile from where she'd been born in Whitechapel and wasn't a bad place to work. The girls joked that the gloves were worn by cheating spouses to cover wedding rings – an idea they liked as it gave them a chance to talk about their own boyfriends. Nettie pretended not to listen as she walked around assessing the garments. That she was in charge of quality control filled her with grim humour – it was an odd title for someone whose life seemed full of unfinished stitches and edges waiting to fray.

Nettie ordered them Coca-Colas and resisted gulping the syrupy drink.

'Is this what young people do now?' Edith asked, watching the crowds dance.

34

From the ceiling hung a lone mirror ball that cast reflections across a face, an exposed leg or a motorbike jacket slung in the corner. The sisters were soon pushed towards the back wall which felt damp against their elbows, and Edith stepped from someone's path. No doubt she'd later insist on bathing before bed, the water in the pipes waking the neighbours. West Berlin was no less dirty but she'd have her ways of coping, her circles of female friends including a woman named Greta she mentioned. They never spoke about men. When their mum asked, Edith said no man quite matched the one in her head and there was no point in settling. Nettie might've said the same thing if anyone asked. And so the three of them sat together at cousins' weddings, their mum pleased to have the company and Nettie feeling the same. But being in this basement was like watching life pass around her, the unknown friends and couples something to be glimpsed through the smoke.

'Shall we dance?' Nettie asked.

'If we must.'

They shuffled from the wall and, although at first careful not to bump against the group of men, their bodies soon loosened. No one seemed to care or watch and even the Coca-Cola tasted better, their fingers sticky around the glasses. The next song was by Small Faces and Nettie grinned that she knew the words: *yeah yeah, it's all or nothing for me.* A man was coming over too. He tapped Edith on the shoulder and for a second Nettie hoped he was trying to get past Edith to talk to her. But no, he spoke to her sister, who gave a shrug in response.

'Do you mind?' he asked Nettie.

'No no, it's all right.'

Returning to the wall she watched them dance. The man's tweed suit didn't fit, his trousers stopping short of his ankles to show an expanse of sock. He was gangly but soon his feet moved in a fluid motion across the floor. Edith in turn did the required steps, copying the man as though she was being tested. He moved his hips jokingly although he clearly loved to dance. It was almost like Edith wasn't there. As he closed his eyes it seemed another world waited in technicolour. Nettie wanted to swim in it with him and found herself mouthing the words, *yeah yeah, it's all or nothing for me.* A song could take you any-where – after a few beats you could be in Greenwich Village, in a smoky coffeehouse or in the din of The Underground Cavern. Where was this man? Too soon another song cut in and Edith walked over, the man giving a final twist before he trailed behind. Up close, he looked older than the other people there.

'Hello,' he said in Nettie's ear, his hand hot on her shoulder. She was surprised by the sudden contact and thought what to say.

'Small Faces are the best, aren't they?'

'An interesting opinion.' A slick of fresh sweat shone on his neck as he began to say more. But another man waved him over and he gave them a final smile before disappearing into the crowd.

'What a bore,' her sister later said. They were waiting for a bus in the fog, watching for the shine of headlights.

'I thought he was quite fun.'

'Arrogant I'd say. Dancing like that.'

They said no more as they waited in the cold, Nettie shiver-ing in her dress. If tonight had been a chance to be different, she didn't care if it'd passed her by. All she thought of was the man's hand on her shoulder, so sure of its place. She craved the weight again but huddled into her sister for warmth.

The next morning they went to see their mum who'd moved into a flat further east in Bow. Market stalls were being packed up for the day, the sellers padding across the ice. Nettie and her sister clutched each other so as not to slip. 'We'll just drag each other down,' Edith said, though neither of them let go.

Their mum appeared at the door, breathless in a red shirt dress pulled tight across the waist.

'Hello, Lizzie,' said Edith, using their mum's name as the woman had insisted since they were young (Nettie refused – people didn't get to choose their own name, you accepted what you were given).

'Hello, Edith, love, it's been too long,' she said, opening her arms for a hug. Lipstick brightened her otherwise bare face which was still pretty, the lines faint from the endless concoctions of oats, lavender oil and cucumber slices she slathered herself with, a filter cigarette sticking from her mouth.

'And, Nettie, come on in,' she said, smiling and turning to climb the stairs. Her curls weren't neat at the back as if she'd given up halfway through putting her rollers in. At least she'd been looking after the flat. They found a clothes horse of washing in the kitchen and the oven already on, exuding warmth. Inside glistened a partridge from the butcher she'd been seeing. Even if the man had questionable ideas about Vietnam, Nettie was pleased her mum was getting out of the flat.

Their dad's medal rested on the mantelpiece in the living room. After he hadn't come home from France, their mum had got into bed and not got up again for a week. Nettie was eleven years old at the time. She'd carried on and made the sandwiches, dressed Edith and walked her to school each morning. Later their mum supposedly took over again but regularly deserted chores to stare out of the window, her cigarette burnt down to a stub. Her lipstick was often smudged too, so she appeared as an imitation of a woman and mum, going through the motions without quite meaning any of it. At least she kept up her part-time job at the shoe shop on Hackney Road. When her manager said people liked how jolly she was, Nettie wondered if they failed to see what she did or if they chose to ignore it.

Helping to make the gravy, Edith stood at the counter beside their mum who wanted to hear all about where she'd been despite the frequent phone conversations the General paid for. Having heard all her news already, Nettie slumped into the rocking chair in the corner. The tilting made her feel sick but she carried on rocking as the windows fogged with steam.

She wondered when she'd been overtaken by Edith. Surely she'd done a lot as a big sister and yet, looking back, all people said of Nettie was that she was a peculiar creature.

Peculiar creature. The words made her think of something that hid in shadows, something deformed, with a beak and wings. Overly large too. No one explained what made her this way or how she could change; it was merely a fact that everyone knew and accepted. When Nettie was fifteen her mum suggested some herbal pills she'd read about in a magazine. She said nothing, hot to her stomach, but later searched chemists for the name. *For hyperactive or anxious minds ...* read the label. Since then she'd taken them every day, unsure what might happen if she ever stopped.

They sat at the fold-out table in the living room where Edith carved the partridge, the flesh sliding away to reveal bone. Talk continued about a family holiday in Scotland. They'd not been the past few years but their mum was keen to go away. 'I need to relax with my girls.'

Hearing this, Nettie focused on spearing peas with her fork. She'd meant to save the past year but she'd spent money on various things for the socialist club.

'The same caravan as before?' Edith asked.

'Oh yes, it's all got to be the same.'

Nettie cleared her throat and asked after Robert, seeing her mum immediately sit up at the mention of her boyfriend. 'He's a good man,' she told Edith, who nodded. 'I never thought I'd find someone after your father and here he is.' Her fingers flitted about the cutlery she'd placed on the side of her plate. She never ate much and mealtimes felt more like a performance where she was concerned.

'He gives me crackling half price. Plus he's taking me to the greyhounds.'

Edith shot Nettie a look which she ignored, knowing what was implied: she should be looking after their mum. Not letting her bet away her earnings with a man she barely knew. Nettie came round often enough, bringing the shopping, listening to Edith's letters read out loud as though they were poetry. She even said nothing when Robert placed a hand on her thigh beneath the table one afternoon. Now the memory of this shocked her. Had she reacted or even walked away? She didn't know.

'I might get Robert around later,' said their mum. 'After pudding.'

The meat passed uneasily down Nettie's throat as she turned to her sister, hoping to communicate something.

Edith frowned. 'Do you think that's a good idea? We're having a nice time the three of us.'

39

'After your father died I was alone for an awfully long time.'

'That wasn't for our sake,' said Edith gently.

The room fell silent as they continued the meal. The idea of Robert in the flat made Nettie queasy. 'We could have a smoke after this,' she said, picturing the three of them in the courtyard.

'Oh no,' their mum said in her breathy voice, the one she heard on the phone. 'I smoke less these days. Robert says smoking's for old women, it reminds him of Bette Davis.'

As Nettie pushed away her plate, its edge knocked her cup of tea and sent a brown tide over the table.

'I'll fetch a cloth,' said Nettie but Edith was already hurrying to the kitchen. 'I'm sorry.'

Her mum's face pulled into an odd smile. 'I'm going to bed,' she said, clutching her stomach as she drifted away, her plate still full.

Once the spilt tea was cleared the two sisters carried on eating. It felt fitting that it should be just the two of them, time an endless paper-chain doll folded back into place.

The following month she met the man from the dancefloor. She had been at a socialist meeting, sitting at the back as usual. The only other woman had stopped coming the previous month after calling it too much of a boys' club, though Nettie suspected the real reason was she wanted to focus on getting married and being a commie wasn't a turn-on. She'd stopped telling people about it herself, not mentioning the meetings to the factory girls. The men in the group sometimes looked at her with narrowed eyes if she asked a question. That evening they were organising another rally for nuclear disarmament. National interest had long declined and it didn't do them any favours to have just a few dozen people holding placards, but she kept quiet as a man spoke at length.

As soon as the meeting finished, Nettie pulled on her coat and hurried out. She wanted to catch the 7.45 bus to Bethnal Green. She almost didn't see him.

'I know you.' It was his voice. He was dressed in a suit, though it was different from the one he'd worn that Friday night. Now he looked like an entirely new version of himself – serious, his hair slicked back – though his grin was unchanged.

Nettie paused as other men passed by. 'You danced with my sister,' she said.

'How short-sighted of me.' Although it was a line, she smiled and stored it away. 'I have my class now, but how about I meet you later?'

As the two of them stood in the corridor a stern-faced lady appeared. The working men's club lent its rooms to various night classes and groups on the condition of good behaviour.

'Well?'

The teacher lingered.

'I don't think so,' Nettie muttered and stepped out into the street.

Huddled on the bus she realised how hardened she'd become. Since breaking things off with Morris she'd not seen anyone. And even that was an affair briefer than the lifespan of a jar of gherkins. He was a married man, a supplier at work who took her to the cinema, claiming his wife refused to be away from their children. Although she knew it was wrong she liked it when he started turning up at her flat. How he checked the lock at night and kept a pot of Brylcreem in the bathroom. But whenever he left she scrubbed herself pink in the bathtub and thought what her sister would say. There'd been no one since, much to the dismay of the girls at the factory. Tea breaks were dominated by talk of going out, so she began sitting on her own, pretending to read. She carried on wearing nice clothes but changed her gloves to a dark maroon pair that seemed fitting for an ageing spinster.

Over the next days she couldn't help looking out for this new man. She thought of him on the dancefloor, how he closed his eyes to the music, and pictured herself with him. Two weeks passed before she saw him again outside the meeting room.

'I'd like that drink,' she blurted out, then realised he'd not asked her for one. It didn't matter, she told herself, suddenly brave. 'I'm Nettie.'

'Harold,' he said. A smile spread across his face as he straightened his suit jacket. 'A drink it is.'

She waited for him in the Dive and Bell pub, where tinsel shone from the ceiling. It was where the men went after meetings sometimes, not that she'd ever joined them. She was precious about who she spent time with yet here she was, sat on a stool, picking at wax spilt on the table. Christmas carols played from the jukebox and she bought herself a brandy. What did it matter if she made a show of herself? It was hardly like anyone was watching.

At a few minutes past eight, Harold came through the door. After spotting her he called over to the barman saying he'd have 'the same as the lady' and sat himself down as though they'd known each other for years. She was taken back, although, in truth, it was she who'd invited him. And he was a handsome devil too. She wasn't sure how Edith could have been so quick to dismiss him, or what she'd say to know Nettie was here.

II

The next morning she tried not to fully waken. All she wanted was to stay beneath the covers with Harold beside her. None of it seemed real. In the pub she had drunk too quickly. Gabbled about the factory and told borrowed stories from the girls' nights out – someone's heel caught in a drain, a photo with a policeman's horse. All overheard. The next thing she knew, the carpet was swirling about her feet, the two of them arguing about the upcoming election, about council rates, her howling with laughter as the final drinks bell rang.

Now they laid in her bed. As he reached over to open the window, his shoulder blades glided beneath his skin decorated with freckles. He'd told her he liked adventure stories – the bigger the lions the better – and she'd suggested he didn't admit that in polite company. Now she grimaced and clutched the blankets around her as cold air slipped between them and kids shrieked in the street below. Seeing the print of make-up on her pillow, she felt the puffy skin of her bare face, the grate of brandy in her throat. How was she supposed to slip to the bathroom without him watching? The factory girls would no doubt have their methods. But then what did it matter? Grabbing her robe from the chair she was briefly chilled before going out of the door and running along the hall.

It was a relief to find the shared bathroom empty and she whipped the door closed. So much of the time someone knocked while she was halfway through washing but today the building was quiet. As the bath ran she performed her usual inspection in the cabinet's mirror, seeing first her breasts that sat minding their own business. What if there was nothing peculiar about her after all? She groped her body as if clues might be inscribed on her ribcage or in the shape of her thighs. But it was something that couldn't be pointed to. Something that evaded medical charts. Once in the bath she scrubbed the flannel across herself, then thought she should give Harold time to leave without any awkward conversation. But though she listened for footsteps the only sound was the slop of water as she scrubbed every inch of herself.

Twenty minutes later she found him smoking in the kitchen, tapping the cigarette ash into a saucer. The sight of him among her things – his shirt unbuttoned – was like something from a daydream.

'Are you hungry?' she ventured.

'Hungry?' The notion tickled him. 'No, I think I'll survive.'

Wanting to hide her flushing cheeks, she tidied the mess off the coffee table. How stupid that she'd left out her flyers from the socialist club. The list of things to talk to her sister about.

'But I do need to buy some matches,' he said, stubbing his cigarette. 'Walk with me?'

Harold suggested they head towards the park and she agreed, putting on her best coat and leather gloves. Away from the outhouses with their piled up rubbish, the streets were quiet. The tracks of kids' carts formed lines down a slope where snow claimed large sections. It made her feel strange to know another winter was already here. But still, she was lucky to be out with this man who dipped into a corner shop while she watched from outside. He looked nicely dishevelled as he spoke to the owner. Hard to imagine he'd care about his rumpled hair. He was so much himself.

'I enjoyed last night,' he said on returning, then laughed a little. 'You have quite a few opinions, don't you?'

'I suppose.' She expected him to make fun of her but he kept on walking across Weavers Fields as if the two of them were simply out for a stroll.

The Italian cafe stood on the other side and he headed towards its custard-hued panels and steel frame. While Nettie often passed by, she'd never been inside and now pictured the two of them sharing a bun or pastry in the warm little room.

But he merely appraised the place. 'Is this where Jack the Hat goes?'

'No idea.' She had little interest in where those thugs drank tea.

Harold lingered another moment before setting off again.

'Where are we going?' she asked, annoyed to realise she was trailing after him – the man she'd invited into her bed despite him barely noticing her that first night.

'Well I need to go to see a client.'

'Oh right.' She clutched her scarf tighter. 'Never mind then.'

'But I've got a few minutes.'

He took her arm and pulled her up a slope towards some

45

chestnut trees. At the top a patch of snow was melting beneath the branches. Someone had drawn a love heart and some initials and so he found a fresh patch, then held her in a waltzing pose.

'Oh come on,' he said when she pulled away. 'It should've been you I danced with that night.'

Seeing the contented look on his face, she let him hold her, swinging side to side on their own little stage.

The next weekend they spent all of Saturday together. Despite not living in the city – but Northampton with his parents – Harold knew places she'd only heard about. At the greyhound races he chose the dogs with the funniest names, claiming they should embrace the sheer chaos of the game. *Some people work out odds*, she teased. But he just grinned and placed two bob on Crazy Sister. It was partly that he was flush. His family business of selling car parts had taken off and he bought her ales and peanuts. He shrugged when he lost, though during one race he hollered at the dog in an American accent, 'You sold me down the river!' and the crowd laughed.

Afterwards they went to a dance hall where the band thrashed out songs with raucous drums. Without enough space, his movements were haphazard and he knocked into a lemonade stand. But he still wore a grin as she pulled him further into the middle and began to dance. She could be different around him, his jokey way protected them both, the crowds becoming a blur as they spun in their own technicolour.

In the run-up to Christmas she kept asking to see him, keen to discover an underground lair that awaited them in Soho. Some of these places were new to him too and together they found Soho coffee bars like the 2is where men wore sunglasses. Jazz clubs with songs that didn't let your feet stop. Compared to rock 'n' roll, the rhythm and blues always kept you guessing. A bit like Soho itself. At times she was shocked by what she saw – the youngsters in spangly outfits, Carnaby Street glowing with neon lights to expose half-dressed men. Phone boxes plastered in adverts for 'French Lessons' and 'Naughty Girls'. But she stayed anyway, happy as long as Harold followed.

Of course she didn't tell the factory girls. She knew they'd worry about how she was the one who'd asked him to the pub, not the other way around. How she kept doing the asking too – something that amused Harold, but didn't stop him turning up at her door. This wasn't how dating was supposed to go. Especially with a man she hardly knew anything about, only that his father was unwell and that's why he lived at home. And that he had an appetite for life she'd never before known in someone. Lying in her bed, he played jazz notes on her belly, a glint in his eyes as they hatched a new plan.

Keeping the secret wasn't hard. Long ago people had stopped asking what she did at weekends. She began to relish hearing the girls talk about letting a man hold their hand, knowing what she'd done. Or finding a smear of ink on her wrist and remembering the crowds. After years spent listening to their stories, now she was the one tired at her machine the next day, hiding a yawn but giddy to remember how late she'd been out. Far later than the other girls, with their self-imposed rules and curfews.

Nettie spent Christmas Day with her mum and boyfriend, who bickered about the pheasant he'd plucked in the kitchen. Leaving before it got dark, she pretended she was expecting Edith's phone call early this year but, once home, only drifted about the flat and looked at the card that arrived yesterday.

Dear Nettie,

I can't see you for New Year's Eve but I'll make it up. Promise!

Your fellow dancer, Harold
xxx

Later she stood in the telephone box and spoke to Edith.

'Good wishes for next year,' her sister said. 'Best of luck.'

'Yes, you too,' she replied, wondering if her sister had always been so restrained. 'Any wild plans for the new year?' Nettie asked.

'Perhaps.'

Frustrated by the silences, Nettie told her about Harold and – suddenly panicked to hear the response – gripped the receiver.

'That man from the basement? With the gangly legs?'

'Yes.'

'Right.' Edith cleared her voice. They'd hardly spoken about men before – almost as if there was a pact whereby men had no place in their relationship. Spinsters together, Nettie once assumed. Now she felt breathless.

'You realise what you are?' Edith asked carefully.

'No?'

'You're his good time girl.'

She started to protest but stopped herself. The dancing. Him in her bed. She didn't even have his address. But no – it didn't feel that way. Did it?

'As long as you understand that,' Edith continued. 'Just remember to be careful. You don't want to end up like Mum.'

She was about to ask what Edith meant when she heard voices

singing on the other end. 'I'd better go, merry Christmas,' her sister said and the line cut off.

Stung by the words 'good time girl' Nettie spent the next few days toying over whether to throw away Harold's card. Whether the three kisses he'd drawn meant anything. It wasn't until the end of January that she saw him again. She'd taken to waiting at the working men's club where they'd first seen each other, even on nights when she had no meeting. The whole thing was embarrassing really – perched on the cold plastic seat, pretending to read. But she refused to sit alone in her flat. Of course this thing between them couldn't be called love – it didn't fit the ways love should go. He wasn't a proper boyfriend or a fiancé. It was a clumsy sort of thing that'd left her bruised and wanting to dislike him. And yet she'd done it to herself. And she wouldn't take it back. Even if her sister was right – she was just his good time girl – she needed to see him again.

At last he emerged from a classroom one Tuesday evening and she tried not to return his grin as he walked over. They went to the same pub as before which was now empty, the jukebox silent, no coins pushed through its slot.

'Why didn't you drop in after Christmas?' she asked.

'You wanted me to?'

She flared with heat but refused to look away. 'I did.'

'Well I didn't know,' he said, frowning. 'Do you think I have all the time in the world to guess what you want?'

'I think I've been pretty clear.'

Laughter taunted them from behind the bar, along with a waft of brandy.

'Sorry.' He shook his head. 'I should be at home with my dad.' Nevertheless he remained sat with her and they drank their half pints until only dregs remained. Unsure what was happening between them – why he didn't just leave – she watched him sink another full pint. He was a greedy man. Someone people never said no to, though they should. For a minute she hated him, knowing if she seized the feeling for long enough she could walk away. When she finally stood, though, he rose with her and they ended up walking in the same direction.

'I'm taking the bus,' she told him. 'I can't afford taxis, like you can.'

'Fine. Can I come?'

She lightened to realise he was waiting beside her. Even if his eyes were downcast, it was the same pavement they were staring at. After some time it became too cold to wait and she said they'd have to walk the hour's journey. As they crossed a scrapyard where rubbish whipped at their ankles, she almost felt bad he was following her. He had better places to be, she knew. Places where the women didn't work in factories and have manic hair expanding from the damp.

'I'm sorry,' she said.

'It's okay. I like being with you.' He frowned as he said it and they carried on across the rusted bridge over the river, the water dark beneath. After a while the fog enveloped everything in a silvery mist, vague shapes replacing the Nissen huts left from the war. When a policeman on a bike stopped and asked if they were okay they agreed they were.

'Ugly, isn't it?' He motioned to a yard where a rag and bone man was packing away his cart of broken toys and crockery.

'This is how a lot of people live.' The two of them had been part of a fantasy, she realised. The dancers and youths of Soho were only a fraction of London. Harold gave the man a coin but refused any of his wares. 'The bloody poor,' he joked when they were out of earshot. Then he lit a cigarette and took an angry puff. 'I have no right.'

'Pardon?'

'To be sad about my dad.' He motioned to a metal hut where a pair of child's boots were left outside. 'When families are living this way.'

She'd not been aware he had been thinking about his dad. 'Of course you can be upset. It's bizarre how we try to weigh our own sadness against other people's.'

They walked the rest of the streets without a word, their silent reflections in the wet, silvery ground.

When they got back to her flat, he stood fidgeting in the lounge. He told her his dad was now in a wheelchair with no hope of getting better. 'You can't cure an illness like his,' he said, describing how his dad's leg muscles were seizing up. The doctors unsure what to do next. She sat on the settee and listened.

'Everyone's in denial. Even now I'm running the family business, Mum insists he just needs rest. My friends don't understand and I can't see them any more. They all lie.' He seemed distraught and she rose to hold him.

'No,' he said, backing away. 'Don't tell me it's okay because it isn't.'

'I won't.' She swallowed. 'People die and it's horrible. Sometimes there's nothing anyone can do.'

For a moment he was aghast and she expected him to shout or tear down her posters. But he curled into her arms and sobbed, an animal-like sound which filled the room. That night she held him in bed, realising he wasn't as large as she first thought, his chest rising to a gentle mound. She understood where his appetite for living came from. Why he wanted to experience as much as he could. Life was more fleeting than a heart drawn in the snow.

As she was stroking his hair in the lamplight, he pulled away. 'This might never go anywhere. Between us, I mean,' he said, looking at her with bloodshot eyes.

She felt a lurch of sadness but it was enough to have him with her and she nodded. 'I don't need any promises.' They made love but not like the times before. Their bodies huddled together and he whispered, 'For as long as this lasts.'

III

_____

It was a surprise to realise what had happened. The doctor soon confirmed with a grave nod. Pregnant. *Almost nine weeks gone.*

He appraised her age – thirty-two. *You might just be fine.*

At a certain point she'd accepted she wouldn't have kids and felt relieved as other women turned grey chasing after children, their bodies swelling beneath elasticated clothing and becoming shared property. Now she reappraised the idea and, that February morning, was impatient to be back home. Maybe the kids screaming in the yard would sound different to her now. Or maybe they'd still make her want to bung up her ears and that'd be her answer ... although what was the question? The thought of having the operation made her head swim.

She was expecting Harold that evening and knew everything had to be right: a casserole served on her nicest crockery. Her bathed and scrubbed to a soft pink. The plan was to eat first but as soon as he arrived, she blurted out the words. 'I'm carrying your child.'

Without saying a thing, Harold placed his satchel by the door and drifted to the window. She waited for him to react but he merely gazed into the yard, searching for answers in the paving slabs.

'Well?'

'I ... I'm not sure what to say.' He lit a cigarette. For a while the news sat oddly between them as they ate tea and spoke about the forecast rain.

'You need to tell me what you're thinking,' she said when the bowls were empty. A smile crept around his lips, a secret he couldn't keep.

'I don't know,' he said before he pulled her onto his lap, placing his hands across her belly as if he was discovering a whole new world. 'We'll have to think of names.'

For the rest of the night she felt breathless with luck. This was what happened to other people. Edith would be shocked and she played out imaginary conversations between the two of them. Yes, she'd be a mum. And she'd be happy as a lark.

But in the morning he was gone, leaving behind only an empty cigarette packet. She hurried down the street without any clue which direction he'd gone in. Three days passed and it was agonising not to visit his building; yet she knew he needed time to think. After a whole seven days, she felt weighed down with the knowledge of what was growing inside her. Perhaps her sister was right, she was just his good time girl.

Unsure what else to do, the following Monday she sent a telegram to West Berlin.

Later Edith's voice was gentle but unsurprised. 'This is what I was worried about. As much as you'd love that baby it wouldn't be fair. You earn so little. And Mum's still getting her life back together.'

'What can I do?'

'I can send you some money.'

The dark street around her was desolate. 'No, Edie.'

Her sister's voice lowered. 'Don't use bleach or crochet hooks. Go to a proper place on Harley Street.'

'And tell them what?'

'That you're mentally unfit to have a baby.'

'Mentally unfit?'

'Of course you're not,' she added quickly, then: 'I'd come home to be with you. I really would but the General has cancelled all leave.'

'It's all right.' Her quickening breath clouded the glass, her forehead knocking against its cold surface.

The next week she left the Harley Street practice, phased at how easy the conversation had been. Her sister had called ahead and explained the situation, though Nettie couldn't think what might've been said. The nurse had spoken in a slow voice and she'd left clutching a letter with an appointment time. None of it felt real and as a wave of nausea made her sway, she thought of the child forming, its tiny fingers and heartbeat ... What if she could raise it alone? The answer slipped like a balloon string from her fingers.

The rag and bone man had been, a single child's sock lay on the pavement outside her flat. She clasped its soft wool as she let herself into the building. More items littered the stairs: a cracked plant pot, a set of weighing scales. It seemed cruel they'd be here. The parts of a life fallen apart. Who had left them here so carelessly? She passed Number Three and thought of knocking but the stairwell blurred behind a veil of tears. At the top she found Harold waiting. Dressed in his work suit he was bundling various items into his arms.

'What's happening?' she asked, wiping her eyes.

He shrugged and gestured to the odds and ends around him. 'Harold?'

A smile flickered between them as he said, 'If this is real life, I reckon I'll spend mine with you.'

Even after that she didn't know much of what would happen. They kept the weighing scales and baby clothes, then gave away the rest. It was just like Harold to buy the whole lot without thinking and she laughed every time she weighed flour in the scratched dish.

He still seemed distant from the notion of being a dad, even as the days passed and they slipped into a routine of him visiting several times a week. 'Never thought I'd have them, that's all,' he said one night; she'd found him sat on her building's step staring into the distance. He pretended he'd had an impromptu meeting but carried a near-empty briefcase. He mentioned her meeting his parents too but was fuzzy about dates. It was only when she later brought up a possible christening that he changed. It was in passing, really, a girl from work having gone to one that weekend.

'Of course he'll be christened,' Harold said.

She'd not pegged him as religious. He didn't seem the type and she herself had been raised in a mostly faithless house, her mum treating God as a form of home surveillance better not mentioned. Harold on the other hand was quiet on the issue, shrugging when she brought it up but not apologising either. He told her how his mum had begun to pray for his dad's recovery and he might as well 'give it a try too'. Nettie suspected it was more than that. She noticed the moments he was a pensive, altogether different man. The adventure book he'd been reading would go limp in his hands, and she'd wonder if he was thinking of his dad or the baby. Once again she couldn't get inside his mind, but what if she had their whole lives together to try?

The day they got married the Kray brothers were in the newspaper, the men photographed outside their Soho club. Their hair slick, a crowd around them, they looked like businessmen when only the year before Ronnie had walked into a pub and shot a man in the head. Nettie refused to read the article her mum pored over at her kitchen table. The two men were violent criminals but people didn't treat them that way. It was like early death was glamorous until it was someone you knew at the wrong end of the gun.

'Put that away, can't you?' she said.

Her mum left the newspaper open but got up to fetch her cigarettes. Outside the three of them stood in the courtyard in their dressing gowns, even Edith not complaining they should dress first. No one else was around, or at least their windows weren't open, and the sisters smiled at each other. They'd stayed the night with their mum, supposedly enjoying a hen do although the hours were mostly spent listening to her talk about Robert – how he'd admitted to being with other women, a man too. Nettie hadn't minded listening. She was merely grateful her sister had been allowed to visit, something she was yet to explain.

'I wouldn't mind the Krays dicing him up, you know,' Nettie said and registered their surprised faces. 'Put him in a pie for tea.'

'Oh, was that meant to be beef and potato in the pie later?' asked Edith, joining in. 'Because I put Robert in there.'

Their mum cackled and they did too, the sound echoing around the courtyard. But the next moment she stopped and let her body fall against the wall. 'I just thought he loved me. Is that so unlikely?'

Nettie's reflection stared back at her in the taxi's window – the flowers in her hair were wilting in the July heat but at least her cheeks were rosy. As the other two chatted she leant into the pool of sunshine so her dress bleached of colour and detail to leave only this promise of life beneath her fingertips. Even the idea made her hands so damp they stuck to the lace.

'I hope he'll turn up,' said their mum.

'Lizzie!'

'I'm just saying. A kiddie on the way is enough to frighten a man off.'

Her sister and mum bickered in the back as Nettie closed her eyes. Despite Edith's earlier protests, Nettie knew she was somehow disappointed in her and tried not to care. When they ground to a halt in the traffic around Shoreditch High Street someone knocked on the window. A lanky guy with dreadlocks spilling from a beanie peered down. For a second she was a sham, a version of her mum wanting to be loved. Harold hadn't asked her to marry him. She'd suggested they get married as he was working one night in her flat. He had carried on typing, then stopped and showed her the typewriter. 'Okay, old bird' was written at the top of the page. It was what he'd started calling her. His old bird, like a pet rescued from the farmhouse.

But the dreadlocked guy grinned. 'Have a great day, yeah?' It seemed a genuine question and she felt her mouth drop open, not sure what to say.

Once they arrived at the town hall Edith raced off to check everything was running on time. Nettie had suggested a church to Harold but in the end they'd settled on an informal wedding with a dozen guests. Through the window Nettie could see the rows of chairs, people fidgeting and fanning themselves with papers, but no Harold.

'Where is he?' asked her mum.

'I'm not sure.'

She went into the bathroom to grip the cold edge of the sink. Stood in a mound of white – the delicate fabric pulled beyond its design – she squeezed her eyes shut and thought herself the old bird. *Peculiar creature. A black fold of wing, grasping claw...*

But the door opened. 'Harold was just in the back room. Ready?'

Nettie pulled down the lace sleeves, made sure her high collar was clipped. 'I think so.'

'Even if I had my doubts ...' Edith pursed her lips. 'I'm happy if you are. Truly.'

The room was decorated with a single ribbon tied around the lectern and a bouquet to match her own on the piano. Waiting for the pianist to see they'd stepped into the room, Nettie glanced about. A couple of Harold's friends had come, along with some girls from the factory who'd insisted on being there. Linking arms with her mum, she took a breath and waved at Edith who turned round in the front row, sat beside an unknown woman with raven-black hair and a camera. Nettie was working out who she might be as the music began – a version

59

of Pachelbel's Canon but played too fast. A few giggles went around the guests and her mum clutched her tighter as they strode down the aisle. The only person not smiling was Harold. It was rare to see him tense and she couldn't help but grin.

The registrar's words began and she held hands with Harold, who was dressed in the same oversized tweed jacket he'd worn the night they met. It'd been only eight months ago but she already knew each of the freckles that mapped his nose and cheeks like stars. The angle of his jaw that now ground as he searched her eyes. When it was time for his vows he produced a piece of paper and cleared his throat as the room fell silent. Without his hands in hers, Nettie felt oddly apart from him. He stepped back as if not sure whether to address just her or the room.

'I didn't want to love you,' he began with a frown. 'I didn't want for this to happen. Because I was fine without you and doing well. And you came along.' As he stared at the paper Nettie shifted. Someone muttered in the back. He continued, 'And you made me weak, you found my fault lines. I was confused at first. But now I understand.'

The registrar waited for more but he folded the paper and shoved it back in his pocket. A silence drifted that left only the memory of his palms, the heat of his skin.

'I love you too,' she said and the crowd erupted with laughter and applause before they walked outside into a shower of confetti that filled the sky with colour.

As a flash turned the scene white she felt Harold's arm around her and heard cheering. Then the camera lowered to show the dark-haired woman. 'Congratulations,' she said in a German accent, and reached out to shake Nettie's hand. 'I hope you don't mind me coming,' she added with a serious face. 'Your sister thought you might like photos.'

'This is Greta,' said Edith, appearing behind. 'I invited her along. You don't mind, do you?'

They all went to the Crown, the pub at the corner of Nettie's street. The landlady clapped as she walked in. Nettie realised she should be with Harold who was chatting with the men. She went to call him over but noticed how Greta was sizing up shots, photographing her sister as she set about unwrapping the trays of pies. Their mum was observing her too as she pretended to listen to the factory girls.

'She's very stylish,' Edith said, pointing to Greta's cream suit jacket, peaked with crisp shoulder pads. 'She chose that dress I gave you.'

'Oh!' Nettie thought of how clearly the beaded mini-dress wasn't picked with her in mind.

'You've got to appreciate her eye for fashion.'

'I guess so.'

'Edie,' said Harold, who appeared behind them. 'I hope I get another dance tonight?'

They hadn't seen each other since the night in the dance hall and Edith gave a little nod. 'Why not? Although I never could dance. That's why we need Nettie.'

'We do, don't we?'

She'd never considered herself a good dancer but liked the idea. He pulled her in for a kiss and they linked hands, wedding rings softly knocking, until someone by the bar called him over.

'Actually,' said Edith. 'I wanted to tell you something. Not that I mean to steal your thunder, it's just I might not see you for a while.'

61

'What is it?'

'Greta and I have been planning a trip,' said Edith. 'To America.'

'What do you mean?'

'Greta will be working for *Time* magazine and I could look for a job in an office.' She studied Nettie's reaction before she glanced to their mum.

'Isn't it exciting?' their mum said, scurrying over with a tray of sparkling wine. They each took a glass, including Greta who clutched her camera in the other hand. It was a bulky thing with a lens that pointed to Nettie so she saw her face reflected, a frown stretching across its glass. She'd barely heard of this woman who was now taking her sister across the ocean. So that was why she was able to come today – she wasn't working for the military any more.

'To new beginnings,' said their mum.

They all looked at Edith, even the barmaid. Nettie's wedding dress felt heavy. Her sister off to America for how long? She wanted to ask but didn't trust herself to speak, a welling inside her.

Talk had turned to the Krays and people passed around a different newspaper, the wedding party merging with normal punters, some of whom Harold had bought glasses of Babycham. Aware it was already six o'clock, Nettie wanted to call him over to dance or do whatever it was newly married couples did. Just as she searched the room he appeared behind her.

They went to sit in a booth while the others carried on drinking, even Edith seeming unsteady as she stood with the factory girls. 'My folks gave us this,' he said, taking an envelope from his pocket. His parents weren't in the room. They had pulled out the day before, his father stuck in bed. But then maybe they'd never planned on coming, their unspoken notion that he should find a different wife. Not some ageing spinster from the factories.

'What is it?'

Inside the envelope was one hundred pounds. A surprising gift for people who'd not even made the day. Maybe they weren't so disapproving after all.

She felt the cash in her hands and almost wanted to smell it. For all the corners they'd cut that day, the single ribbon, here was enough money for a lavish do.

'See? I knew you weren't such a socialist,' he said, grinning.

She laughed but then put the money back in the envelope. People at the bar were still talking about the Krays and she suddenly felt dirty. There was no card with the money.

'We'll give half of it away,' she said.

'We bloody well won't.'

'It's my money too, isn't it?'

Just as he went to grab the envelope something outside exploded and a man ran past the window. Harold pulled her under the table as if the Krays might appear at any second. But it was just a car's exhaust and they laughed, staying under the table despite the envelope deserted above, her mum and sister already chatting about the noise. It didn't matter who else was there or what plans they made, only that they were together. And in that moment she promised to keep him close for as long as she could.

2

2015

4

July 2015

She doesn't rise as soon as she wakes. Sometimes she is surprised to have woken at all. She tries to register an appetite for breakfast. It's easy to imagine life itself as a meal: you can enjoy the experience but, on nearly finishing, not want another plateful. And yet here she is, satiated but still breathing. A final visit from her granddaughters and she'll be full to the brim.

'Rufus,' she calls and he pads up the stairs and into her room. Performing their morning ritual, the dog pushes his head into her outstretched hand and she feels his shock of warm bristles. After making a fuss of him she'd usually go downstairs in her nightgown to put on breakfast. But perhaps she should dress today, what with another person in the house – a near-stranger, no less. She pulls open her top drawer to rummage among the petticoats, the gloves, the underwear. At the back a spoon knocks against the side – what is this doing here? It needs returning downstairs except she won't do that in front of James; people are quick to label old women doddery or demented. She'd rather avoid both those labels, thank you very much. After shutting the drawer she listens for sounds from the next room. Is James out of bed?

Finding the house quiet, she decides to just slip on her dressing gown. In the landing, the door of the spare room is open and the single bed already made, its sheet tucked tightly under the mattress.

'Maybe he had an early start,' she tells Rufus.

The dog peers up uncertainly. She knows he wants his breakfast and makes her way down the stairs. It's an effortful thing, the creaking of the bannister reminding Nettie of her weight. No point in dieting, though. Food is such a pleasure.

Singing starts up when she's halfway to the bottom. 'Strong and white edelweiss, every morning you greet me.'

It's too late to turn back to dress – she won't give him the satisfaction of knowing she cares – so she continues down in her dressing gown to where he sits at the kitchen table. He's drinking tea but the Moroccan set is back on the shelf. Instead he's opted for the wedding china they bought with the money from Harold's parents, choosing a set with gold rims and dots across the handles. A cup is balanced on the fold of the morning newspaper, the milk jug out too, as if it's normal chinaware and not what she's carefully tended to for the last forty years.

'It's too much,' she says. Without her stick her hand judders in the air, fingers pointing at him. It's the motion of an elderly woman but she doesn't care. 'How dare you.'

'What's all this?' He stands. 'I'm sorry, Annette.'

He seems genuinely upset. His slight paunch touches the table edge before he steps back, apologetic.

'It's my best china.'

'Oh, I see.' He gathers the teacup and jug off the newspaper and almost doesn't want to touch them again. They then sit in a dull shadow and seem overly small, the gold dots muted. It's all she really has any more, though. The last remnants of her marriage.

'I was thinking,' he says, still standing away from the table.

'Yes?'

'I could ask Catherine to come here.' He studies her reaction to the name – a currency he knows is worth something.

'Really?'

'Maybe she could bring the girls too.'

'You met them?'

'Oh yes. Such lovely girls.'

'I know they are.' She means to speak more tersely but already she's picturing them sitting at the table. Blonde hair shining in the light like dandelions as they talk about school. 'But I'm not sure they'll come.'

'Oh, I'm confident they would.' He lowers himself into a chair. 'If I asked Catherine. We have something important to discuss, you see.'

'What?'

'It's an AA matter.'

Unsure whether to believe him, Nettie walks over to the table and picks up a teacup he's left out for her. It's surprisingly sturdy in her palm.

'I wouldn't mind a little more,' says James with the makings of a smile.

The cup is already dirty and it seems churlish to deny him.

'You really think she'll come?'

'She was talking about how she missed the farmhouse,' he says and holds the cup below the spout. 'Probably only needs a nudge from the right person. I'll give her a ring after this.'

So she relents and pours more tea into her best china.

After getting properly dressed, she shows him the phone in the dining room. He takes in the space with its piano and oval table surrounded by four chairs. A light falls through the window to show the dust that thickens the air. But at least the table itself is clear, decorated with just candlestick holders and a salt pot, as if her family are expected at any moment.

'Over here.' She taps on the phone that sits by the window ledge and it lets out an excited ding. James waits for her to step out of the way before he dials Catherine's number. It *is* 667 – his fingers nimbly turn the dial before he tucks them into a pocket, then meets her gaze as they wait.

'Maybe this afternoon, if she can make it?' Nettie says.

'Possibly.'

'Or tomorrow? I could cook lamb.'

She grips the table edge and feels the fur of dust slide away. What if the girls might soon be having lunch with her? Suddenly the thought of another meal alone makes her despair – the crack of an egg or rough smear of butter on toast. She studies James's face for signs of what he's thinking. Whether Catherine will pick up. Maybe she's already on the phone, chatting with a friend. Does the woman have many friends these days? She hopes so. Her daughter can keep people at a distance but then she's a lot of fun too, always keen for a party.

'She's not there.' He places the phone in its cradle.

'Oh?'

'We'll try again later,' he says and almost puts a hand on her shoulder before she can step back. She knows he could be lying about having any sway over Catherine. He probably is. For all she knows the two have barely got to know each other – the fact he mentioned her own supposed socialist values doesn't mean much. People often know things from the past that surprise her. The internet contains all sorts and she dares not ask what circulates.

She is weighted by these thoughts as she walks through the back door. The concrete is a barren land of grooves and scratches, tainted by her shadow. The chickens are slow to emerge from their house even as she curls her fingers into the feed.

'That hole needs fixing.' James has appeared behind her and is pointing to the gate's splintered wood.

'I'll get round to it today.' She motions to the barn where there'll be supplies.

'May I?' He opens the barn door and out wafts the smell of dried grass, and a familiar, rotting sort of sweetness. It's hard to tell where it comes from, whether it's thanks to the red onions she used to string up. She hardly ventures inside any more, not having bothered to replace the lightbulb when it went. Now darkness claims most of the clutter although she can see the boxes, a glint of Harold's car and a sit-down mower, another technological device that needs endless servicing and trips to the industrial park outside town.

'I can't find any spare wood,' James says but carries on moving around in the dark. Seeing the barn open, Rufus trots across the yard and slips inside; he used to always root around in there and occasionally got trapped if she closed up without realising. He's not one to bark even when he should. No kind of guard dog.

*

71

'This place could use some work in general.' James has gone upstairs to wash his hands of the barn's dirt and she hovers in the hallway.

'It isn't that bad,' she mutters, not wanting to shout. She'd been on the way to her bedroom but stopped, it feeling too intimate with the two of them up there.

'I might be able to have a tinker.'

'No thank you.'

'To repay you for letting me stay last night.'

Never mind the house, Nettie thinks, *get my daughter to visit*. Without even hearing footsteps, she knows he's inspecting the landing window, the view of the field marred by its silver cracks. The glass should hold a while longer, though.

'Let's at least fix the gate today.'

Ten minutes later they're stood by the front door where she pulls on her gloves. She shouldn't begrudge him really. The man is merely trying to help and it's only a trip to the local timber yard. Plus if they can get this place looking respectable, Catherine will have one less reason not to visit.

Outside the day has brightened and the air is filled with the hum of a hedge trimmer, the commuters gone now it's nearing ten o'clock.

They journey into town, past the pubs' hanging baskets that overflow with pansies. Bunting arcs between shimmering white cottages. Romsey takes pride in its appearance. Too much at times – the idyllic English town not something that actually exists. Or at least not without the poor being pushed out, a hush over certain topics. Someone looks at them and she is self-conscious beside this younger man. Seemingly oblivious, James whistles and peers into the newsagent's window. Nettie is grateful to stop and take a breather, wondering if he is pretending to look for her sake. She can't help notice the scrape of hair over his scalp. How he's wearing the same denim shirt as the day before, its resewn button hanging by a thread. Why would he want to be here with her? He has nowhere else to go perhaps, but he seems industrious, competent. If he's lost a job he should be working out some sort of plan. He shouldn't be here with a woman more than twice his age.

'Where to?'

'The post office,' she says. 'Although you don't have to come.'

'Of course I will.'

There's a queue but he doesn't seem fussed and chooses a chair by the window as she takes her place. Her usual monthly routine to collect her pension feels different now. She can't hear the whistling from where he's sat behind but is still conscious of him.

'Mrs Ravenscroft?'

The young woman is waiting. She's not even got her pension book out and rummages in her handbag. 'Sorry,' she says. 'I was a hundred miles away.'

'Looked more like a million.' The woman's garishly pink lips part in a smile.

'Yes, well.' She flushes. 'I'm sorry.'

Afterwards she slips the cash into her purse and wonders if James is watching her. Maybe him being here is all an elaborate hoax; he'll rob her then move on to the next house. He'll earn the money first, she thinks darkly, motioning the way to the timber yard further out of town.

Wood shavings scent the cavernous building where people in matching T-shirts push around carts. Two old men are talking by the rows of paintbrushes. Apparently last night a vat of oil was dumped in the river, down by the memorial park. A peculiar thing to do, one says, adjusting his flat cap. They're having to rehome some of the ducks. The other man reckons it must be bored kids and Nettie is relieved not to be the only person troubled by those youths. But still she notices how the men stop talking as she approaches, the larger of the pair stepping into her path. For a second she assumes it's an accident but he meets her eye and doesn't move, staying close enough that his cigarette breath sours the air.

'Excuse me,' she says without stepping around him. She's never known what to do in these situations.

The man sucks his teeth and remains fixed in place.

Feeling herself tremble, she refuses to give in to them yet is unsure what else to say as the other man steps nearer. They close in tight and a sickness curdles, expands, shuddering through her arms into a curled fist.

'Nettie?' It's James whose voice saves her. They all turn to see him at the end of the aisle, holding a cutting of redwood. 'How about this one?' She floats over to him. Did he notice what just went on? Maybe not, he seems preoccupied. 'Whatever you like,' she says.

At the till she doesn't mind handing over the £5.99. Although she's been saving money for the grandkids – the ice creams and lunches out they'll want – this is a small price to pay for the chickens. And for help from James.

He turns down the offer of delivery and, instead, rests the wood on his shoulder before the two of them walk out together, past the old men who mutter at the sight of her new friend.

The gate is easily fixed. After James twists the final screws, he shakes the whole thing and, sure enough, it holds. As she opens the coop, the chickens run out in a riot of orange feathers and she smiles as they dance around the yard. James, on the other hand, is less content. 'What I am really concerned about,' he says, 'is your roof.'

She squints in the direction he is pointing but, despite her glasses, can only see a hazy terracotta mass. The missing tiles have long been felt in the house, though – through the draughts and the spread of brown on her bedroom ceiling like the tide washing in.

'It'll only take me a day or so. Besides, it'd be expensive to get someone in.'

'You'd know what to do?'

He's removed his shirt to leave just a vest beneath. Hair curls out from the fabric and when he bends his arms his biceps protrude. 'I was in the army for a few years and we didn't always have much to do in a town. A friend taught me stuff about building.'

'Oh. You're not trained?'

'Well maybe there's someone else in Romsey who can do it for you?'

She can't tell whether he's goading her. His face is straight as he appraises the roof again. 'A friend who won't charge an arm and a leg?'

'There isn't, no.'

By mid-morning he's not done much. The ladder is leant against the wall and there's a growing stack of tiles from the barn. He sorts through them on his haunches, finding the ones that aren't broken. Everything is shrouded in cobwebs and he asks her to clean them with a damp cloth. 'We might as well do it properly.'

While he goes to find more tools in the barn she hovers.

Really she should be fetching these things but it's dark in there without a working light. At least her house is being fixed. With every glance of him in the darkness, though – the combed hair, his boots beside Harold's car – she tenses. Even Rufus is slow to walk into the barn. He keeps his nose to the floor, his tail suspended. It goes quiet. The darkness becomes too thick and she wants to know what he's doing. But she daren't move.

'James?' she says and there's no reply. 'Hello?'

'What is it, Nettie?' he calls back, his face appearing. Holding a toolbox he lets it clunk on the ground, then smooths his hair. 'Why don't you let me get on with things, eh?'

5

Nettie hasn't been to choir practice for years; it feels uncomfortable with too many people squeezed onto the stage. Now the idea keeps returning. For hours she's been listening to scratching above, as if an intruder is finding his way into her house piece by piece. All the while she sits at the piano. The notes aren't enough to blot out the sound of James wandering into parts of the house no one has seen for years – the attic for one. She plays louder, a Satie sarabande that builds until her fingers slip across the keys, adding too many sharps as she stumbles onwards.

Another bang upstairs makes her pause.

James is moving something around in the attic and she gets up to find her handbag and stick. 'Keep an eye out, won't you?' she tells Rufus who's picking at a piece of wood he must've found in a nearby field. Sometimes he escapes and drags things back but she's given up trying to stop him; the farmer never comes by to complain.

'I'm going out,' she calls up into the dark square of the attic hatch. The ladder has been wiped clean although a trace of blood stains a rung. There's another knock and a cough and she almost heads for the stairs without waiting. But James's face appears.

'Where are you off to?'

'Choir practice. At church.'

'I could drive you,' he says, then sucks at a finger. He seems tired, his hair rumpled out of place, and sits down with his thighs splayed. 'You don't want to walk back in the dark alone.'

'It won't be dark,' she says curtly, then regrets her tone. He's only trying to help. 'To be frank, the car hasn't worked in years.'

'That's a great shame.'

'Yes, well.' She drifts towards the stairs and he calls after her.

'It'd fetch a decent sum. Must be a collector's item.'

In the yard she passes the barn door. She knows the car is worth something because one year Catherine asked a man round to look at it and he was impressed, whistling when he saw its engine. As she lingers by the entrance Nettie has an idle wondering: would she be upset to have the car stolen? Not particularly. She always hated the thing.

At first the church seems unusually shadowy and she is slow to make her way to the front where groups mill. People are surprised to see her and assume she's lost or looking to pray on her own. But after telling them she's here to sing they make room and one smiling red-haired woman hands her a book. She's glad to see they're singing Brahms today. A requiem she knows so it doesn't matter the notes are too small to see without bringing the book to her face.

Marianne emerges from the vestry and gives her a wave.

'Hello,' Nettie calls and grins, pleased to have come. The voices then merge around her in a great swirl of sound, no single person demanding more attention than the rest. Even though her vocal cords are dry she lets herself release the words without worrying. Someone's perfume sweetens the air and she lets her arms touch those on either side. It's only later she notices the woman sat in the audience, four rows from the front. Her pale face is almost featureless as she sits without singing and without clapping when they reach the end. A visitor, Nettie assumes, or someone thinking of joining, although she can't imagine her unclamping that mouth to release song. The funeral march perhaps.

Afterwards Nettie goes to talk to the vicar.

'I'm glad you came,' Marianne says as she collapses the music stand.

'Even though it's so busy?'

'The church always has room for more.' She leans in to confide. 'Most of these people don't actually come to services, so you get bonus points for that.' Her capped tooth slips into view and Nettie returns the grin. At last the veil of manners has slipped, they're sharing a joke. She's about to mention her idea of the fete when the woman from the audience stands up, watching them. Dressed in an oversized pink sweater she's the sort who should seem harmless and childlike. But the way she lingers unnerves Nettie and she lets Marianne go and speak to her.

The honeysuckle curls itself around a fence, pink encroaching in all directions. Walking through the park, Nettie knows she shouldn't be jealous of the woman Marianne spoke to, especially if she was upset. Maybe she could ring tomorrow and ask if everything is all right. It's hard to know where to start; she doesn't know much about Marianne's home life. Whether she's met a partner in Romsey or even got to know her neighbours. Surely she must ring now. Marianne could still become her friend.

Walking in the swaying grass makes her feel better until she reaches the bridge and remembers how the river was polluted by kids. In the low water weeds are exposed in gnarled coils while remaining oil clings to the surface. A shuffle of feathers announces a duck which tries to swim by. Nettie silently apologises. She should really have reported the kids a long time ago. Helped put a stop to this sort of carry-on.

The light is fading by the time she arrives at her gate and she grasps its rusted metal top, glad to be home. Although purplish shadows fall across the yard she can see the ladder has been put away. The barn doors are closed too. Perhaps James has finished the work and gone. The house will be hers again, its whispering draughts for her ears only. But as she approaches the back door she hears voices. A girl's laugh, is that?

Finding the door unlocked she steps into the kitchen. A jazz record is playing – one of her favourites from when she met Harold. She hasn't played it in years, worried she'd wear the song out. Now this man has put it on. What else has he looked through?

In the living room he sits in her armchair, his boots still on, unlike the girl who's barefoot as she prances around, half-dancing, half-exploring the room. Her top rides up, ribs visible below the tanned skin. She speaks in a loud voice about some ex-boyfriend. An all right guy apparently. 'Loved himself too much though and that wasn't healthy.' Rufus sniffs her legs, then pads about the rug for crumbs. It's rare to see him this lively – usually he's a knot of brown fur from evening till morning.

'At least he never touched me,' the girl says. 'Not like my cousin's boyfriend who gave her a black eye. But then again I'd smack her given half a chance.'

Nettie lets her stick clatter against the floor.

'Hello,' comes James's voice from the living room. 'Anybody there?'

Nettie refuses to answer – who else would be walking into the house? – and waits for him to appear.

'Apologies for bringing over a guest.' His face fights a smile aimed at the girl behind. Remembering himself he smooths his hair and carries a glass to the sink. 'I would have rung but I assume you've not got a mobile.'

'No.'

'That's what I thought.'

Nettie waits for him to introduce the girl who's stood in her living room. She can see a short skirt. Bare feet on the rug. The girl can't be more than seventeen or eighteen. Certainly too young for James. 'You've multiplied.'

'Maybe you know Tara? She works at the Hope and Anchor in town.' His complexion has turned ruddy with sunburn, his chest still uncovered without a proper shirt.

'No,' Nettie replies, not having set foot in a local pub in years.

'Come here and introduce yourself,' he calls.

Tara walks in. She's wearing earrings that twinkle and a skirt that cuts across her waxy brown thighs. The girl strikes Nettie as doll-like but then she's no good at recognising fashions any more; maybe all young women look this way.

'Hiya,' she says, her arms crossed. 'We'll go if you like. This place is ...' She looks around the aged kitchen, at the dog bowl on the floor. Hers is a babyish face of full cheeks. 'Well, we could go back to the pub.'

'We could,' James says before he turns. 'How was choir?'

'Fine.'

'Oh good. I am pleased.' His eyes study hers. 'Would you like us to leave, Nettie? Leave you to your own devices?'

She hesitates, knowing the answer should be yes. This man has brought back a young woman for Heaven knows what. And he's been rummaging in her record collection that had been stowed in the trunk. But the music's rhythm is soothing as it fills the air. 'I don't know. I'm hungry.'

In the fridge she finds some cheddar cheese and a packet of beetroot. Several bottles of cider are parked around the bin, a lipstick stain on each. Even if James isn't drinking he's remarkably tolerant of others who do. Catherine could barely walk past a pub without craving a visit.

Nettie finds some salted crackers and sits down to eat. It's only Tara's voice she can hear over the music. She's giving a monologue in that way some young women do, as if to cease talking would be to cease to exist.

Trying not to listen Nettie slices the beetroot into layers. What would Catherine say if she knew they were here? Anybody's guess.

The last time she came to stay – five years ago – she let Nettie do everything while she lounged around having baths and painting her toenails a film-star red, sleeping until midday and reading magazines while spread across the settee. They should've carried on like that the following summer instead of deciding to go away for a holiday. It'd been Nettie's idea to travel towards the Scottish border to where she went with her sister and mum as children, then with Harold. She'd pictured Catherine and the girls in the fields, lighting fires, collecting pebbles to weight pockets ... Such a reckless idea. Why couldn't she have been content to carry on as normal?

Nettie now realises the beetroot has spilt its juice across the table. It stains her fingers and drips onto the floor.

Just as she's rising Tara appears. 'Watch out,' she says. 'It's gonna get on your clothes.'

'It's only beetroot juice,' Nettie says.

Tara watches her move to the sink where she washes the purple that spreads across the metal bowl, slow to disappear. The girl is right – several drops have already stained the hem of her skirt.

The phone rings and it's Catherine's voice on the line. A tingling awakens her cheek as she grips the receiver. It's been too long. Far too long.

'How are the kids?' Nettie asks. She can hear one of them talking in the background. Maybe the younger one, Grace, who's turning ten soon.

'Hard work. They want me to take them to Harry Potter World. Like I can afford that.'

'We could go when you visit.'

'It's the wrong direction, Mum.' Catherine gives an impatient sigh. 'I was just seeing if you were all right. I had a missed call from you earlier.'

'Oh yes.' Nettie lowers her voice although she's not sure why. The music is playing loudly and through the dining room doorway she can see his boot, where he sits in her armchair. 'I've got a visitor – a man named James.'

'James who?'

'James from your AA meetings.'

Catherine sounds confused. 'He's in the house?'

'Yes.'

'Right this minute?'

'Yes.'

A silence stretches so Nettie speaks again, clutching the phone tighter. 'He's not dangerous or anything is he?'

'No, I'm just surprised he's gone to see you.'

'He didn't. It just turned out this way.' As she says the words she questions whether they're true. Perhaps the man did intend to visit although that makes little sense. Her daughter tells one of the girls not to take something from the fridge before she returns to the phone. 'He was trying to stay here too. I think he's lost his job, turned into a scrounger. I kind of felt sorry for him and one night, well … I'm pretty sure he's gay.'

'Oh.'

'Probably why his wife chucked him out.'

Nettie doesn't see how all this is relevant. 'He's not a bad man, is he?'

'Harmless as a bloody butterfly, I'd say. But I'd get rid of him, Mum. Otherwise he'll never leave.'

'Right.' Nettie curls the wire around her finger as she thinks how to ask Catherine about a visit. So many times she's hinted. 'When will you be coming to see me?'

'I don't know, Mum.'

'It really needs to be this summer.'

'Why?'

Nettie frowns. 'It just does, okay?' She suddenly feels weak as though the room is pulling away from her. She barely hears

84

as Catherine mumbles something half-hearted and says she needs to go.

Lowering herself onto the settee Nettie feels how its springs have gone. Usually she prefers her armchair but she might as well let herself sink here, her eyes closed, with James's and Tara's voices around her. Really she should tell these strangers to leave, but at least they want to be here. People talk about old folk needing quiet but she gets too much of the stuff. Spaces where memories flood. Sometimes she turns up the television or Radio 4 but tonight she needs neither. Cracking open an eye she sees James is back in her chair while Tara bounces between the kitchen and here, bringing more drinks or bags of Kettle Chips she's produced from somewhere. It's hard to hear what she's saying since the music is loud. What does it matter if they play her record? It was easy to think of a song as your own. To resent other people muddling your memories. Now, though, it's nice to hear it again. A floorboard is loose and she moves a sandal to feel it shake.

6

The next morning voices drift up the stairs. Nettie puts on her earrings though she is tired, the clasp fussy. The night before she lay awake, aware of the noises from the spare room. It was only the occasional squeak but in a way the silences were worse – where her mind filled in the shadowy details: Tara regretting staying over or even visiting at all. She pictured the girl edged up to the wall. She's far too young for James. Too young for anyone except some adolescent to match her own thin limbs and a body she's just beginning to understand.

But downstairs she sees Tara's jumper on the settee where a cushion has been used for a pillow. Relieved, Nettie watches the girl apply make-up in the mirror above the fireplace – she wipes away the dust in one corner to check the layer of lipgloss, practises her pout, then frowns. There's something vulnerable about her – maybe the bare feet with a solitary thread around her ankle. Or the way she smiles at James who's sat at the kitchen table absorbed in breakfast. He lets a spoon fall against an egg so the shell cracks, exposing the white beneath.

'Good morning,' Nettie says.

Tara turns but says nothing.

'Good morning, Nettie.' James looks pleased with himself as he saws off the egg's top. 'I hope you don't mind me eating without you.'

'That's all right.' He's not made the girl anything but left the day's newspaper in Nettie's place, plus the egg box that's been filled. 'You've seen the chickens already?'

'I always thought country life was rather provincial, for the simple-minded, if you don't mind me saying so. But there's something quite fun about this, isn't there?' He chuckles to himself. 'Seeing any friends today?'

'No, I shouldn't think so.'

'That's a shame. It's important to get out.'

After breakfast he goes to fix the roof. For all his knocking about yesterday he's a diligent worker, setting out his tools across the yard. He calls down to say he needs to order more tiles – it's a bigger job than he thought – and they can be delivered to the house.

'How much will this cost?' Nettie asks from the bottom of the ladder.

'We'll settle that later.'

He disappears onto the roof and she sees just the edge of his boot. It seems a bad idea not to agree the amount up front. For all she knows he'll charge a heck of a fee like the rogue traders on those television programmes. What does she *really* know about this man? Still, she's not got the energy to shout up and get him to stop. And things do need to be fixed.

Nettie drifts towards the back garden in search of something to do. Who is James to suggest she needs to get out more? Letting her mind turn blank she pulls at the weeds that are tall enough to reach without bending. Rufus lies in the morning shade. She almost doesn't notice him cock his head.

'What is it?'

When he continues to stare she returns to her weeding, humming a tune. Then she realises: it's 'Edelweiss' that comes from her lips. James's song. Maybe she has been too trusting of this man who's slipped so easily into her home. And now he's brought a stranger too.

Tara is hanging around, engrossed in her mobile phone. It's not clear whether she's had breakfast but Nettie doesn't ask. Apparently her pub shift isn't until later so the girl sits on the chair with her legs stretched out. She chirps on about herself as Nettie wrestles weeds from the ground.

'I won't be working in the Hope and Anchor much longer,' she says, sitting up. 'My mum named me after some actress. I'll be going to auditions in the West End. That's in London.'

'Where is your mum?' Nettie asks.

'She lives near Southampton with her boyfriend and his brats.' She drifts over to look at the well, her nose scrunched up even though the lid has been tightly on for years. 'I either crash above the pub or stay on a couch.'

'That doesn't sound very comfortable.'

'It's not like I can get a flat. Mum reckons Romsey is for yuppies and rich old women.'

Nettie dares to think she's right. Here she is with a large house that's mostly empty and the garden she can hardly look after any more. The girl might well have cause to blame her but she's more interested in her phone that's just beeped.

'I suppose you've got friends to see?' Nettie says.

'Yeah. My mate's got a thing. She'll want me there.' Despite her words, she doesn't leave, only drifts back to the seat where she twists the dirtied anklet.

They do some gardening together after Tara agrees to pull out the lower weeds that've crept among the lavender. At first she complains about the feel of soil but soon busies herself in the task and carefully lays the uprooted plants on the grass. It's only when she edges closer to the oleander that Nettie stops her. Although a vivid flourish of pink, its petals can irritate the skin and cause a rash. When the girl says she doesn't care, Nettie agrees they can pick a few offshoots to prune it back into shape.

Afterwards Tara carries the pink petals indoors. By the time Nettie has caught up, the girl has arranged them in an old jam jar with water, the buds staining the air with their strange perfume.

They're back in the garden when the whispering starts.

'What's that?' Tara says.

'No one.' Heat rises in Nettie's cheeks as she edges round the house, thankful the girl doesn't follow. In the glaring white concrete of the yard she can't see much at first. Then a shape emerges. Small. Hair an electric mass. It's the little blonde girl and she's shaking a spray can while the freckled boy watches. The last message was years ago but can still be seen on a bright day across the house's back wall, behind the weeds she's let grow. The council promised to help remove it but no one ever came.

'Stop that,' Nettie says at a distance. 'Please.'

The girl tests the paint in a cloud of orange. She wants to spray another message of hate, never letting her forget. A line stains the ground. She sprays another.

89

This can't go on. Everything sharpens as Nettie approaches. The girl raises the can, as if to spray her in the face, and she trembles. Swipes an arm.

'That hurt,' says the child, clutching herself.

'I'm sorry,' she answers. Surprised at her sudden strength. She'd merely meant to take the can, hadn't she?

It now rolls away over the ground. Towards the boy, who reaches down. Except she's moving towards him. The yard blurs. Turns hot white.

'Hello?' comes another voice. James appears and looks from Nettie to the others, not knowing what to say. The children run towards the fields and are soon gone.

'I'm sorry,' Nettie breathes, unsure what just happened. She's still shaking and for a second he doesn't reply. It seems he's weighing something in his mind before he says, 'Don't be. You've got to stand up for yourself, Nettie. Or they'll tear this place apart.' He frowns. 'Why target you anyway?'

Still confused over what happened with the kids, Nettie is relieved when no one says anything more. Tara isn't interested it seems. Rather, she sunbathes on the lawn and opens an eye to see if James is looking. He isn't. Instead he calls Rufus and tries to get him to roll over using a series of hand gestures the dog doesn't understand. He merely collapses onto his front legs and won't twist, his body grown stocky.

'He gets too much food,' says James.

She does feed him scraps but then again he's old and there's no point in pretending otherwise. From the shade of the back door she watches the man struggle and grow agitated, grasping Rufus who becomes a dead weight as he's turned. Maybe the pair of them are simply too long in the tooth to change their ways.

After another attempt, however, Rufus pushes onto his feet and awaits more instructions.

'See? He's got strength in him yet.'

Nettie frowns and watches the dog roll again. Maybe she will phone Marianne and ask about that tea. If she's going to organise a fete it'd need to be before the town park gets booked up with other summer events. In fact, there's all sorts to organise and discuss.

'Tea? This afternoon?' Nettie blurts.

There's a pause before Marianne replies. 'I'm not sure.'

'One cup.'

A gentle laugh. 'All right then. I'd like that. Where and when?'

The cafe is all white surfaces with large glass lamps over-hanging the counter, every flake of the pastries illuminated. Echoey music plays and Nettie absently hums along, sitting at the table waiting for Marianne, who's in the queue. A young couple has just come in, the woman pushing a buggy set on huge wheels surely designed to charge down a dirt track. The man trails after her and tries to help. Nettie likes listening to them quibble over what to order. The dynamics of a couple who've been together for years: how each takes a little of the other, always adding to and subtracting from a sense of self. The woman negotiates the baby's position on her lap while the husband goes to order from the counter. A relationship con-tinually builds layers which shift and occasionally break apart, plunging you into boggy ground before the next moment it's great again. You miss all that with new acquaintances. The fact Harold has been gone for more than twenty years makes her feel empty, the memories only kept by her, one half of a locket. Still, she has a new friend to share coffee with. To plan a fete with too if she's lucky.

'Feels a bit like a laboratory in here,' Marianne says as she passes over a coffee in a tall glass. 'Will they do testing on us, do you think?'

'I hope not,' she says, playing along. 'I'm not sure I'd pass.'

Marianne's laugh is surprisingly loud, like a secret trap door within her. She's bought three macaroons which sit in ruffled papers, more artwork than something to put down the gullet. They both stare at them as if thinking the same thing.

'Blow it.' Marianne takes one and bites it in half. 'Have a taste.'

'They're a little sweet for me. But thank you.'

It makes Nettie smile to see her in a different setting. Usually it's just the abbey or the occasional time she'll pop in to check on her at home, usually with the air of getting a job done. Now the woman wears a summery outfit: three-quarter-length trousers and sandals emblazoned with velcro, the kind for hiking or at least pretending you're off to the New Forest. Her face is dewy like she's been in the sun. But something is off – she's cut her fringe overly short, a theatre curtain not fully raised for the play.

'How are you finding it here in Romsey?' Nettie asks.

'I admit it's been nice to have a new start in this parish. You saw my friend yesterday.'

'I did.' Nettie waits for more but the third macaroon is being pulled from its paper. 'Everything all right, I hope?'

'Yes, good.' She swallows an ambitious mouthful. 'Pauline is just a slightly … difficult person. A troubled soul, as they say. We met at my old parish.'

'Troubled in what way?'

'It doesn't matter,' she says guiltily. Then: 'She can never leave anything be, that's all. I've tried to move on to give us both time and space.' She absently fingers the capped tooth.

'Pauline did that?' Nettie is shocked. She can't picture the pink-jumpered woman lunging forwards with a raised hand. Or maybe she can, thinking of how she hovered until the end of choir, desperate to speak with Marianne. 'You poor thing. What happened?'

'It wasn't all her fault. The two us, well, there came a point where we didn't know how to look after each other. I tried to care for her but …' She shrugs. 'It wasn't enough. I needed space. *We* needed space.'

Nettie didn't know she had a female partner. Thoughts of Edith rush through her and she wraps her fists in the spare fabric of her skirt. It's been years since she had so much as a birthday card. But now is not the time to dwell.

'That sounds difficult,' she says. 'There's never cause for violence.'

'No. Well.' Marianne sips her coffee, eyes cast down. A blotchiness is creeping up her neck and jawline. Does she regret confiding? Shifting in her seat, Nettie tries to think of something reassuring to say. The cafe is turning cold with air streaming down on them from a vent. The empty papers rustle. 'I'm here if you ever need me. If she keeps bothering you.'

'She's not bothering me,' Marianne says carefully. 'The woman is just intense. She rings and leaves rambling voice-mails. Emails. Sends Facebook messages. It's a pain more than anything else.'

'But now she's turning up in your new parish?' Nettie wonders what the woman is capable of. Hard to tell, the same with anyone.

'It'll be fine, I'm sure.' She tries to smile, brushing her blunt fringe. A paper falls onto the floor but she doesn't notice and sits lost in her head, receding from Nettie who sips at the coffee, trying to know where to take the conversation next. The cafe is emptying out though it's not yet five o'clock. A few minutes later Marianne apologises and says she needs to go. She's got a few things to do around town.

'Will you be okay getting home?' she asks, reaching for her handbag.

'Ah yes, I'll be fine.' Hearing herself overly stiff, she wants to confide something more. 'James is still here, by the way.'

'Oh?' She perches on her chair. 'It seemed the two of you weren't ...'

'We're hardly best friends but he needed a place to stay.'

'That's kind of you.'

'Not really. I mean, he's fixing my roof so it's not exactly scot-free.'

'Still.'

As Marianne talks about how nice it can be to have company, Nettie realises she agrees. For a long time she's thought herself a solitary person but what's wrong with filling the empty rooms of her house? And isn't James the reason she's sat here now?

'It's like that quote,' Nettie says. 'The love you make is equal to the love you take.'

Marianne looks blank. 'That's not the Bible.'

'No, it's the Beatles.'

Marianne laughs and gives Nettie's hand a brief squeeze before leaving.

Once alone Nettie listens to the pop music as she finishes her drink. On her way home, she finds families in the park and is distantly aware of their chatter as she walks beside the sunflowers that merge in a swathe of gold. Further along the path stands a man; he keeps walking off but stopping, turning to argue with a woman behind him. Some relationships are never quite finished, like trails of spider webs you feel on your skin long after they're wiped away.

Nettie ambles along enjoying the warm air. Past the bowls club she sometimes watches from across the fence. It's only when she's almost on the main road home, she realises she forgot to ask about the fete. Maybe it was inconsequential in light of their conversation but then again it was half the point of the trip. What a silly woman she is.

In the yard she finds the back door locked and – after rummaging in her handbag – realises the keys aren't in the folds of fabric among the tissues and biros.

'Honestly, Nettie,' she mutters as she peers in. The kitchen is dark but music is playing – the same jazz record as last night.

She knocks on the door.

No one comes and all she can see are James's stretched legs with the boots removed. He's back in her armchair although without Tara.

She knocks again but maybe the music is too loud for him to hear. The legs remain stretched, fixed in place.

'James,' she calls.

There's a soft sound as Rufus runs over from inside the barn.

'Have you been locked out here too?' She notices his tail is smeared with oil, the smell of petrol a dirty aura.

Her breathing quickens as she tries the handle again. The

music is muted from outside like it's not hers to be listened to. The trumpet riff is almost indiscernible. She's stuck out here and what if he can hear her knocking? What if he'll keep her outside all night? It strikes her now: he might have done something heinous. He might be on the run from the police. A criminal in her home. But no, it's a stupid idea; if that were the case he wouldn't go wandering around Romsey.

She makes her way to the front door. Past the living room window. She sees him sat in the armchair, his face in shadow. Maybe his eyes are closed, asleep. Or maybe he's looking right at her. It's hard to tell – the mauve cascades of wisteria scratch as she tries to get closer. At the front door she almost doesn't want to knock for fear he won't answer. To know he's keeping her out. She raps once and holds her breath, hand still gripping the metal. Then she goes to bang her fist on the paintwork except the door is opening.

'You've not been there long?' James rubs his eyes as if just woken.

'You locked me out!'

'I did?' His hair is rumpled, the usual grubby vest over his torso. 'I never meant to.'

Seeing him loiter, blocking her way, she gives a testy gesture. 'May I?'

'Sorry.' He steps aside and she's back into her hallway, her home. 'It was the vandals, you see. I heard about the river and thought better safe than sorry what with locking the doors.'

'They're my doors!' she says hotly. 'And I'm no vandal so why are you locking me out?'

He pulls back, open-mouthed. 'Apologies, I fell asleep …'

She wants to say more, hating that he might've planned this

whole thing. But her key is on the hook where she left it. He's washed the lunch dishes too.

He now skirts to the kitchen where he's left out the gin. The bottle is still almost full with an unfinished glass beside it. He scoops it from sight but it's too late. She's clocked him. No one who struggles with drink would manage half a glass before stopping. They wouldn't hang around in pubs either. As she watches him slope upstairs, she realises the whole notion of AA must've been a lie. A ruse. But for what end?

1974

IV

September, 1974

The first time Nettie stepped into the farmhouse she knew it was where they should live. The walls had been freshly plastered and new plumbing installed, while the rest spoke to the place's age with beams of oak and nook-like hideaways for reading. Only a single cottage sat up the road so it'd be just the three of them and the spread of land. By the window a cabbage butterfly flitted and Nettie smiled to hear its wings against the glass. Outside, Harold waited; he'd been humouring her in even visiting after they'd agreed somewhere around north London made sense. This area was much further from his office. But she knew once she called him inside he'd understand.

'I won't be able to do much,' he said, peering down the long hallway. 'What with work.'

'I can handle it.'

When he looked at her doubtfully she showed him the kitchen where someone had left a bowl of fresh tomatoes.

Made him close his eyes and listen to the silence. In that second she remembered him in the dance hall – what had he been dreaming of? She hoped it was somewhere like here.

They moved in the last week of September when Catherine was almost seven years old. Days later Nettie still liked to wander around the empty rooms, imagining their lives taking shape at last. Granted, she had a lot to learn. Even her mum pointed out she knew nothing of looking after a farmhouse, the acre of land out the back or the coop ready for chickens. Nettie was naive, of course, but everyone had to start somewhere. By the second week she had learnt to break up the soil and bought a mower. She started painting the walls in shades of cream and pale green. And if she felt overwhelmed by the work she took a herbal pill and felt better.

Harold invariably came back from work to find the house in a mess, and Nettie streaked with colours, her hair in a tangle. He would crack his usual smile but would be tired, wanting to read some of his adventure novel before tea.

'What's in that book that isn't right here?' she joked one evening.

He laughed and stood up to grab her hands. They danced around the kitchen in their clumsy, lilting way, the only sound their shoes on the stone floor. Dancing like this was a habit they'd formed when words didn't seem enough, and instead their feet slid together and apart in conversation. Their first few years hadn't been easy. Nettie's Bethnal Green flat was cramped with the three of them, knocks on the door of the shared bathroom interrupting Catherine's baths. Some afternoons Nettie forgot the new colour television and simply stared out of the window, waiting for Harold to return from whatever business trip had stolen him away. As soon as he returned, things brightened to a full spectrum of colours and they laughed at the mess of themselves. His crumpled shirt, her eyes sore from not enough sleep. They went for walks through the park or even to a Wimpy bar for a treat. Often, though, they teetered on the edge of an argument: he'd complain of immigrants flooding the area and she'd ask when he grew so conservative. His parents had grown up as working class Labour supporters but he'd started reading the *Sun* and bad-mouthing the Wilson government.

There were other shades to their arguments too. He'd ask why she no longer saw the factory girls or went to political meetings as if the measure of someone was how much they socialised. *Because I'm stuck here*, she'd say, though really she'd not apologise for being content at home. Sometimes she enjoyed arguing with Harold – so much of a marriage was the cut and thrust of an argument, the clashing of screams before falling into bed in a clutch of limbs. It seemed people were most themselves when they argued – Harold's serious side appeared for once, as rare as a solar eclipse. But other times it was simply too exhausting and Catherine awoke in cries that would echo through the building. This farmhouse was their promise to make a better life for themselves. For Catherine.

That night it was their daughter who prompted them to finish their dance. She was shouting from upstairs and Nettie discovered the girl's room strewn with half-read books and far more toys than Nettie had ever had. Catherine stood with balled fists, forever sticky from where she sucked them. The teacher claimed she'd settled in during her first week of school, not counting the tantrum; Nettie had gone to pick her up and, as always, was amazed at the noises the girl produced. At least now she had the outdoors. She could run herself ragged. Nettie was mesmerised by how her daughter swung from the oak tree in the field, how she shrieked into the wind as if grateful to have lungs.

For the girl's seventh birthday they had a little party in the garden. Yet to know many of the locals, they just invited the woman from the nearby cottage and Mrs Gough turned up with a bowl of blackberries and stories of the war. They sat around drinking gin, while Catherine played on her new space hopper, content in the hazy sunshine. It was a relief to see Harold back to his old self. At times since moving here he was strained in a way she couldn't put her finger on. Tired, too, although he pushed on, spoiling Catherine with endless games of chase and boiled sweets which sprung from pockets. That night she and Harold stayed up late, intending to play rummy, but leaving the cards untouched and simply sitting together under the sky riveted with stars.

The next week the chickens arrived, just before Harold returned from the train station. He wheeled his bike into the barn and stared at the birds: noisy things with reddish feathers that turned golden in the light. Catherine sat on the concrete among them.

'Boiled, scrambled or poached?' Nettie asked.

He leant in to kiss her forehead, then ducked down to see Catherine who presented him with a feather.

'All three.' He grinned and held it in his palm. 'Good practice for her.'

'What do you mean?' Nettie said.

'Creatures dying. The cycle of life and all that.' His dad was now permanently in a wheelchair, unable to use his legs. Harold rarely spoke of the man himself but of the family business, and how he needed to learn about the contracts and clients, in a flurry that saw him work long hours and weekends. Even then his dad complained it wasn't enough and the men bickered. 'We shouldn't name them,' he said.

'Why not?'

'It'll be easier for Catherine to accept their deaths.'

Nettie retrieved their daughter from the floor and dusted her down. 'The point isn't to never love something. It's to know that one day it'll die and love it anyway.'

When Harold was late home that Tuesday, Nettie waited by the kitchen window. She'd talk to him and arrange a trip to see his parents whom she still hadn't met. Too many arguments between the men over the family business – Harold supposedly elbowing out his dad – had meant their meeting had been delayed for seven whole years. Shared holidays were not even up for debate. But it was important for Catherine to meet her grandparents, not in a hospital but in their home where things could seem normal.

A distant noise turned into a growl and she ran outside. A large brown car was waiting on the road. It was a Ford Cortina, as far as she could tell. He tooted the horn for her to open the gate.

'I'm about to sign a new client,' Harold said once it was parked. 'And it's time we got out more.'

'Out?' Nettie had thought this house was their 'out'. Their adventure. They had long planned to buy a new car but nothing so large and expensive.

At the weekend she found herself in the passenger seat as Harold steered down the country lanes. It felt wrong to be away from the farmhouse with so much to do, having left instructions with Mrs Gough next door to feed the chickens. But Nettie tried to relax as the hawthorn bushes slipped past. This was something her husband needed and he already seemed different. He let his hands hold the steering wheel near the bottom and chatted about the office. About a new assistant who was really very clever and had some contact at a supplier's.

'I really think we should visit your parents on the way through,' Nettie said, making the most of his good mood. 'Catherine should meet them.'

'And *you* should too,' he added. 'It's just we've got a long journey to Scotland – maybe it should wait.'

'Harold.'

He said nothing as he turned for the Northampton exit and twenty minutes later parked outside a large house. Despite its size there was something overly neat about the place with a garden of shortly trimmed grass and not much in the way of flowers. Even the windows seemed bare.

'I'll go in first to make sure Dad is out of bed,' said Harold.

While waiting in the car Nettie ran fingers through her daughter's hair as the girl squirmed into a hot twist of corduroy. Soon giving up, she checked the mirror for her own appearance, wondering if she should apply lipstick. On glancing out of the window she saw him: the man in a wheelchair by the front door. It was Harold's dad who she recognised from photographs – a white-haired man shrunken but with a hard stare. Expecting him to call her inside she started to get out of the car. But he continued to stare as if not trusting his eyes or else the opposite: seeing something in Nettie that everyone else had missed. She raised a hand, then quickly lowered it again, and told her daughter to stay put. A second later, Harold appeared behind his dad and wheeled him back inside.

'We'll come properly one time soon,' he said on returning to the car where he ignited the engine. 'That way we can make a proper weekend of it. Mum says she looks forward to planning something.'

They spent five days in Scotland, near the caravan site where Nettie had visited with her mum and sister as kids. While Harold pulled out a book at every grassy spot, she ran around chasing Catherine through marshy fields, swimming in the lochs. As Nettie plunged herself under the cold water, she tried not to think about his dad's glare. It was easy if she carried on – doing so much she slept deeply at night. They bought a second-hand camera and took photographs of Catherine to give his parents. They wrote postcards too, as if sharing pieces of their holiday with the family. It was only back home that she began to wonder. In return for the photos she sent, Harold's mum sent their own sets which Nettie framed above the fireplace. Several times she caught herself studying the dad for that same stare, hoping it was something inherent in his features. But it seemed his glare was reserved for her.

V

_____

The soup kitchen was Harold's idea. Or at least one he'd helped to bring about. When she complained of him being away on work trips he pointed out she needed something of her own. Away from the farmhouse, the chickens, Catherine with her endless need for apples without peel and grass stains scrubbed from skirts. A small part of her did miss the city. It surprised her to yearn for the clang of factory machines, the smell of leather and cigarettes on a warm day. And on reading about another cut to welfare spending, she decided it was time to do something.

The local primary school allowed her to use its kitchen and dining room every Tuesday evening. Various people had offered to help, though it was usually just her. She didn't mind. It was a simple enough routine of making soup from any cheap produce she could lay her hands on: potatoes, leeks, sometimes the parsley that grew in scraggly bushes in the garden. She'd judged Romsey a wealthy area but every time a queue formed: many of them elderly and wanting company; others single mums who ate in silence, resenting the handouts they needed. Nettie tried to make small talk as best she could. To enter into conversation about Edward Heath's policies on the three-day week back in March. Or the next round of coal mining strikes. But really, it was enough to put a slice of bread on someone's plate.

One evening in November an unfamiliar man sat at the back. While others clustered in groups, hunched over bowls, he rested plump arms across a newspaper. He was about her age or slightly younger with thick brown glasses. She carried on serving the queue, trying not to mind when he looked up and caught her eye. The soup kitchen was intended for everyone but he could at least say hello if he was going to take up space. Catherine was at the next table along – leant over her scribbled drawings – and she wondered whether she'd been right to bring her. Sometimes Mrs Gough babysat but tonight she'd wanted her daughter close. It was enough that her dad was absent, let alone her mum too.

Soon the man was walking towards her. He was younger than she first realised with a faint scar across his cheek, though the rest of him was smart, his double chin sitting above a buttoned-up shirt collar and blazer.

'I just wanted to say well done for this place,' he said, his voice gentle. 'I saw a poster and thought I'd drop in. I hope that's okay.'

'Of course. Would you like something to eat?'

'No thanks, my mum will be cooking,' he said, blushing.

Not sure what he wanted she went back to stirring the soup. He didn't move away. 'Do you ever go to a group?'

'Pardon?'

'The Young Socialists of East London?'

The spoon scraped against the side of the pot. 'I did.'

'I thought I knew you.' He glanced around the room as if now seeing it differently. The space had become stuffy with bodies, raindrops dappling the windows that overlooked the playground. Catherine was within earshot although hadn't yet looked up. 'It's a pity you left.'

Nettie lowered her voice. 'Yes, well. I'm doing work here now.'

As he wiped his glasses against himself, he blinked in a rapid flutter, then took a breath and leant in. 'I should tell you, there are bigger movements afoot.'

'There always are.'

'The world as we know it is changing whether the politicians want it or not. Like I said, a shame you're not part of it. We need people like you.'

'Like me?'

He slipped his glasses back on to stare at her again. Despite his obvious shyness his expression betrayed something else. 'People who genuinely care.' He stepped closer. 'Pretty rare, don't you find?'

'I don't know.'

'I'll give you my number,' he said and when she didn't take the card from his outstretched hand, he left it on the table. After he was gone she scooped it up along with the dirtied pots and bowls. She had no plans to ring but dropped it to the bottom of her handbag.

Later, Mrs Gough showed up and eyed Catherine, who'd since deserted her drawing and was ambling around yawning. After pointing out she should be in bed, the old woman took the girl's hand and said goodbye. Nettie grimaced when she waved off her daughter. At least she was trying to do something good for the town. The rain threw silver streaks on the pavement and she dragged a cloth across the tables, suddenly tired. She wanted to phone Harold to hear his voice, a need she felt more and more these days. He often told her a joke or something silly from his day but could be short-tempered too. After finishing up she saw it was still raining and was relieved not to have to go home yet. The place was too quiet once Catherine was in bed. Instead she drifted around the school and found an upright piano in a classroom. It was the first time she'd ever played and she liked how the notes absorbed her. If her mind turned to thoughts of the man's number, or her husband away, she played louder until everything had been replaced with a blundering sort of music.

VI

Since moving to New York, Edith had made the occasional visit but mostly sent letters which Nettie kept in drawers with bags of lavender to protect them from mice. The names inside – of people, galleries and restaurants – meant little to her. Edith's latest portrait sat beside their others on the mantelpiece, a poor replica of the real thing. But then Edith telephoned to say she was coming to stay the following week. Her voice rose as she said it and Nettie instantly started to make plans.

She decorated the spare bedroom with the help of Harold that weekend. *You can't just choose the wallpaper based on what she likes!* He'd laughed and she had too before selecting a pale blue design printed with doves, a bird her sister mentioned seeing in the park. The two of them spent the afternoon applying it, struggling to get the wings quite aligned but not minding a slight wrinkle. They spent time in the garden too, clearing away weeds and Harold planting oleander, apparently his dad's favourite plant. On Monday he left for some work conference but promised to get back in time to see Edith. *I'd like to see my two favourite people in the same room!* she said before waving him off.

'What a sweet place,' commented Edith as Nettie showed her the farmhouse: the chicken coop; the vegetable patch with its beetroot and cauliflower; even the wallpaper earned a smile and nod. As they traipsed across the field, grass silky at their ankles, Nettie watched her sister surge ahead, her skirt hitched to show a pair of delicate wingtip shoes. Apparently she and Greta had *gone their separate ways*. So far that was all she'd said, complaining she needed air after a long flight. No doubt she'd later say *these things happen,* among other clichés. Across the crowds at the airport she'd seemed gaunt, like someone else's sister. But as Edith give her a pat and a tight smile, sure enough it was her sister again.

At midday they visited the high street. Middle-aged couples milled around with bags of shopping and family dogs like terriers or spaniels that sniffed the cold air.

'Oh look – a farm shop with proper Cheddar,' her sister said as they strolled along. It struck Nettie that the town was more Edith's kind of place than hers. Despite her travels, Edith had certain standards of appearance and would relate to the women in their floral prints and neat pussy bows, who aspired to shop in Laura Ashley and complained of the new estate bringing traffic. Feeling out of place, Nettie wished she'd brought her pills as they waited in line for cheese, surrounded by wheels covered in thick wax, stilton moulded blue. It wasn't all bad. Maybe her sister could be convinced to move here if her life in New York had come to an end.

They went to a pub. It was the fashionable kind with thick carpets and wet-look mock leather, but it still displayed a picture of the Queen behind the bar. A television showed London crowds filling the streets. Students mostly. Young people with scarves knotted around heads, placards held aloft to show the cameras: *Help for Immigrants* and *Black and White Unite*.

Nettie was transfixed. More often than not, these days she switched off news reports halfway through, unable to stand any more talk of rampant inflation and IRA bombings, Edward Heath almost lost to one. But now she stepped closer to the television screen. To the footage of people pooling into streets with determined chants. Was this what the man in the thick glasses had been referring to? The reporter said the 'spirit of anarchy may well spread', though didn't say where to or how. It seemed unlikely in this pub, which was empty except for two elderly men sat separately at the bar.

Edith had taken their lemonades to the corner table where she perched on a stool. Nettie knew she should go over. But first she dug in her handbag to feel the man's card, pressing its corner against her finger. *We need people like you*, he'd said. It was no doubt a line; he barely knew her.

After gesturing to the other stool, Edith took off her floppy hat, her own little revolution.

Nettie went over. Still aware of the flicker of television lights, she tried to focus on how her sister twisted the glass of lemonade on the sodden paper mat.

'I suppose you miss Greta,' she said, sitting down.

Edith studied the lemonade bubbles that didn't quite rise to the top. 'I do. And our apartment was gorgeous. You should've seen it.'

You never invited me, Nettie thought but waited for her sister to say more.

'We found this little Italian place a couple of blocks away. It sold spaghetti – have you tried that?'

'No.'

'And I was getting to know this woman who worked for an embassy. There was work apparently. Lots of it.'

'So why did you come back?'

'No reason,' she said and twisted the glass again.

'Sure you don't want to talk about it?'

'There's not much to say.'

Nettie sighed. The noise of the riots came from the screen but she couldn't make out the words. She pictured the fists again. Crowds charging in streets.

'I didn't want to leave,' said Edith, speaking in a tight voice. She shifted her weight and Nettie was surprised to see that her sister's eyes glistened, the upper lashes wet, though no tears fell. She'd never referred to Greta as her girlfriend or talked much of her at all. For everything Nettie told her sister she knew little in return. Her sister's knee bobbed up and down beneath the skirt, catching the table so lemonade spilt from her glass. 'I did love her, you know.'

A roar came from the television but Nettie didn't turn. She put her hand on her sister's. 'I'm sure.'

They spent the next day around the house, feeling no reason to leave. While Nettie cleaned out the chicken coop she glanced through the kitchen window to where Edith stood cooking lunch. She had long suspected her sister loved other women. The word didn't seem to fit right for her, though. The women and men who drank in underground bars to avoid police raids, who had started to wave flags during city marches, seemed nothing like her sister.

On the Tuesday evening they ran the soup kitchen together. Not having been granted any of the council funding she'd applied for, Nettie could afford to run the kitchen just once per month. Now she kept her eye on the table where the man had sat, telling herself she was glad when he didn't return. He'd only distract her. The temperature had dropped overnight, and it was a busy day. They focused on making sure the soup spread to enough bowls. Afterwards Nettie asked Edith to follow her through to the classroom.

'Aren't you tired?' her sister said.

The piano was waiting in the corner.

'What am I looking at?'

'I've started to play.'

'You are full of surprises these days. Go on then.'

Nettie hesitated. She'd not played for anyone before. The first note sounded timid before she fell into a slow, lilting melody. It was a song she'd made up or maybe borrowed. A familiar refrain that her sister hummed along to, her voice thin but hitting the right notes.

The next morning Edith said she should get a piano. 'I'll pay – it can be a late Christmas present.'

'It'd be too much.'

'Well, I'd like to pay for half then. I'm not sure how much they cost.'

Nettie wasn't sure either except they were most likely expensive. Usually she discussed all big expenses with Harold, who'd just telephoned to say he was delayed and would miss her sister.

They found a music shop down an alley. Despite being

packed with instruments, it was silent except for a stout man tuning a violin. He eyed them as they walked in but said nothing as they headed for an upright piano.

'How about this one?' Edith whispered, then gawped at the price tag.

The next one was aged with sticking keys. Nettie's attempts to play softly failed with each note.

'Shhh,' Edith said as the man shot them a scowl.

'I can't buy the thing without playing it,' she said and gave it another plonk. *Plonk plonk.*

The man trudged over. 'Can I help you, madam?'

'I'd like to buy a piano. Possibly this one.'

'A gift for your husband?'

'No.'

He sighed as if life's regrets could be expelled through the nose.

'I think I'll take it.'

'To play yourself?'

'Oh no,' she said sharply. 'To cook on, I expect. Or do the ironing on.'

From behind she heard her sister inhale and, flushing, regretted her sarcasm. But Edith hurried to the other end of the shop and – a moment later – let out a great titter.

They cleared space in the dining room and admired the upright.

Still in a giddy mood Edith suggested they sing 'Always in My Heart'. 'Do you know that one?' she asked, gesturing to the keys.

'Oh yes.' As Nettie launched into the song it soon became clear she hadn't the foggiest what the notes were. Her voice warbled over the top.

'The man was right to worry,' laughed Edith. 'You are terrible.'

Nettie was merely pleased they both remembered all the words from childhood. It was a racket but for the next hour they sang tune after tune, neither voice louder than the other.

Romsey train station was near empty the following morning. The waiting room's shadow cooled the ground so they stepped into the sun. All the way here Nettie had tried to find the right words: that Edith could stay a while longer; she needn't go to London now or ever if she didn't want to. It was easy enough to picture the two of them about the farmhouse and running errands in town. There was plenty of space and she'd said how much she liked the spare room's wallpaper.

Her sister was looking in her purse when Nettie said, 'Why don't you go tomorrow instead?'

'No, I don't think so.'

Edith found a pocket mirror and checked her lipstick – a bright red she'd not worn since arriving, a city look, as if she'd already left.

'Just one more day,' Nettie said.

Edith smiled and clicked the mirror shut. 'We've had a nice time. Let's not end things on a bad note.'

The way her sister peered past her, down the platform, incensed Nettie. Why couldn't she stay just a little longer? 'Don't you want to talk more about Greta and everything?' It felt like a box had been opened between them. There was so much to pick out and share.

'Greta?'

'I like that you told me.'

'Told you what?'

'Who you are,' Nettie muttered, her cheeks warming. Her sister looked around them, then stepped closer.

'And what am I exactly?'

'You know.'

'No, I don't. Please tell me.'

Nettie was determined not to be embarrassed by the word. If that's who her sister was she'd proudly announce it to anyone within a hundred yards. 'A lesbian.'

'Never quite had a grip on reality, have you?' said Edith, her breath hot. 'I love you, Nettie, but you should really take a look at your own life before trying to fix mine.'

'Trying to fix it?'

'Inviting me to stay here. Because life in the sticks is the answer?'

'Well ...'

'You ran away from London. From the awkward girl you are. Thinking this would be it. The answer. But let me ask you ...' She took a breath, hitching her bag closer. 'Where is Harold really?'

She sat at the kitchen table, eyeing her husband's empty chair. A crumb was lodged in a groove of the wooden surface. She scraped it beneath a nail. Felt it sting. The table was one of the few items of furniture left from the previous owner and she liked its gnarled texture, the comfort of old stories told in its pattern. But the house's draught began to whisper. And she knew exactly what it was saying.

VII

Nettie watched the countryside shoot past. She hadn't been surprised when Harold hadn't come home the previous evening. It had seemed inevitable that she eat tea alone. That she would be cold without him. Now on the train to London she gripped the seat as the carriage knocked from side to side, as if about to steer off the track.

At Waterloo endless crowds stared back. It'd been less than a year since she left but she felt like a different woman – her gloves torn, clothes shapeless beneath the coat which was one of Harold's. Why she'd flung it on at the last moment before leaving the house, she wasn't sure. A claim to her husband, she supposed. A way of showing this young woman *who* had the real pieces of him. Not just a lighter or a matchbox stolen from a cheap hotel. No, the clothing from his back. Light-headed, she was barely aware of the direction she took through the station, joining the flow of people until she found herself descending to the underground.

Harold's office was as she remembered: the basement floor of a building in Hoxton, a smattering of dirt across its floor. At the bottom, a figure stood on the other side of the window – his new assistant. She was plain-looking but young, with a cardigan pulled over a small chest. Without letting herself think, Nettie strode through the door.

'Morning,' the girl said. A plaster was wrapped around her forefinger. Freckles up her wrists. Nettie studied her for a second, trying to see what her husband did.

'Where is Harold, please?'

'Out seeing his father.'

'Do you love him?'

'Pardon?'

'Do you love my husband?'

'Mr Ravenscroft?'

'Well?'

She gave a quizzical look, determined to understand what Nettie meant. 'He is a nice manager, yes.' Her eyes flicked behind to where someone shuffled. It was a young man holding a thermos and a paper bag.

Nettie muttered an apology before trailing away, knowing the two would later exchange comments on the mad woman in the oversized coat.

It wasn't over, though. She couldn't return home without knowing where Harold was. Could this other woman really be worth all the hurt? As she sat on another train she held herself and wished Catherine was with her. The carriage was near empty – it being just past lunchtime – but a woman stared, then offered a tissue. She wore a smart red coat and matching lipstick, her hair losing its colour but nevertheless groomed to a delicate curl. This was the sort of person she might've become had she not married Harold. But no, she'd always been a weird shrub of a girl. If anything, he'd saved her.

It took another taxi ride before she was finally in front of the house. Already she was worn out and negotiating with herself how many days to wait until she could forgive Harold. It'd started at a month and was already down to half that. Because, really, what would she do without him? He was everything to her. The bricks that built her home.

At the front door things seemed normal, a watering can on the step beside a clothing catalogue. She pushed the bell and heard voices.

It was the woman from the photographs who answered. Harold's mum except with her hair pulled back to show creamy skin and a neck bare of pearls. 'Can I help you?'

'It's me, Nettie.' As she waited for the woman to recognise her, she suddenly wanted simply to come in for a coffee and chat. To pretend she was here to catch up after all this time.

His mum was distracted by someone behind – a voice from the kitchen where a marble counter gleamed. Maybe Harold was there drinking tea. 'Hello, Nettie.'

'Can I come in?'

The woman looked blank. 'I'm sorry, do I know you?'

'Nettie,' she stuttered. 'Harold's wife. From all the photographs I sent.'

'I'm not sure I follow.' The woman clutched the door. 'Who did you say you were?'

Harold's dad appeared behind her in his wheelchair, the same incredulous look on his face as when they'd visited before.

'I don't understand,' said Nettie to them. 'You must know me.'

They were impenetrable. The man motioned for his wife to close the door, which she did, saying, 'My son's wife is called Martha.'

It wasn't possible. She spent the train journey home numbly shaking her head. His parents were mistaken. They were getting names mixed up. Old people did.

How stupid of her not to ask more questions.

Martha?

She turned the name over in her mind. It was a name from someone else's life although it stirred a memory – her mum had suggested it for their daughter and Harold had said no, *not that.*

Nettie was late picking up Catherine who was standing red-faced in the classroom, snot crusted on her cheeks. All she could say was sorry but the words didn't seem enough. At home the chopping board on the side beckoned her to carry on as normal. To make them their tea and maybe practise scales on the piano once Catherine was in bed. She could easily be coaxed into an hour or more of playing, up and down, down and up. In London she was forever aware of the noise she was making but here no one knew or cared.

Martha.

Martha.

Martha.

She first went to the room they'd chosen as the study. The boxes stacked in a pile by the window were crammed with Harold's motoring magazines. Apart from these, there wasn't much else and it sunk through her to realise they were token boxes, the stiff sides betraying their recent purchase.

Somewhere out there he had a whole other life she knew nothing about. Neither did Catherine, like a loose part in the world. Would her daughter grow up like her? No, they'd have each other at least. A pair of oddballs.

Knowing she needed to look harder, Nettie went up to the attic. It was the only part of the house that was Harold's domain – where he stored the things they didn't need for everyday life. The air was dusty and wooden beams groaned as she moved around. Her torchlight found the collapsed boxes from the move, an elderly suitcase her mum had lent them. In the corner a satchel slumped.

The catch refused to open but she tugged, determined not to go another minute without knowing. Finally it relinquished its grasp and she pulled out a handful of papers. Most seemed like work contracts with talk of engines and a supplier in Germany. A set of deeds to the house were clipped together. Except they weren't deeds to the farmhouse but to a house in a village named Little Brington, the postcode Northampton.

For the buyers:
Mr Harold Phillip Ravenscroft
Mrs Martha Anne Ravenscroft

It was dated 1955 – ten years before Nettie had set eyes on him. The satchel lay like a shrivelled skin. She was Harold's second wife by umpteen years. Officially the extra.

After throwing up in the toilet she felt no less dizzy. Sitting on the cold floor she waited to cry and instead realised Catherine had been quiet since getting home. The girl was out in the garden grabbing fistfuls of grass beneath the silvery sky. How would she cope with all this? As an engine chugged along the road Nettie braced herself for Harold but the motor passed on by. Would he ever return? Seed fell straight to the floor as she fed the chickens who squabbled around her legs, feet scraping against the concrete. She was married to a man who'd lied all these years. Who'd never told his parents about their granddaughter although his dad must've guessed. She remembered his glare from the wheelchair that afternoon as she sat dumbly in the car. And Harold had just got back into the driver's seat and carried on chatting with them, his token family. They were objects to collect.

It was almost dark by the time the key turned in the lock and he appeared, his face white like a spectre.

'I'll make us tea,' he said.

'Fine.'

'I know you saw my parents earlier. My mum apologises if she was rude.' He might've shaken his head – it was hard to tell in the darkness and neither of them went to turn on the light. 'She didn't mean to be.'

Seeing him wait, she nodded.

'It's not their fault, of course. It's mine.' He fidgeted with the lid of the milk bottle. Clenched it between his fingers. 'We married too young, me and Martha. She was from the village, we went to school together and we—'

'*We?*'

'Well …' His mouth gaped. 'After the marriage I put some of the company deeds in her name. It seemed sensible at the time, my dad suggested it and I went along. Then when things went south between me and Martha she wouldn't let me end it. But I didn't love her, Nettie, I swear.'

'When things went south?'

He dragged a chair and sat down, hands groping for hers

though she tucked them in her lap. 'It was over ages ago. And yes I should've just called it quits but it didn't matter till I met you. That first night in the pub with you I assumed that'd be it between us but we kept seeing each other.' He searched for more words. 'I haven't been the best husband, I confess.'

'You're a cheater, you mean,' Nettie said. 'It's vile.'

'Yes but it didn't go anywhere with anyone else. It wasn't meant to go anywhere with you except you got pregnant and I loved you, Nettie. I loved you more than was good for me and told Martha we needed to live our separate lives. She almost agreed for a while, then changed her mind. But she'll agree now, I'll make her. The house is no place to spend time – she's always complaining of being alone.'

'The house.'

'Yes but …'

'And you still have that house?'

He frowned. 'We do but …'

'Your home! It's your home. Not this one.' She stood up but didn't know what to do. Harold's fingers trembled on the table as if still waiting for her hand.

'Please say something,' he said.

The kettle began its shrill cry and she closed her eyes. 'Why me?'

'Sorry?'

'Because I was easy? Because I didn't ask any questions. Because I'd feel lucky, a man like you should look twice at me. And you didn't need to bother telling me the truth. I never asked.'

'No, that's not true.'

She felt a sourness rise. Overly tall, clumpy shoes. The factory girls laughing at her, turning away. 'I'm gross, so gross,' she said, wanting to be rid of herself. In the hallway a doll lay on the floor, grinning at nothing. 'Like a toy to be picked up, then put down again when you realise it's broken.'

'You're not broken, Nettie. You're …' She waited for more but he couldn't think of anything. Silence lodged between them. The teacups remained untouched as the room turned cold and she shivered, having no idea how late it was.

'I'd like you to stay somewhere else tonight,' she said, her voice sounding like it belonged to another person. A secretary perhaps. How easy it would've been if he'd had an affair with a young woman from work. How much easier to file away in her mind. 'Should I go and fetch your toothbrush and flannel? Though I guess you have a spare set.'

He looked at her searchingly, then decided something and walked to the door. 'I do love you, Nettie. I love you and Catherine more than everyone else put together. And I'm not going to just leave for ever, okay?'

From the bedroom window she later watched his car in the yard. He'd turned it around, ready to drive off, only to sit for a while. Eventually the engine cut out and she saw him lean against the steering wheel. It wouldn't be too late to go down and ask him inside. Even to make love. But he was someone else's husband. Not hers.

In the morning the yard was empty, with a broken tree branch lying on the concrete. The wind was picking up and whistled through the plumbing. She shouldn't have chosen this house and land. It'd been her dream, not Harold's, her chance to run away from London to this hiding place. Now she needed to decide what to do next. She could phone her sister, tell her she'd been right and ask for some kind words. But really there was only one woman who could give her answers.

VIII

Martha laid a blanket over her knees as she sat down on a leather settee. It was the rigid type, more stylish than comfortable. Nettie took in every detail of the room: the pale blue rug beside the electric fireplace that wasn't on, despite the chilly day. The ledge above with just a single photograph in a silver frame: a little girl on a horse. It was like trying to put together Harold's other identity, an alter ego he sent out into the world. And of course there was Martha herself who fitted so well within the room. A slender woman draped in cashmere, she'd been waiting by the front door as Nettie arrived with Catherine. *We'd better talk, hadn't we?*

Nettie's throat was now dry. She said nothing, only perched on the chair opposite, wondering where Harold sat. Whether he listened to the jazz records by the player. Of course he did. This had been his home since he was nineteen. It still was.

Outside, Catherine's shrieks filled the air as the two women negotiated the silence.

'Well,' Martha began. She had large eyes with spiked lashes, placed within an otherwise unmade-up face. Her blouse, though expensive-looking, seemed bulky as if she'd lost weight. 'I have to say, all last night I was wide awake thinking what to tell you. Now you're here I haven't a clue.'

'You knew about me and Catherine?'

'I did.'

She flared with heat but merely crossed her legs, aware of the chair's wooden arms pressing into her. 'The girl ...' She gestured to the photograph.

'My niece,' Martha said. 'Not ours.'

'Right.' She waited for her to say whether they did have children but she merely adjusted the blanket over her knees. Maybe they had several, all lively things he drew into his arms in a bundle of podgy little bodies. She couldn't be angry with children, though.

'Catherine is seven,' she said.

'Oh I know how old she is.'

Martha abruptly rose, as if to wave to the girl from the window, but edged past and said she'd make them coffee.

'I could never have children myself.' She put the two cups on the table. 'The doctors didn't know why. One of those things,' she added.

'I'm sorry,' said Nettie. 'That must've been hard.'

'Well. There's more to life. Harold was supposedly never bothered.' She walked towards the settee though remained standing. Her slender feet were in ballet-pump-like shoes, fussy strings criss-crossed up her ankles. 'But as soon as you fell pregnant he was giddy. Boy-like.' She clicked her tongue as she turned to the window, her back to the room. For a second it seemed she might be crying. She became very still and Nettie wondered if Martha spent as long staring into their back garden, as she did in hers.

'When did you find out about me?' Nettie asked, her skin prickling. 'I'm trying to get this all straight in my head.'

'I've known from the start, I'm afraid.' The woman didn't turn. 'Harold thinks he's clever and in some ways he is. At school, he was head boy. Good at cricket. Grades to match. He's always been ambitious and not afraid of work. His dad being ill made him greedy, I think. He could never stop wanting things and people rarely said no. He's lost friends because of it. Annoyed his best friend Thomas over some girl. And I've been the one all these years, with him, knowing him.' She turned at last with reddened eyes. 'So yes, I knew all about you. The dancing with your sister. The debates.' Her voice sharpened. 'Such fun.'

'He told you?'

'I had to pretend to drag it out of him but he was eager enough. Almost boastful.'

'Even when we were getting married?'

'You had him there with that one, didn't you?' Her jaw stiffened as another shriek came from the garden. 'Soon enough he was leaving a ring in his bedside table drawer. He'd long stopped wearing his actual one.'

'I don't understand.' Nettie rose to her feet. 'Why did you let it all happen?' It seemed like she was missing something. That she was the butt of a joke. She went to call for her daughter who was now lying face down in the grass. A scream rang out.

*

130

As Catherine cried, Nettie struggled to clean the wound and the grass stains. 'I'm sorry,' she breathed.

Martha waited outside the downstairs loo. 'I've phoned Harold.'

'You didn't need to do that.' Nettie was damp under her dress. Tears stung her eyes as she held Catherine.

'It's okay,' said Martha softly. 'Let's go outside for some air.'

They went to the porch where Nettie sat on the step with Catherine, an arm around the sniffling girl. The front garden had a rockery filled mostly with dandelions that flittered in the wind. Stood to one side, Martha took out a gold cigarette lighter. It was one Nettie recognised as belonging to Harold but she kept quiet. At least the cold was clearing her head.

'We could have Harold arrested, you know.'

Nettie laughed, surprised at the noise. 'What an odd notion.'

'It is rather.' The woman smiled too and angled her smoke away from them. 'You know why I let it happen? Because I had no real choice other than to lose him. He wanted a child I couldn't have. And in exchange he gave me his complete honesty. That's all I could ask for.'

'That's more than I had.'

'Yes but he does love you, Nettie. And the family you gave him.' Smoke curled from her lips. 'More's the pity.'

When Harold arrived, Nettie should've refused the lift home and made her own way except it'd started to rain and she had no more money for a taxi. In the car he was quick to reverse, giving an awkward wave to Martha, and soon it was like old times. Within the car's warmth, Nettie rested her head on the leather seat and closed her eyes to feign sleep. She felt how gently he steered round the corners, the hymn he sung under his breath, thinking no one could hear. Back at the farmhouse she invited him inside.

'Just for a drink, I mean.'

'I need to go back and see Martha.'

'What?'

'Things are complicated.'

'No they're not.'

'Oh come on. If it wasn't for her we wouldn't have this house. This acre of land. Our daughter wouldn't be playing with these chickens.'

Nettie grimaced and turned to see Catherine stare back.

'And it's not like you didn't know. You're telling me you never suspected a thing?'

'No.'

'You never asked me any questions, you said so yourself.'

'I never thought this would be the answer.'

'Oh come on.' He lowered his voice. 'You wanted this life, okay? We both made choices.'

As Nettie scrambled from the car his words were quick to sink in. She'd been so swept up in being loved by him. So shocked that they'd got married she hadn't even looked closely at the man beside her.

'Maybe I should come in,' said Harold. 'We'll eat something. Talk.'

It would've been easy to say yes and feel his arms around her. What was another lie if it made them all happy? But she was no longer able to swallow his words. For once she was saying no and, after sending Catherine inside, watched him drive away, leaving her beneath the darkening sky.

3
2015

7

July 2015

The calendar says it's nearing the end of the month, when the roses need deadheading and vine weevil grubs can infest plant roots.

Not long is left for her grandchildren to visit for one final summer. Nettie keeps ending up by the telephone, tempted to dial Catherine's number. She needs to think of something else to say, though. A fete or event that'll have her grandchildren asking to come.

Meanwhile James has been in the house for three days. She needs to find out who he is. What he wants from her. But every time she tries to ask he's up on the roof, which is now half-stripped of tiles. Or talking with Tara who seems in no hurry to leave either. It isn't as if she has much to steal any more. Only the wedding china but she's hidden that in the cupboard. Plus a few other things like the shotgun – still stashed beneath her bed – and the car.

The car is where James and Tara are now sat, in the barn. They've removed its cover, which lies abandoned on the floor, and are laughing together as he clasps the steering wheel. Stood in the kitchen Nettie can't hear what they're saying. Maybe they're talking about her – the doddery old woman who doesn't know when she's being fooled. The idea makes her face swell, her vision turn blurry so it's Harold she sees behind the wheel, Martha in the passenger seat with a cigarette gripped between pale lips.

Walking outside she taps her stick on the concrete over and over, aware of little else but the sound. If he wants to drive off then let him. It's inevitable he'll leave soon anyway. They all do.

James gets out of the car. 'Time for elevenses already?'

'You can have it,' she tells him. 'If you fix it you can have it.' The car is worth more than what he'd likely charge for the roof. He and Tara could drive off together, leaving her in a fog of dust.

'Nettie reckons I can have it,' James says to Tara who's pink-cheeked as she gets out.

'Seriously?' she asks him, then looks at Nettie.

'If he wants it he can have it. But he needs to fix the engine first.'

James runs a hand along its curved bonnet and laughs, a different sound to his usual chuckle, more like that of a boy. He's taken by the idea and smiles at his reflection in the window. But the next moment he walks back to his pile of tiles and climbs the ladder once more.

That he's not interested in her money isn't surprising. The man has invested far too much energy for a few thousand

136

pounds – telling lies about being an alcoholic as a way to slip into her and Catherine's lives. Pretending he's simply here for some time away. No, real thought has gone into this. She later watches the man from her bedroom window, the scene like a TV show on mute. Tara peers up at James on the roof, a one-sided conversation held by the girl who wears glittery sandals that sparkle as she fidgets. When no reply comes she carries on, auditioning for the part of girlfriend and not getting far. Why James brought her here Nettie can't understand. Despite everything, she wants to offer her lunch or enough biscuits to put a layer of fat over those ribs. It's not the girl's belly that needs feeding though. Tara catches Nettie's eye and gives a half-hearted wave before leaving for her shift at the pub. Maybe later she'll ask about her mum again and remind her to keep in touch. That's if the girl comes back.

A scuffle above is followed by the sight of James as he descends the ladder. At the bottom Rufus waits with his tongue out and soon follows the man's hand movements, rolling across the concrete. He wants to go again but James roots in his pocket, finding a phone that he points at the dog. She finds it strange, this impulse to photograph her dog – Rufus is hardly the most silky-haired creature. Some people insist on cataloguing everything, trying to convince themselves that they own each moment rather than the other way round. The thought holds her until she notices he's turned the camera on the house. Its lens is pointed right at her and she skitters from view.

Back in the landing it's cool and she stands for a moment, noticing how a line of light spreads from her own room but not from James's. His door is closed, unlike on the first morning. Pausing outside, she tells herself not to go in and pushes the door anyway.

The single bed is made, the corners so tightly tucked they make her think of a soldier impressing a drill sergeant. A smell of soap tinges the air and on the bedside table lies a comb next to a nest of hair which sits there as if waiting to be reattached. On top of a pile of clothes rests a notebook. It's an expensive-looking one with a thick navy cover, the type that slows your hand as you try to write something worthy.

After a glance outside to the empty yard she takes the book and flicks through its pages. Only the first few are filled, with what looks like names of train stations, times ... one to Romsey and then no onwards train listed. Catherine's number is there too, plus the names of her girls and their birthdays. Then a line of something Nettie said yesterday, *Memories can be tricky things.* It was in relation to his questions about the car and why she let it rust. Why not sell the thing? But Nettie couldn't think and why should she answer to this stranger? She had gone to bed early and squeezed her eyes closed as he moved around below.

A thought hooks her: maybe he's here for something others have wanted in the past. For years they knocked at her door with tape recorders and supposed credentials from local rags, some from national newspapers too. She turned each of them away without spilling a single word. And yet she's letting this man sleep in her spare room. Inspect the car. Ask endless questions.

Finding nothing else in the diary she puts it back and – as boots tread floorboards – staggers out of the door.

From the bottom of the stairs he calls up. 'I'm off into town.'

'Right you are,' she calls back, unsure whether he saw her emerge from the room. 'Have a nice time.'

'I'm going to see Tara at the pub. Are you off out?'

138

'I shouldn't think so.'

'I'll take the spare key in case you change your mind. It's not healthy to be hidden away all day.'

Once the back door has closed Nettie exhales and goes into Catherine's room. It's where she sits sometimes, among posters of bands like The Human League and Brown Sauce, the rosettes for horse-riding frayed at their ribbons. Her daughter says she should update the space. *No thank you*, she thinks. Sometimes it seems the past can be contained in a room; within four walls, time fixed. It's the comfort of a museum – the illusion of understanding the past one cabinet at a time. Except history will always be in motion, its many versions warped and fought over. Gazing about, Nettie notes the usual stretch of cobwebs, a singer's face crinkled with damp. But something in the room has changed. The rug is at a different angle or maybe the china pot on the window ledge has moved. Has James been in here too? Poking around outside is one thing, it's another to invade someone's room. She pushes herself up from the bed, the metal springs creaking in revolt. Enough is enough.

The phone is cool against her cheek. She's not rung the police in years. Not even when her upstairs window was damaged. They do good work, of course. But it's hard to know what they'll be able to do in this situation. Perhaps a background check on a man who's been staying in her house. She's feeling harassed and only needs to know who he is and where he works. A tabloid newspaper or another organisation? She reaches a finger to dial the number but hesitates. *It'd be easier to explain in person*, she thinks. They'll remember she is elderly and frail and might take pity. Sometimes old age is a card to be played.

The midday sun casts deep shadows beneath the horse chestnuts, their leaves fidgeting in the breeze which is warm and thickened with dust and premature seeds. She crosses the car park to the bus stop for Andover, the local police station having closed a few years ago. Funny that the town has grown, land filled with housing developments, but there's still not enough money for the police.

She hovers inside the bus stand although it's no cooler. The plastic is scarred with the white lines of penknives and compasses, the protests of teenagers without enough to do. She's quick to board the bus and watches the town disappear: the cobbles that look so idyllic, the cluster of mums with prams. Something pink catches her eye – it's Pauline who's hovering on the pavement outside the newsagent. What is she doing here? It's too late to worry, though. Today she must find out who James is. Even a single detail would help.

The police station is quiet except for a fan's whirling blades.

'I'd like to speak to someone,' she tells the woman on reception.

'Name, please?'

Her voice dips. 'Mrs Ravenscroft.'

'Sorry?'

'Annette Ravenscoft.'

Seeing the woman's mouth twist, Nettie shrinks in on herself. People are used to her in Romsey – here she is a shock to the system. 'Right,' the woman says, raising her chin. 'Are you reporting a crime?'

'Not exactly.'

'Providing information on a crime?'

'No. I have a house guest who I'd like information about.'

She stops. The woman's face has hardened. 'Please, I just need five minutes of your time. I don't feel safe.'

'You don't feel safe?' She guffaws and a young man beside her leans across. Nettie braces herself for his words but he asks if she'd like to follow him to a meeting room.

Inside they sit opposite one another at a desk.

She explains as best she can. 'I think he's a reporter. Can you look him up on some database?'

'Not really.' The man is young with a nick from shaving. 'Let's have a go with Google, though.' A mobile phone appears from his pocket. 'What's the man's name?'

She watches as he types in *James McCullum*, his fingers fast. 'There's a few results here. How old is he?' It takes several minutes to exclude various people and then he shows her a screen. James's face stares back in a black and white headshot. He's in a suit. His work history is given beneath: a stint in the army, followed by various finance positions and a senior analyst role at JLT Finances until January that year. Not a journalist or anywhere close.

'Could that be a lie?' she asks.

'Possibly but he's got a considerable digital footprint.' The officer taps the screen. 'Loads of references, links to other stuff. And photos too. Him at graduation with his mum, looks like. Here's one with his dad ...'

'Can I see?'

The image shows an older man stood stiffly beside James who smiles with dimpled cheeks, mortar board at a comical angle. He seems a better version of himself – brightened by the hope of youth.

The officer shows her another, more recent photograph of him outside a glass building. 'The guy seems legit.'

Nettie's confused. 'He did lie about being an alcoholic though. Why?'

The man shrugs. 'People lie all the time. I've been here a year and that's already plain to me.'

After thanking him, Nettie drifts out of the station until another thought catches her – if James left his job in January what's he been doing these past months? She returns to find out but now an elderly man is leaning against reception and the woman shoots her an exasperated look. *Fine.* She'll get no more luck here but there are other ways to dig.

Back in Romsey she heads towards the abbey. Marianne might still be tidying up from Holy Communion and, if not, she could go straight to the vicarage. She knows the woman has a computer and it's presumably plugged into the digital cosmos.

Outside the abbey it occurs to her that Pauline might be here. A heated conversation could be going on. Or something worse. Nettie steers herself towards the door and nudges it open. Inside it's cool, the air flavoured with the savoury smell of tea leaves. She checks but can't see Marianne or anyone else about, so sits down to rest.

Being in church feels like a way to clear the fog of her mind. She is just one woman who sits beneath the stained-glass windows which shine out in powerful greens and blues. While she can't fully see him, she knows how God sits on his throne. Except something has changed. There's a hole in the stained glass.

Hurrying along the aisle she hears the gentle strokes of bristles. Marianne is alone. She stops and stares at the broken shards, the broom limp in her hand. Although her shoulders are stooped she doesn't seem upset. Nettie shakes her head on the vicar's behalf. Someone has violated the Lord's home, all for the sake of a cheap shot, two fingers to the town.

'Let me help,' she says.

Marianne turns and gives a thin laugh. 'It's fine.'

'No it isn't. Who'd do such a thing?' she says, then grimaces. It's not up to her to tell the vicar how to feel. She gestures for the broom and Marianne releases it, letting her shuffle about collecting the pieces. There's a stiffness to the woman, as if she's afraid to move.

'It's quite beautiful in a way,' Marianne says.

'What is?'

She points to the pattern of shards whose deep greens glimmer. 'The violent act can be one of beauty or grace depending on the circumstances. We break up the old and something new emerges.'

'I suppose that's sometimes true.' Nettie feels out of her depth. 'But can we afford a new window?'

'Maybe with some fundraising.'

She wants to mention the fete – how it could raise money – but maybe now isn't the time. The vicar drags her fingers through her fringe as she moves to the table. 'The vandalism is getting worse. Even with fundraising, it'd be a lot of money we'd need and ...' She's distracted by a thought.

'Are you all right apart from the window?'

'Oh sorry,' says Marianne, wiping her face. 'Something else happened this morning. I got a phone call from her.'

'Pauline?'

'Yes, Pau-line.' She stretches the word as if trying to understand it. 'That's the fifth this week and it's only Wednesday.'

'I saw her earlier in town,' Nettie admits, wondering if she should've told her straight away.

'She likes the shops apparently.' Marianne digs in her pocket for a phone. 'Another call.'

'Did she do this?' Nettie asks without thinking.

'Do what?'

She gestures to the window.

'My word. She's not a thug, Nettie!' Marianne laughs but then walks away. 'I shouldn't have told you.'

'Don't say that. I'm sorry I spoke out of turn.'

'No, it's my fault. I always do this. I open up and …' Her eyes glaze over as she thinks, lost in her head as they stand below God and his missing pieces.

They leave the church together after Marianne locks up. Nettie wants to ask to use her computer but, afraid her request will be declined, offers to buy lunch first. They pass kids in a front garden who shoot their hose at an elderly dog, their shrieks cutting through the air. *Devils on earth*, jokes Marianne and Nettie tries to laugh. They'll go to the Hope and Anchor perhaps. Tara's pub. Neither of them have been before and, on reaching the side street, loiter outside. It's a dark kind of place with a smell of beer that wafts from the open door along with the roar of TV screens. A deep red carpet that hides all manner of stains and sins.

Tara is standing in front of the bar talking to a group of balding men in near-matching checked shirts and jeans, a uniform of sorts. Nettie realises James might be there too. But no, it doesn't look as though he's around. Tara lets out a half-hearted laugh for the men before she stoops to collect empty glasses.

'Shall we go inside?' Marianne asks but Nettie isn't convinced she wants to say hello after all. Tara clutches the glasses in tight fingers before she puts them down again and wipes her hands as if her palms are sweaty. Another roar breaks out and the bald heads bob up and down in front of the screen.

Nettie raises her hand in a wave. Momentarily it seems like a gesture at a witness stand. Her pledging to tell the truth. About what? She dismisses the idea just as Tara meets her eye, holding it for a moment that stretches and warps, the two of them locked together in some indefinable way.

Marianne's voice is distant. 'It's not the nicest of boozers, not for the faint-hearted. But I never say no to fish and chips.'

The girl turns and disappears behind the bar.

'Nettie? You've gone all pale.'

'I'm all right,' she says as she drags herself along the pavement. It's tempting to turn and ask Tara if there's something wrong. An argument with James maybe? Why look at her like *that* all of a sudden, though? They hardly know each other, she tells herself. There's no point in guessing what's in someone else's mind.

8

They eat lunch in a cafe, choosing a table near the back. The chips are silky with grease and they eat in companionable quiet while the other diners chat away. Finishing long before Nettie, Marianne then tells her about becoming close to Pauline. Apparently the woman never had many friends but not because she wasn't outgoing. She could be the life and soul, the one telling jokes to a crowd, and people in the parish spoke affectionately of her wit and intelligence. How she could've been accepted by Mensa if she bothered taking the tests. Pauline, however, was a fussy befriender. She spent long periods on her own, not speaking to anyone for days. To an extent it was what she needed – the woman started working in academia and spent time in the library – but often it became a state of depression as she cut herself off from her family and those who loved her.

'When she took an interest in me I was ...' Marianne pulls

a face. 'Flattered I suppose. I'd never even considered loving another woman. Not like that.'

Nettie is surprised by how frank Marianne is being, like a dam has been dislodged in a stream. 'When she acted like I was the only person she wanted to spend time with, I almost felt honoured. Which sounds so needy.'

'We all want to be loved,' says Nettie.

'That's true but arguably I should've known better. It's just, I've never known anyone as intense as Pauline. In my own way I became intense as well. We'd talk till we were blue in the face. Argue over the smallest things, the biggest things. God. The Tories. We screamed at each other about whether we needed a royal family. But I saw things differently when she was around, like everything was in sharp focus. I felt God more too – in the town, in the grass, in the reflection of a puddle. It sounds stupid.'

'No, I know what you mean.'

'It couldn't last though. It was hopeless.'

Marianne invites Nettie back to the vicarage and as they walk together, a queasy feeling glides around her stomach. A part of her expects to see Pauline waiting by the porch but no pink figure looms. Instead it's just the two of them and she wonders if her company is enough. There's no replacing a lover. All you can do is speak into the gulf.

Marianne's computer is in her bedroom and Nettie feels awkward as she pads in. 'Thank you,' she says, noticing the scent of talcum powder.

'What is it you want to do?'

She could tell her everything. It seems appropriate, what with her being in this intimate space, knowing about Pauline.

But it's more than just a tricky situation. One question will lead to another and this woman is her only friend. 'My family tree,' she says.

'How fun. I did mine a while back. I'll show you a good website.'

Soon the screen is filled with various boxes. Self-conscious, she hesitates to type in James's name.

'I'll let you get on,' says Marianne and then she's alone. It takes her a while to get the hang of it, the red text that keeps appearing, but she tries again and is shown a list of people with his name. Born over thirty years ago ... she looks through them and finds the entry that fits.

Name: James McCullum
Born: 1979
Parents: Mr and Mrs N McCullum

No family address or phone number is given and it doesn't seem enough. Next she puts his name into the computer's main search box. A list of words appears, some parts highlighted or underlined. Nonsense really. She clicks on the top entry and a page shows her various James McCullums, one of them a younger James. There's not much on the page apart from some photographs of him as a boy playing rugby and him in a posh school blazer. She scrolls through some messages – the most recent is someone asking, 'Mate – all okay??? Text me.'

Three question marks? She's wondering why the excess when his voice startles her.

'Hope it's not a bother,' says Marianne downstairs. The front door closes and he says something too quickly to hear.

It seems unreal as she edges into the landing where James's sharply combed hair comes into view.

'Here she is,' the vicar says, peering up. He seems agitated about something and gives a forced smile without replying.

As she makes her way down the stairs, her friend explains, 'I thought it'd be nice for you to have company for your walk home.' She turns to James. 'I hope you don't mind me ringing.'

His voice has a forced brightness. 'Well, Nettie would never ask herself, would she? Too stubborn.' He tries to smooth his hair and his fingers tremble. 'Always telling herself nothing bad will ever happen. Not true, though, is it? There are heinous people in the world.'

Marianne nods and squeezes Nettie's wrist as she approaches; she doesn't want to go but can't think how to explain. The vicar passes her stick. Then there's nothing for it but to walk over to James who holds out a stiffened arm, ready to clutch her against him.

9

A pitter patter sounds above. Rain is falling on the exposed ribs of the roof, too many tiles stripped away at once, surely rendering the place vulnerable to damage or rot. The early evening sky is light yellow, the colour of a fresh bruise ready to turn. Nettie watches James from the same spot through her bedroom window. For the last two hours he's been stalking about. Waiting for the delivery of tiles, apparently. It has been delayed *as these things often are*, James muttered as if he has great experience of building work. What a strange fish he is. At times it seems he's looking for something again – maybe the same thing he wanted to find in Catherine's room earlier. A clunk from outside makes her shudder. At least with this man fixing the roof she won't be left to freeze in the winter. She has no savings to draw on and refuses to sell up – the idea of sorting through each room is too wearing. Maybe it wouldn't be such a bad thing if she did freeze but then what about Rufus? The dog wouldn't survive on his own.

After locking her bedroom door, she has an idea: find out how long he'll keep up this act. Downstairs she takes out the bottle of gin. Then a glass for him. A glass for her. His reaction might be the first slip in the charade.

She doesn't drink much herself these days, especially not if she thinks of her daughter. Considering it now, though, she thinks how nice it'd feel to be softened by the gin, to obliterate her mind for a few hours. She has no more clues about what this man wants and is tired of the perpetual worries that hook themselves into her thoughts, burrowing in deep. *Let them be gone.* She pours herself a little and smells the fumes, scented by juniper, citrus and another ingredient she can't identify. The heady mix takes her back to the olden days before she met Harold, when she was still just dancing around her flat alone. Maybe things would have been simpler if they'd never met.

Floorboards creak and there stands James by the kitchen door, the forced grin on his face exposing his small teeth. 'Having a tipple, are we?'

'Let's pour you one, too.'

'No I can't. Remember?'

'Go on. Be a friend.'

He raises an eyebrow, surprised when she pours him a glass. A moment passes before he takes a sip. 'Pretty shameful to encourage an alcoholic, wouldn't you say?'

She doesn't rise to it. Only watches him replace the near-full glass before he heads upstairs. Tempted to call after him, she instead sips her own gin. Of course – the sweetness of flowers is the third ingredient. An image of crushed petals appears in her mind and she puts down the glass, twists it from side to side.

By the time James comes down again she's on her second glass. 'I don't want to drink alone,' she tells him.

'Fine, whatever you say.' He picks his glass up to clink against hers but hesitates and puts it back down. 'Can't drink on an empty stomach, though, can we?'

She makes them both a cold supper of Cheddar and salted crackers, the remaining eggs and ham. The fridge is almost empty, with no milk for breakfast, but she's feeling reckless as she plonks everything on the table. Some days it feels there's no tomorrow, as though a field of long grass is pulling her into its swathes and all she can do is sink back and be engulfed. But now is not the time to be maudlin. She'll wait for him to eat, then start the drinking. It's not clear what'll happen between them but something has to change.

'Take whatever you like.'

He seems perturbed by the spread, narrowing his eyes at the beetroot whose bulbous shapes glisten purplish-red. Nevertheless he sits down and fills his plate. He eats tentatively, in small bites. He starts to ask her something, then stops as though he's not got enough puff. He builds towers of cheese and ham carefully on the crackers. One caves in and he grips the butter knife as he tries again. His hair is less smooth than before. Smears of dust sully his thighs.

'I can't get the dirt off, it's everywhere.' He's repelled by what's under his nails and gets up to scrub them. It's like he wants to run from her kitchen and never return. She half expects him to and her heart shudders. Would she want him to go? Of course she would. Nettie scolds herself. This all needs to stop.

But he just sits down and builds another cracker. She nudges his gin glass towards him and he takes a sip. She pours herself a little but soon he's stopped noticing what she drinks, too absorbed to care. What she's doing might be devious but it seems the only way to needle the truth from him. She bides her time and they munch through the food, both eating more than usual. He's still piling cheese onto crackers so she tips more gin into his glass, over and over again.

'Trying to get me drunk?' he says.

'I suppose I am.'

He smirks – as if to say *try your hardest* – and downs the glass.

Once the gin bottle is empty he stands, rankled by something. It seems he wants to accuse her and is grappling with the exact words. But it's her turn to speak.

'Who do you work for?' she asks, clasping her face.

'Careful now.'

'What?'

'You do that when you're anxious – knock your cheekbones.'

She stops. This man doesn't know her, nobody does any more. She pushes herself up to his level and begins to ask him again. Only there's a bleating cry: a phone is ringing upstairs and James is walking off.

Shoving dishes into the sink, Nettie is growing impatient. The gin has made her woozy and she sweats as she runs the water. In the room above comes James's voice – maybe he's talking to someone about her. *And I'm missing it*, she thinks, hurrying to the bottom of the stairs.

James's voice has sharpened. 'This is just something I need to do,' he says. 'But when I'm back I want to see you. Both of you. Please.'

She clutches the bannister.

'You can't stop me from seeing him. He's mine too.'

As James continues to plead, she trails away and – now overly hot – goes outside for some air. It feels wrong that she heard him upset. Sunlight haunts the evening, a glow across the far corner of the field. Wanting to be rid of the sound of James's voice, she calls for Rufus but no tinkle of collar answers. He'll be off in the surrounding fields no doubt, always such a wild dog. She wishes he'd come and curl around her ankles. She's wondering whether to go back inside when James appears.

He drifts towards her, his eyes not really focused, and stops opposite the barn, a few yards away. Even from a distance she can feel the drag of air into his lungs. He's still recovering from the phone conversation and yet stands in the yard with her.

She speaks softly. 'Were you talking to your wife? I heard you argue.'

'Soon to be ex-wife,' he mutters. 'Ever felt surprised at how your life turned out?'

'I suppose I have.'

A silence takes hold as he peers at something in the distance. A hot air balloon sinks in the sky. 'We were fine for a while, the three of us. Happy almost. Then I couldn't handle it. I hated my job. Hated the suits. The lies, pretending it was what I wanted.'

'And now she's punishing you?'

'I don't know. We punish each other.' He gives a sad chuckle. 'I wanted to be a poet. Can you believe that?'

'You still could.'

'I make notes, scribbles. Try to pay attention. Who knows.' He's despondent, the drink weighing him.

'It's not too late. You're young.'

'My folks would love that, wouldn't they?' He looks at her incredulously. 'Anyway, what does it matter? I have nowhere to go, no one to write for.' His hands fling up, then land with a slap against his thighs. He takes them together as if ashamed, one hiding the other.

She wonders whether to feel sorry for the man staring into the distance.

He acts nothing like Catherine does when drunk. One afternoon several months after their attempted holiday in Scotland, they'd had a conversation where Nettie moved the phone receiver from her ear as the shouts started, painful things that ripped from her daughter's throat. The raggedy sounds of her struggling for breath. Aware that her kids were in the next room, Nettie had tried to quieten her. *We can't just forget it happened*, Catherine cried. *It doesn't work like that.*

Shuffling back indoors, Nettie wants to go to bed but knows she won't be able to sleep. The sight of Rufus's bowl makes her frown. It's still full of dog biscuits. She returns outside and calls his name more loudly than before. In the dimming light James watches as she opens the barn and peers into the darkness which seems thicker than ever. An odour of something wafts towards her and she holds her breath. 'Rufus?'

She doesn't want to move further in but forces herself to skirt around the car. There's a rooting sound before Rufus pads into view. He's panting slowly, ribs showing beneath fur blackened by an oily residue. 'You poor thing.' She wants to blame James for trapping him inside but she is the one who should've checked. 'Let's get you clean.'

James waits by the door. For a moment his eyes glisten before he crouches on the floor and wraps his arms around the dog. Rufus almost disappears beneath him as the man talks into his dirtied fur.

'Lovely to have around, aren't they?'

'Yes,' she says.

'When everyone else leaves, the dog will stay.'

Nettie sighs, glancing at her empty farmhouse. 'Very true,' she admits and walks over to help the man up from the floor.

10

—————

The theme park isn't yet open so Nettie sits on a bench to wait. Without any people around the place feels desolate, the only life a row of saplings in plastic containers. Her head clouded from last night's gin, she thinks of how fragile James seemed. If he isn't a journalist then who is he?

That morning she rang Catherine and Elly, her eldest, answered the phone. Said they were visiting the theme park and she couldn't talk because they were late for the train. *Which train?* Nettie asked but the girl didn't know. Now she waits, sitting in the yellow summer dress she hitched on in a hurry, only to find it was too small. Never mind. Her appearance doesn't matter, only that she finds out more about James. Granted, she can't help looking forward to seeing the kids too. A group of teenage girls have arrived in a commotion of chatter. One elbows her way to the front, dressed in a tatty skirt, leggings and plimsolls with a broken lace. Is that clothing what they call 'vintage' or simply a cry for help?

Nettie checks her lipstick and waits. Minutes pass and the park opens with a crackle of pop music, a queue forming along the railing. It's a warm day with greenfly that settle on her clothing and make her itch. By the time Catherine and the girls show up they seem like a mirage, colours wavering through the hot air. Nettie smooths her dress as they walk over and waits for them to notice. Perhaps it's sneaky she didn't tell them she was coming but then, seeing Elly and Grace, none of that matters. They've grown of course – Elly must be almost twelve and is stretched tall with large, watchful eyes. She clutches the hand of her little sister who still has dandelion-blonde hair and ambles along in trainers that flash.

'Catherine!' says Nettie.

Surprised, her daughter pulls back, tugging a handbag around her expanded frame. 'Mum?!'

'I thought it'd be fun to come along.'

'It's nice to see you but …'

As Catherine falls quiet, Nettie opens her arms to hug the two girls. At first it's an awkward motion but they quickly squeeze her back, their soft hair against her cheeks and the scent of their raspberry shampoo the world's best perfume.

As they all queue in silence Elly peers up at her mum, waiting for the women to talk. Catherine merely tugs at her blonde hair that's become brittle from too many home colour-jobs and soon the girl is distracted by the people behind. It seems they are part of their group; a man waits with three girls, each with shiny black hair and matching striped T-shirts.

'This is Jav,' Catherine says and the man leans forwards to shake Nettie's hand. He has a bright smile and glasses that hang from his neck, along with a pink child's rucksack that causes no obvious affront to his masculinity as he pulls the straps tighter.

'I'll get this.' He steps forwards to pay but Catherine dismisses him.

'No, I'll get ours and my mum's. I'm the one who asked you here.' She's brusque and he recedes into place with a nod, ruffling his eldest girl's hair.

Nettie wonders if there is something between her daughter and this man. As far as she knows Catherine hasn't had a boyfriend in years. The fathers of her children have each married other women, although they're all on friendly enough terms. Is this what people mean by a modern family? A rubik's cube of family arrangements – constantly changing to find the right design? Disrupting her daydreams, Nettie reminds herself of why she's here: to find out about James. Whatever fun she may enjoy now is nothing compared to how much she'd enjoy having the children at the farmhouse, the two girls all to herself for a few final days.

Crowds are filling up the park, where speakers hang from wires and fast-food vans are already open, deep-fat fryers popping with oil. Nettie feels a tugging on her dress.

'Will you come with us?' says Grace.

'Of course. Where to?'

Nettie smiles as she watches them on a ride of plastic cars that spin around in whirls of pinks and oranges. Funny what society deems pleasurable. It's nice to see Elly throw her arms in the air, though. At the entrance she seemed overly serious as if – at twelve – she was already weighted with problems of the world. Now she shrieks with the others. Catherine and

Jav go to check the park's map but she stays and waves each time the girls pass. They don't know what's ahead of them in life. What they're hurtling towards or running from. The job market. Housing crisis. She wishes she had more to leave them in her will. At least Catherine is a good mum. A little short-tempered, yes, but committed to AA and to her family. Nettie now observes how Jav points to the map and Catherine shrugs, before he says something and she curls a hand into his, the shade from a birch tree dappling their faces.

'How does it work?' Elly says afterwards, pointing to the ride.

'Heaven knows!'

'Why don't *you* know? You're the grown-up.'

'Well, if life's taught me anything it's how little any of us really understand.'

The girl isn't satisfied with this answer but, seeing she'll get nothing better, catches up with the four other kids.

As they wander around Catherine calls to them to stay together. They'll get lost otherwise. It *is* a maze of places with paths leading in all directions, queues spilling across tarmac and even a pond of swans that stick together in a puzzle of white. Nettie tries to keep up with the group. She wants to talk to Catherine about James but her daughter is preoccupied with tasks – tying shoelaces, solving squabbles … It feels endless and the air sucked of oxygen. At one point Nettie asks Grace if she's having fun but the girl barely hears.

'Don't worry, Mum,' Catherine says. 'They're always like that.'

'Oh yes, it's fine.'

'Do you want to stop and sit?'

'No, no. The girls are having such a nice time.'

The hill inclines and her sandals scuff the ground. A waft

of wind carries ice cream wrappers and the smell of hot urine. Nettie can't help thinking it wouldn't be like this at a fete in Romsey. It'd be dignified, with fewer queues by half.

'Come on, let's stop here.' Catherine waves over Jav and the girls who peer at some machine with a handle, a clown's face spinning on top. At a wooden shack a man sells toffee apples or at least enormous things covered with chocolate and sprinkles.

'I'll get these,' Nettie tells her daughter and afterwards – as they stand around, the kids absorbed in the treats – Nettie asks about her visitor.

'Is he still there?' Catherine's open-mouthed. 'Seriously, Mum? It's been days.'

'He's helping to fix the roof, only I'm still not sure why he's come.'

'I told you, he's a scrounger. Kicked out by his wife.'

'He said he had something to discuss with you.'

Catherine pulls a face. 'I don't know what that'd be. He stayed on the sofa one night after a meeting and just went on about missing his family. Acted all polite at first. Till I caught him poking around in my bedroom. Pervert.'

Nettie considers telling her about the lies. Him not being an alcoholic. But she knows her daughter will be furious at her for not throwing him out sooner. In the distance laughter erupts as a metal box shoots into the sky, a line of legs dangling beneath. 'Why come stay with me, do you think?'

'Because you're a soft touch. You let people do whatever they like.'

Caught out by these words, Nettie feels dizzy. In her mind she's back watching Harold drive away. Knowing how many years she thought them married when it was all a sham. It's tempting to collapse on a picnic bench but the children are trailing off again, talking about some ride in distant-sounding voices.

A gorilla walks past wearing a baseball cap. It growls and beats its chest but the kids barely notice. They're nearing the top of a hill that's crowded with people waiting for a cable car. Endless people. Endless heat. Then something is digging into Nettie's back. She's leaning against a fence which holds her up and for a moment no one notices as the others continue. She wants to call but her throat is as dry as dust. The next thing she knows, teenagers are leading her somewhere and she's letting them. Soon she's sitting in a trailer that's dark and warm, her swollen feet the only sight.

Catherine appears outside the door and asks the attendants if her mum is all right. Whether she's annoyed or concerned is anybody's guess. Jav hovers behind and tells the kids to be patient. As Elly comes over to hold her hand, Nettie should be embarrassed but merely squeezes the girl's fingers and tries to sit up in the chair.

'You shouldn't have come,' Catherine says after stepping inside as Jav ushers the kids away.

'I hardly had much choice,' Nettie murmurs, her hand newly empty. 'You won't visit me.'

'Sorry but don't pretend you don't know the reason for that.'

'Maybe I don't.'

Catherine exhales and plonks herself in the seat opposite. 'After the accident that summer, what happened on the road, it ...' She shifts her weight. 'It gets to me and I just need to follow the programme steps. Be around the right people.'

Anyone but me you mean, Nettie thinks but knows how her daughter suffers. Four years later and it's still difficult for her to lead a normal life. What price must be paid?

She remembers driving along the motorway that afternoon and playing games with the girls. Singing along to the radio. A whole week's holiday ahead of them. She remembers driving through the village and arguing over directions to the cottage. Arguing over Harold. Everything. Then a jolt of metal, the glass scattered across the road and the kids screaming in the back. The other car with the little boy wide-eyed, red trickling down his forehead, red that surely couldn't be blood ...

A lurch of movement brings her back to the room. Jav is all eyes in front of them. He says he can't find Grace. And then there's a screech as Catherine launches herself out of her seat and runs outside, calling *Grace Grace Grace*. Nettie tries to follow but the park seems doubly chaotic. The clown's face stares back as if taunting her. Red lights swivel behind. She trails after her daughter as the others search.

'Go on without me,' Nettie calls. They already have. She sees just a flash of striped T-shirts as they disappear ahead. Her heart hammers a rhythm – *it's your fault, your fault*. Where can the girl be? Is this the price they'll pay?

Everything turns hazy as she looks down at the tarmac.

She's back on that road. Staring at the boy with blood on his T-shirt. The mum who emerged from the car and struggled with his door. The dad who couldn't even get out, he was too stunned.

Park attendants appear again but this time she waves them away. She's not the one who needs help.

A few minutes later, however, everyone returns to where Nettie is standing, Grace fine as she's pulled along by her mum. The others smile with rosy cheeks and Jav pretends to wipe sweat from his forehead as he laughs with them.

'Please don't do that again.' Catherine hugs her daughter, then turns to Nettie. 'We'll go home soon.'

It's not even lunchtime, she wants to say but remains quiet as Elly picks grass from her sister's shoulder. They amble towards the exit and share a joke about Grace's lightning legs always getting her in trouble. Glad of this reputation, the girl springs about so her trainers flash. Still, they're going against the tide as other families are arriving and slip into single file.

'I'm sorry,' she tells Catherine by the gates. 'I would really like to see you properly. With no heatstrokes or drama.' She attempts a grin. 'We're organising a fete.'

'A *fete*?'

'Hopefully yes.'

For some reason the word annoys Catherine. 'You always do this, Mum. You get these ideas in your head about what matters.'

'I don't understand.'

'I'm not bringing the girls to yours with James there. Not after what you said about him still hanging around. It's creepy. You need to get rid of him.'

'I'm trying.'

'Well try harder. I don't want some unstable alcoholic around my children.'

'He might not be,' Nettie lets slip.

'What?'

'He might have lied about being an alcoholic.'

Catherine is horrified. 'What are you saying? He lied about it all? Jesus, Mum.' She ushers her to the side, away from the others. 'Never mind about fetes or toffee apples or sunstroke. Why aren't you freaking out about him more? What's wrong with you?'

1977

IX

_____

October 1977

It didn't seem wise to leave the house. To venture onto the streets where the autumn wind shivered through the hawthorn. Every part of her body was begging to return upstairs to bed where she could pull the covers over her head and form her own dark world of dreamy consciousness.

Instead her shoes clattered on the kitchen tiles as she put on her coat and hat. The house was overly echoey these days – empty of the wedding china she had long since packed away, along with Harold's wellington boots and jackets and the curtains he'd picked out. Three years had passed since he'd left but signs of him remained: scratches in the wooden counter where he'd shone his shoes; a mark on the wall where the settee was too large to fit and he'd laughed at her mismeasuring. And then there were the letters he sent to Catherine. Notes of things he wanted to tell her, things they'd missed doing together like when he went to Hyde Park and saw an ostrich.

How he'd seen a solar eclipse and wished he could've held her hand. Presuming it was a phase that'd peter out, she'd been surprised when – every few months – the envelopes kept coming through the door. Each time Nettie read them out loud to their daughter and then slipped them in the drawer, careful not to crumple the paper. He asked her to write back and she'd sometimes relent.

Catherine went horse riding.

Catherine has measles.

Catherine fell from the oak tree.

Catherine misses her father.

The last one she didn't send.

It wasn't as if he didn't see the girl. But he claimed it just wasn't the same. Snatched visits at weekends. An evening here or there between his other appointments.

Now, dressed in her coat and gloves, she told herself to concentrate. When he'd first left, trying not to think of him was all-consuming. As time passed she congratulated herself for every day he'd not been on her mind. Now thoughts of the man were dulled things – recycled memories worn at their edges – but today was their daughter's tenth birthday and his absence stung like a fresh wound.

She made slow progress along the road but found it wasn't cold after all. A smell of bonfire scented the air and a trail of smoke curled from a field, the town's clutch of houses beyond. It wasn't so bad to be out. Funny how she worked it up in her mind. Waiting for Catherine by the school gates was okay. So were trips to the grocer's. Anything more, though, and prickles of sweat betrayed her inner chaos.

Town was busy with a thrum of mums and children. The lollipop lady was already out as three o'clock neared and she hurried past the bakery where a pumpkin sat in the window, flesh cut to form a face. The chemist's bell tinkled as she stepped inside and hesitated among the rows of shelves packed into the small room. Ointments, soaps, pumice stones ... So many things to fix the body's endless grievances. The herbal section was arranged in its usual powders and bottles of tonic. But the pills weren't there.

'Where are your Herbal Health pills?' she asked the boy behind the till.

'We're expecting a delivery later. It'll be an hour or so.'

She checked her watch but remembered it'd stopped and she still hadn't replaced the battery. 'I'll be back. Please don't shut early.'

Outside the school other mums were chatting. Something about an immigrant family who'd supposedly got a home with no questions asked. Nettie stepped onto the grass verge where she wouldn't have to listen. She no longer read the newspapers with their headlines on the rise of the National Front, which was setting up groups across the country. Instead the television babbled away as Catherine watched show after show, refusing to do homework until after *Doctor Who*. Nettie hardly minded. It felt easier not to read every article or left-wing pamphlet as she once had.

'Happy birthday, my sweetheart!' She wanted a hug but her daughter no longer tolerated such things so she settled for a kiss. 'Did you have a nice day?'

'Where is Dad?' the girl huffed.

'You'll see him very soon.'

Mud stained her skirt like a pattern of its own. Last week Nettie had been asked into school to talk about her daughter fighting with a little boy. It wasn't clear who pushed whom and Nettie hadn't known what to say. To apologise or to insist on no more slaps of the cane. Once again she felt like a girl masquerading as an adult and thought of her own mum's performance of smudged lipstick and hands on hips.

They went back to the shops with Catherine dragging behind, bumping her satchel against her knees. Nettie was sorry to see her scowl, especially on her birthday. The last time she'd seen Harold it'd been at his house. She had meant to only see Martha, who was helping Catherine with maths homework, but he'd been outside washing the car. The encounter was surprisingly painful for a reason she couldn't understand. That his hair was thinning maybe – the strands gradually falling out and lost. She'd waited while Catherine said goodbye to them both but wouldn't step inside even when he asked several times, wringing the sponge. If it was their daughter he wanted to see, she judged there was no point in placating him for the sake of manners.

They hurried down the high street to find the chemist closed. Paint flaked off the door as she banged but no one answered. A whole weekend with no pills. At home she dug into the deepest recesses of her handbag, hoping to find a spare bottle. Instead a card fell out – the one from the man who'd visited the soup kitchen with his nervous smile and talk of social change. She clutched it in her palm as she hovered beside the telephone and then began to dial.

X

The pigeons picked over the cobbles, wings tight against their bodies. Really she should be sat in the pub rather than out here with her ale. King's Cross wasn't an area where a woman waited alone but it was crowded indoors with smoke choking the air. So she stayed on the bench, peering along the alley where the shadows of birds merged into a black pool.

She'd learnt the socialist's name was Winston (*after Churchill himself, would you believe?*) but he called himself Sam. He was teaching social politics at a polytechnic in north London and living with his mum. It'd been an awkward conversation, her ringing out of nowhere like that. He'd assumed she was someone from the council and she took a while to explain herself. At the end, though, he'd invited her out for a drink or two that Friday afternoon.

She wrapped her coat tighter. They should've met somewhere more central except she'd insisted it was fine to come here. *I used to live in the East End*, she'd told him. Now she was self-conscious and doubting the long skirt that rose up in the wind. The peach thick on her lips and the hat she clutched over her hair. Earlier in the pub toilet's mirror she'd assured herself the outfit was fashionable enough, attractive even. But as she turned to leave, she saw it as an odd assemblage of parts. Nothing quite wrong. Nothing quite right.

Some minutes later – she hadn't yet fixed her watch – Sam appeared along the alley. Another man was with him, taller and wearing a serious expression as they strolled towards her. Had she misunderstood in thinking this was a date? Was she too old for such a thing?

'Hello, Annette, this is my friend Christopher.'

'Hello.'

They stood like two schoolboys with windswept hair and hunched shoulders. Only Sam's glasses – mended on one side with tape – pegged him at his real age, surely no younger than forty. His unwashed shirt and trousers made him look like a fisherman and, remembering his previous smart outfit, she wondered whether this was how socialists were now supposed to dress. Christopher announced he'd stretch to some drinks and pointed to her half-drunk ale.

'Oh no, I'm fine, thanks.'

Once his friend had gone into the pub, Sam sat down opposite. 'I hope you don't mind me bringing him. He was at a loose end.'

'Of course not.'

'I was surprised when you rang,' he said. 'Nicely surprised, I mean.' The correction spoke of a mother's influence. He attempted a smile directed at the pigeons who gathered closer.

'Well thanks for meeting me,' she said and grimaced. It was

she who'd come all this way – having left Catherine with Mrs Gough next door. The old woman had told her to go and have some fun. *It's not healthy to be cooped up all the time. It puts you on edge.* Had she meant people in general or just Nettie? Mrs Gough must've noticed the way Nettie's hands trembled these days, how her smile was nothing more than the pulling of lips over teeth. It was time to move on. And surely with someone who shared her politics. Even if he had brought another man with him.

Christopher returned with two pints of ale and complained of the price rising since last week. After sitting beside Nettie he took it upon himself to inform her of the socialist situation, as if he'd earlier been instructed by Sam. There was in-fighting among the Trotskyists, with factions forming around different leaders. He rattled off names which meant little to her except the odd one like Tariq Ali. When she looked at him blankly, he was staggered at how little she knew and continued his monologue. Sam listened too, though after a while went to roll a cigarette. His hands were so careful with the paper, it was like he was creating artwork. From the corner of her eye Nettie watched him release wisps of smoke.

'Are you listening?' Christopher asked.

She tried to concentrate on what he said but the whole thing reminded her of the men at the socialist club puffing themselves up in their shirts.

'… And really we need our own manifesto. Then we can start a journal. I've been thinking of names too—'

'I don't know what you mean,' she interrupted. 'As in, I don't understand any of this. And if I don't understand how can you expect anyone else to?'

He scowled before he seemed to decide something. He laid

his arms on the table. 'Look – all any of us have got to understand is that we've been sold a lie. The idea we now live in a classless society where anyone can be what they want. Cover your face in make-up and you're some space oddity? Buy a colour TV and we're all equal? It's ridiculous. The disparity of wealth is as bad as ever. Everything is blamed on the poor, the immigrants. Nothing ever changes.' He shook his head. 'At the last election the National Front almost gained a seat. They've got fancy headquarters. They're probably sitting there right now planning their next rally.'

Nettie nodded. Deep down these things needled her too.

Christopher took her silence as an affront, so downed the rest of his ale and stalked back towards the main street.

'Sorry,' said Sam afterwards.

'No, he's right in a way. I do need to get more involved.'

'Really?'

'It's been easier not to. To concentrate on the everyday. But I need to do more.'

'Well, there are all sorts of meetings, leaflets, journals to write for even. A march is happening next month.'

She laughed. 'A march? It was hard enough coming here for a drink.'

'Oh well, it was just an idea.'

After they finished their ales he said he'd walk her to the station. She had assumed they would stay for at least a couple more. This was supposed to have been the beginning of a new phase of her life away from Harold. A better man to love. Once again words failed her and she rose from the bench.

'I shouldn't have brought him,' Sam said as they took the

long way round the railway arches. 'I thought you were interested, that's all.'

'I am interested. I told you I was.'

Fiddling with her hat's brim, Nettie wondered why she'd not followed the news more. The previous weekend she'd spent the whole time at home, trying to sleep or walking around in a stupor, willing away the headaches. First thing on Monday morning she'd gone to the chemist and, after stocking up on the herbal pills, felt so elated she'd bought the new skirt and hat. As if these were the things that mattered.

They passed a crumbling brick wall where someone had painted the words, EAT THE RICH. Was that her now? No, she could barely afford a new washing machine although her lifestyle was, arguably, middle class. They got to the station and headed towards the stairs for the underground. Nettie wasn't ready to go home and slowed, trying to think of a reason to stay. The daylight was fading but plenty of people milled about. Men slick in leather and studs. A woman clutching a guitar like a lover.

'I want to go see them,' she told Sam.

'Who?'

'The National Front.'

He looked blank and steered them away from a group of teens.

'I just want to see their headquarters, that's all. I'm curious.'

Although reluctant, Sam agreed they could get the bus to Shoreditch for the sake of seeing the building. Her old number 16 was waiting and she hopped on before he could change his mind, then climbed to the upper deck where the city waited in its towering silhouettes: cranes beside new office blocks, factories with chimneys and – somewhere beyond – the canal.

'I was planning to have an early night,' Sam said with a gentle smile.

She could've felt embarrassed but was only pleased to be out with someone. A rumbling heat rose around the bus as Sam spoke about his work and admitted he didn't much like teaching politics.

'It was supposed to be this great calling,' he said, a blush filling his large cheeks. 'A way to make the world better some day.'

She touched his arm. 'You already do.'

They reached Great Eastern Street and he showed her the way. The National Front headquarters were in a four-storey building that seemed overly respectable. So this was where they assembled to discuss their campaigns against anyone not born in the country, to decide on the figures with which they'd fill their newspapers, which cropped up in cafes and bus shelters. Nettie peered through the dark windows, hoping to see something to help her understand. But all she saw were stacked chairs and a broom left in the middle of the floor. She went to the entrance.

'What are you doing?' asked Sam, startled.

She tried the handle. 'It's locked.'

'Let's get out of here, please?'

Not knowing what else to do, she took a final look at the doorway and followed him along the road. He was heading towards Brick Lane. Night had fallen but it wasn't dark, the streetlights giving the shopfronts a tinged sepia look. A pram had been deserted by a pile of rubble, a woollen cardigan left inside. They carried on and he suggested they find somewhere quiet for a drink.

'All right,' she said, her mind still on the building. How

the city was changing at such a pace, a mosque opening and age-old businesses closing, but how not everyone wanted these changes. Paint was streaked across a corrugated metal shopfront and she was afraid to read its message. Around a corner, the yeasty smell of a brewery hung while a group of male students argued outside a pub. With another place in mind, Sam gestured along a side street. 'It's a friendly one,' he promised. 'Has a piano and everything.'

They headed for the green-painted front where lanterns glowed and a man on the pavement stepped back to let them pass. 'Evening,' he said.

'Hello,' they replied.

'Fancy something to read with your pint?'

The newspaper he offered was emblazoned with the words: National Front.

'No I don't, thank you,' said Sam before they hurried to the door, then hesitated. Through the window, they saw the pub was empty apart from a dozen men around a table. They were smiling at each other, many young with hair cut close to their scalps. Braces pulled over white shirts. An older man sat with them and nodded thanks as someone passed around a packet of peanuts.

Sam's voice was low, 'Look at them, just sitting there. Bet the barmaid's too scared to ask them to sling their hooks.' He shook his head, cheeks quivering. It was the same intense expression he had worn the night he came to the soup kitchen.

'How can they be so brazen?' was all she could say. They went to leave but she stopped. It wasn't enough to just walk away and, before letting herself think, she opened the pub door. The men looked up. The old man's face creased with a smile.

'Yes, love? You lost?'

'No.'

'Then what?' The place went quiet.

'Bunch of fascists,' she said and turned on her heel. The next thing she knew, she and Sam were running down the street laughing, air whipping at their clothes. Around the next side street, they carried on before he pulled her into a doorway. After he checked to see if they were coming, finding the road clear, she drew him in for a kiss. His mouth was wet with breath, cheeks overly smooth against her hands. It was off-putting somehow but she carried on.

'Hold on,' he said. Footsteps were slapping at the ground and voices calling but no one reached them. Instead the skinheads had met the other group of male students who'd now spilt from their pub. Sam ran towards them as punches were thrown. It was hard to see what was happening. A couple of skinheads grabbed a young guy and spat on his shoes, only for the rest of the men to rear up. Suddenly someone had a chair and a smashed glass. Sam went to help a lad who'd fallen while she froze in place, yards away. She should be helping, she knew, but it appalled her how animalistic it seemed. The sound of a kick to someone's middle, the skitter of boots. Soon a man came out and announced he'd phoned the police, prompting everyone to flee. As the older man staggered past, Nettie saw his hearing aid had been ripped loose. He gave her a wide berth as if not wanting any more trouble. Maybe he'd not wanted trouble in the first place.

They later crept through Sam's darkened house, a terrace where a woman was asleep on the front room's settee. Feeling ashamed of herself, all she wanted was to slip off home to

Catherine and feel the child's hair against her face. The last train had already left, though, and Sam agreed she could stay at his. He'd seemed shaken on the bus and said little.

'My mum will be peeved if she's woken,' he whispered as they climbed the stairs.

His bedroom was simply decorated with a typed poem stuck on the wall. It was missing its 'e's, the typewriter missing the letter. Some battered shoes were left in a neat row beside the single bed. She took off her gloves and saw her hands bare of the wedding ring. The sight made her eyes itch.

'Thanks again,' she said to Sam who was perched on his bed.

'Are you with anyone?'

'Not really.' She sat beside him. 'I mean, no. Not any more. Although we have a daughter.'

Sam opened his mouth but let it fall shut again. Instead he drew together his thighs, clasping his hands between them. He then turned on the radio – the tail end of a Bob Marley song was followed by the announcer reading the news. Undertakers were going on strike in London, causing a pile-up of unburied bodies.

It was plain Sam and Nettie wouldn't make love and, relieved, she slipped off her shoes and lay back on the bed. The evening had been supposed to go so differently but it didn't matter. Even if Harold had another someone, she couldn't. It seemed a basic fact now, like how night followed day.

'I don't know what I was thinking tonight,' she confessed. 'I thought with a different man I'd be a better person. Everything would be better.'

He watched her for a moment, then lay down too. 'See that poem? It's one Christopher typed out before he fixed his typewriter. He didn't even mean it as a gift, just left it on the table. It's the first verse of *Howl* by Alan Ginsberg. About creating a fairer society. I told myself I kept it all these years because it was an important poem. But really, I kept it because Christopher typed it out.'

'So …'

'So sometimes it's less about someone's particular choice of politics. More about how they are deep inside. The love they give you.'

She laid her head on the pillow and they both settled down to sleep in their clothing, the house warm, a branch skimming against the window. An hour later, though, she was still awake and thinking of the only voice she wanted to hear. Her chest tight, she crept downstairs to where the phone sat in the hallway and turned the dial.

Harold's voice was groggy. 'Hello?'

'It's me.' She was surprised to hear herself so faint. 'Sorry.'

'Sorry for what?'

Pressing her mouth into her shoulder, she tried to muffle the tears but it was like trying to stop the rain.

Harold was waiting in the driveway the next morning. 'I was worried,' he said, following her to the back door. It made her feel grubby to know she'd telephoned him. All she wanted was to scrub herself clean of the make-up and forget the previous evening.

'Good morning, Mrs Gough,' she said.

Without turning, the woman clattered about, shoving breakfast dishes in the sink.

'I saw him waiting.' The woman gestured to Harold who stood inside the door. 'In that car for ages he was.'

'I didn't know if I should come inside,' Harold said, amused by this hostile reception. 'Although I do still have a key.'

Nettie went to find Catherine and stiffened to hear him follow her into the hallway. The man did still make payments for the house. Put money in their post office account every week. It was for their daughter's sake but of course she benefited from it. From Martha, and from the family business that had expanded this past year. 'You didn't need to come at all.'

Harold placed his jacket on the hallway chair. 'You were upset and ...' His voice was half-swallowed. 'It's up to you who you see. But whoever it is, well, I hope he treats you well.'

She began to correct him but noticed him looking up; a series of buzzing sounds came from Catherine's bedroom where she was playing Operation.

'Can I see her?' His face broke into a smile. 'I have something for her birthday.'

He produced a cardboard box from his car boot. A series of miaows escaped from it. A ginger kitten pawed at the side and yawned as he held it in his arms. Catherine wasn't sure at first and stayed back.

'It's a lot of work,' Nettie told Harold.

'Not really. Cats mostly look after themselves. They're pretty selfish really.'

As Catherine dared give it a pat, Nettie knew this was the moment she'd have to decide whether they'd keep him or not. Suddenly the decision was too much. She just wanted to watch as Harold held it easily across his wrist, this sharp-toothed creature a kindred spirit, its ginger hair like wildfire.

XI

It was the kitten that, six months later, was the undoing of Nettie's contained home life. After tumbling over the animal she fractured her ankle and knew she'd need help around the farmhouse. A day passed before she telephoned Harold. She'd hoped her mum or sister would be free but no luck.

'It won't be for long,' she told him on the first morning as he stood in the kitchen. Time had slipped back on itself. His very presence was large and she was reminded of first meeting him. He was arguably as confident, though in the odd moment his body betrayed him. His walk was heavier and when he stood by the window she saw the lines on his face – not just those from smiling but indents across his forehead too. Perhaps they were marks she'd left. His body a map of her own pain.

After rolling up his sleeves he went straight out into the field. Nettie watched how he carefully turned the mower before he began each line. How he wore a serious expression and didn't stop even when the April wind threw the grass up in his face. For another few minutes she watched and then forced herself to go into the living room. She wasn't used to not being busy. There was always something to do around the place or a call from Catherine's school to bring in her gym kit or, occasionally, to learn about another fight; the boy called Joseph taunted her for supposedly having no father. *It can't go on*, said Miss Julie. *No*, said Nettie but without a clue how to punish the child for the pink marks she left on the boy's face.

Now lacking anything to occupy her she sat in the armchair and listened to the house. To the scuffles in the yard as Harold cleaned out the chicken coop. To starlings making nests on the roof. How long would the man stay? She thought of him sleeping in the house that night. Of bumping into him on the landing. Ex-partners weren't supposed to return, a ghost in the household machinery.

At around midday he came in to make coffee.

'Want one?' he asked.

'No thank you,' she said, though her mouth was dry.

'You need a new blade, you know.'

'Pardon?'

'Your mower.'

'Oh. It's been fine so far.'

'Well it isn't going to last much longer.'

He later went to school to collect Catherine, who returned unusually sanguine as she held his hand, something she never allowed Nettie to do. Apparently the girl had kept out of trouble for the day and now presented her with a flyer. It was for a school production of *The Sound of Music* in ten days' time.

'You need to come, Dad,' she said and showed all her bottom teeth in an ape-like smile.

'When is it?'

'The 17th of April.'

He glanced at Nettie, who was still in the living room. 'I'm not sure if I'll be here or not. I might have a business appointment that day.'

'A business appointment?' Catherine puffed out her cheeks. In her pulled-up white socks and tartan dress she looked like a sweet little girl who, after all, only wanted both parents to come to her school play.

She turned to her mum, who said, 'Maybe if he's still here.'

Her face lit up and, with a grin, she went clattering upstairs. Nettie and Harold exchanged glances. Who knew how long it'd take for her ankle to heal. It throbbed as they later watched television – Catherine sat beside her dad on the settee. It was *The Goodies* and the two of them laughed at the men flouncing about in their dungarees. After a while Nettie laughed along too. They were singing their song about funky gibbons.

The house felt different with Harold around. Nettie became more aware of herself. Of the soap nubs by the sink she planned to press together. Of strange little habits like how she used an egg timer that only counted a minute, so she continuously needed to reset the thing. Harold often watched her with a faint smile on his face but when she whipped round to ask what he was doing, said nothing. He, in turn, was frustratingly comfortable about the place. He and Catherine soon formed a routine. In the mornings he had her breakfast waiting: soldiers and an egg, the top already removed. Upstairs the spare bedroom was full of him, too – the latest Wilbur Smith novel left open on the rug, the scent a mixture of musk and dried grass that no chemist could bottle. Nettie lingered outside on her crutches. Really she should open the window to air out the place. It was too much to hobble over though. She was supposed to be resting.

The next day he left without saying where he was heading. Surely back to Martha, Nettie thought. Her deep breathing made her dizzy so she ignored the throb in her ankle as she went around opening every window. In streamed cold air till the doors rattled in the draught and it felt like the whole house was convulsing. When Harold returned she didn't say anything and neither did he. After taking off his jacket he merely laid an object on the table. It was her watch and it was ticking again.

Nettie wasn't sure how grateful to be towards Harold. He seemed to be doing everything right. That was until Saturday morning when she woke to hear voices in the hallway. Martha was here. Had he invited her? The two women had been civil over the years, exchanging small kindnesses in a careful sort of economy – complimenting the other's clothing or swapping weekends of childcare. They never spent time in each other's homes though, a threshold not to be crossed.

Frustrated at the thought of them standing in her kitchen, Nettie made her way to the top of the stairs.

Mostly it was low whispers except for the occasional soprano.

'All I wanted was for you to look at the brochures,' Martha said.

'There's no way.'

'And what about Teddy? Are you going to explain why you won't see him marry?'

'Teddy shouldn't organise such a last-minute wedding.'

The two carried on talking, with Harold trying to extricate himself from the arrangements of who'd drive to the airport if not him, Martha without her licence. Although Harold still insisted they were getting a divorce, there was no easy way to cut all the threads that bound one person to another. Hearing the woman's voice climb in pitch once more, Nettie returned to her bedroom.

After Martha had gone she found Harold in the kitchen holding their daughter on his lap. She was dressed in a mis-matching outfit of brown corduroys and a yellow frilled top, a Brownie gone wrong. The girl was, again, asking him to the school play and he was making light of it, pretending he had all sorts of other things to do. *Lion taming. Or sailing the great seas.* Their daughter laughed along, humouring him, until she eventually puffed out her cheeks, demanding an answer. He said he was supposed to be at a wedding but didn't want to go. *So you'll come?* She gave a pleading grin. *Whatever you say, missy.*

Noticing how Catherine danced around when Harold was near, putting her hands on her hips or showing him the leaps from gym class, she wondered at these new codes of femininity. If girls these days were in fact changing and growing stronger like the women who set off stink bombs in the Royal Albert Hall or railed against their factory pay. What did it mean to be strong, though? To hike yourself up a tree? To slap a boy around the chops? In a way it seemed like nothing had changed as she watched how self-conscious Catherine was. But Nettie could hardly be critical. She too found herself acting differently when Harold was around.

*

186

Over the past few days she'd barely been outside. On the Saturday night, Harold was watching television with Catherine. They spent too much time that way, as though the television was a god who offered flashing lights and tunes at the sacrifice of hours that'd pass without notice. In the yard Nettie went to fetch a handful of grit for the chickens and the cat followed. 'Leave them alone,' she told the animal, making sure it didn't slip through the wire. The thing often prowled about the yard – a ginger flash on the barn roof or along the guttering. Harold's promise of it catching mice was, at least, fulfilled and Nettie would find little offerings by the back door, a shiny bladder or spleen revealed in a messy biology lesson. This time the cat wasn't interested in the cage and instead rubbed its body against her leg. As its silky fur sent a shiver through her she didn't like to think how long it'd been since someone touched her apart from that kiss with Sam. The cat rubbed itself again, then sunk a claw into her calf.

'Honestly,' she said and hobbled back inside. She'd not watch television but have a bath. Arguably the hot water wasn't good for her swollen ankle but the rest of her needed a soak and she'd always treated baths as a form of ablution, as though certain things could be scrubbed away. Thoughts of Harold perhaps. The cat's fur against her skin.

In the bathroom lay Harold's bar of soap, plus the striped towel he'd brought with him. The mat was patterned with two large damp footprints from his recent bath. She edged it to one side and thought of Martha, wondering what she was doing tonight. Her brother's wedding was the following week but Harold insisted he'd come to the play. Not everyone could be happy, she supposed, as if the world only had so much joy and it needed to be doled out in strict portions.

Taking off her clothing, she sat in her knickers to unwrap the bandage from her ankle. The other one had swollen from bearing too much weight. She tried perching on the bath's side to run the taps but the twisted movement was difficult.

'Everything all right up there?' called Harold from downstairs.

'Yes – fine!'

'Sure?'

She'd not locked the door and now, reaching for her dress, felt a sudden thump that sent a hot burst through her. Shocked to find herself splayed across the bathroom floor, she could only listen to the approaching footsteps.

'Nettie? I'm coming in, okay?'

She didn't reply. The mat was bundled to one side. It would've stopped her slipping but she'd been too proud and now he was helping her up and onto the chair. Her breasts sagged as she leant forwards but all she could focus on was not crying.

'Don't be embarrassed.'

His own hair was still damp with little curls at the bottom as he leant across to feel the water. She went stiff as he put his hands under her armpits, fingers pressing into her. The water was too hot or maybe that was just her body, squeamish as she unbent her legs like a child with a parent. It seemed she should cover herself but there were no flannels around and Harold found the sponge and began to wash her back, water gliding over her shoulders. He said nothing as her cheeks dampened with hot salted tears.

'I wasn't with Sam,' she said. 'We're just friendly.'

'Oh,' he said and carried on sponging her arms.

Later he returned to the television with their daughter while

Nettie sat at the kitchen table. The news came on and the presenter announced a naturist beach opening in Hastings. 'That's not very British,' she said. 'We're supposed to be prudes, and there's nothing wrong with that.'

Catherine groaned. 'Mum is so freaky.'

'That's true,' said Harold. 'But that's why we love her.'

Her fingers stumbled across the keys. Most Sundays Nettie practised the piano and that morning she could hardly tear herself from the Chopin. Really she should be preparing for their arrival. Or at least dressing Catherine. They'd be here any minute and yet she carried on thrashing out the music. Despite her sister now living in London, they hardly spoke, as if a hard shell had formed around each of them. Not that Edith had ever been forthcoming. She simply didn't talk about her partners or, really, any of the workings of her heart.

An hour later their mum's voice was filling the kitchen. Edith's too. As they talked to her daughter about how much she'd grown – not having seen her since Christmas – the familiarity was disarming, like a dream half-remembered. Nettie edged towards the kitchen and thought of what to say.

Harold reached them first. The women cooled but not much; in fact her mum was soon giggling at his jokes, the ruffles of her dress flouncing over her petite frame. They had made a sport of talking about the perils of men, listing Harold's faults as a shared mantra. But her mum's emotions had always changed like the wind. She was currently seeing a man named Gerald who she met at bridge club. Apparently he had no strategy and she refused to be his game partner. But he was a gentle soul and a contender for 'life partner'.

Nettie watched the family tableau for a second: Harold

taking coats; Edith complaining that hers needed to be kept on a hanger to avoid creases. Maybe *she* was being cold towards him, hard to tell. Her dress looked expensive but was an uninspired shade of beige, her hair clutched in a bun tight enough to cause a headache.

Seeing her standing there, Harold asked what she'd like to drink.

'Oh, Nettie! It's been far too long. And your ankle!' Lizzie pulled her in for a hug and she squeezed back, enjoying the feeling. She then approached Edith and they managed an obligatory embrace.

'Brews all round for my favourite Cockneys?' Harold was in a teasing mood and she resisted hitting him with a tea towel as he busied about her kitchen. It was awkward with the three of them watching and she suggested they go to the local agricultural show.

'To see lambs?' asked her mum doubtfully.

'Catherine enjoys it,' she lied. Anything to avoid them spending the whole Sunday caught in a dance where no one knew the steps.

'All right.' Edith waived an offer of a biscuit. 'It'd be nice to see the area.'

'You coming?' their mum asked Harold.

'Ah no,' he said, nodding at Nettie. 'My paperwork is calling.'

'We'll need a lift, though,' said their mum, giving him a wink.

Nettie felt heavy in the car as she listened to them chat, her mum and sister in the back with Catherine. They laughed along about Lizzie's new grapefruit diet. Edith didn't approve but Lizzie insisted it was good for her insides even if she needed the toilet every five minutes. Harold shot her a look which she ignored. She'd dressed in a high collar that morning but still felt on show. She didn't want to be a prude except the memory of her own naked skin shuddered through her.

A series of marquees stretched across the estate's lawn, the spring air rich with freshly cut grass and the bleating of lambs. Their mum stole glances at the country house, self-conscious of the crowds in their smart jackets. 'It's hardly Buckingham Palace,' she announced and Nettie smiled. While she might've once felt guilty about living here, now she merely appreciated the expanses of green. How snowdrops emerged from the winter mists, bursting through the ground as the skies lifted. Now even her mum smiled at the children playing on haystacks.

Walking ahead, Edith held hands with Catherine, who tolerated this on the promise of lemon squash.

'She's broody,' said their mum.

'Ah well, she'll find someone, won't she?'

'I'm not sure, truth be told.'

Nettie knew the two women spent time together, with weekly trips to the grocer's and an occasional meal out. Yet she'd assumed their mum was clueless as to her sister's love life, despite the fact she made these comments. In fact it seemed much of her flouncing silliness was for show, and a shrewd woman lay beneath. Was it a generational habit? Or did most women play down their intelligence?

Her mum leant in. 'You realise part of the reason she came home was Greta.'

'Yes.'

'The other part was you.'

'Me?'

'Yes, you!' She pulled her in tight. 'The girl was worried after Harold left and wanted to make sure everything was all right. But you never see each other any more. It's a crying shame. You used to worship the girl!'

That afternoon she watched her sister. At the horse show, the rest of them cheered on the Shetland ponies rumbling around the field. Edith stood silently with a fixed smile and, as the crowd turned rowdy when a boy was disqualified, she left to wander the stalls. Later she spoke with a women at a cheese stand where she re-counted her coins several times but didn't linger.

'What kind of cheese is that?' Nettie said when she returned.

'I'm not sure.'

Her sister peered over at Catherine with their mum.

'You'd make a good parent.'

Edith blinked rapidly. 'Yes, well.'

'But it'd be a shame if you didn't end up with someone you loved.'

A microphone blared. Some prize-giving was happening in the marquee. Beneath the white plastic they saw a line of women's shoes all pointed in one direction. *And the runner-up is . . .*

As her sister made a show of wanting to listen, Nettie sighed. If she wouldn't cast off her hard shell, how could Nettie? Relationships were meant to work both ways.

She was wondering if they should go home when a screeching noise cut through the wind. At the drinks stall their mum was shouting at a man.

'Don't speak to me like that,' she said and staggered away. 'I might be an East Ender but I'm no tart.' The sisters ran over to help, seeing the man push through the crowds to leave. 'What a swine. I was only being friendly and he called me such names.'

Seeing her trembling hands, Edith offered to fetch her a tea.

'An extra sugar, plus cake,' said their mum. 'For the shock.'

They went to a stall. 'Do you think they have grapefruit flavour?' asked Nettie.

Her sister hid a smile. In the background they heard their mother still complain. A passer-by stopped and she recounted her story in dramatic gestures.

They bought slices of Bakewell tart. Once again Nettie couldn't help but watch her sister. Little coils had sprung free from her bun, and she wanted to smooth them back. It was an instinct that surprised her. All these years she'd been desperate for Edith to open up and yet they'd always know each other. Recognise the signs of discord or happiness, as though a secret language existed between them that only they could decipher. Perhaps it was something about growing up together. You'd share things no matter what.

When they returned, Catherine was placing a crown of daisies on their mum's hair. The cake eaten between grins, Lizzie was pleased to see the two of them standing together at last.

'Well done,' Edith told her mother. 'A nice performance.'

What might've been an annoyance only made the sisters shrug. For all her silliness their mum knew exactly what she was doing in life. More than either of them anyway.

'I'm moving in with Gerald,' she later said as they went to call for a lift home. 'The fella from my bridge club?'

'Yes, we remember,' they both said and exchanged a smile.

They chatted about her moving to his bungalow near Epping Forest, a quieter area she was looking forward to exploring.

She didn't need a dozen pubs to choose from. As she described the place to Catherine, the two of them sat on the grassy bank, Edith helped Nettie hobble to the telephone box. Suddenly she seemed edgy, fidgeting with her handbag.

'It's partly because I envy you, I suppose,' she said without introduction, continuing a conversation played out in her mind.

'You do?'

'Maybe. You take risks, like Harold.'

Nettie looked at the weeds that pushed up between the pavement cracks.

'And yes, that's been difficult at times,' continued Edith slowly. 'But it's better than never letting things run their course.'

With that her sister returned to the others. Nettie drifted into the phone box and let herself lean against the glass wall. She wasn't the only one with troubles that burrowed deep. Everyone could be afraid of the future, most of all her sister.

That evening, once her mum and sister left, Nettie looked out her outfit for the school play. She chose her new long skirt but decided against the peach lipstick. Sometimes make-up felt like clown paint. A smile she drew on. She took off her bandage too and noted her ankle was less swollen despite being walked on. Harold would soon be gone. She thought of what her sister had said about taking risks and her heart skittered as if remembering itself.

When the door went she half expected him to appear but it was the cat which slunk through, its fur wet with rain. It'd be too much to trip twice but things would feel strange around the house on her own. What if his coat was permanently back on its peg? Their home complete again?

In the school hall the only seats left were in the front row. Being here with Harold could be nice, she knew, the three of them together. Maybe she would ask him home after this in some romantic gesture that'd make him laugh. It was a dizzying thought. Still, she couldn't help but feel on stage herself. A hand tapped her on the shoulder and a woman from school leant forwards. 'The cheat's home again, is he?'

'I'm not sure.'

She swivelled back to the front before the woman could say anything more and wondered if Harold had heard. Catherine was in the middle of them and seemingly oblivious as she swung her legs. Kids on stage were walking about, half-dressed and carrying wigs or a recorder.

The next thing Nettie knew the audience was murmuring. She looked on stage to see what the fuss was about and put her hands together to clap. But it was a boy behind who pointed at her daughter – Joseph with his hair cut in an old-fashioned mop top.

'That's her,' he said. 'She's the one with no dad.'

Catherine gestured to Harold and yelled, 'He's here!'

'Not for long, Mum says.'

Everyone stared for an agonising moment until Nettie rose from her seat. The boy stared back and waited for her to say something. To tell him to shut up or to leave her daughter alone. Harold waited expectantly too. But the words lodged in her throat and – aware of all eyes on her – she only slid back into place.

After that she struggled to focus on the play. The kids on stage spoke no sense to her, their voices whiny. Other parents around her let their eyes wander. Whispers had people shifting in seats. In her handbag she found her bottle of pills and took two. She'd always thought her daughter's temper was an anomaly. But Nettie felt her pulse throb, ready to turn around and scream.

'You are coming home, though, Dad?' Catherine asked on the way back, as rain tapped against the car windows. She hadn't mention her mum's mute performance.

'No, sweetie. I'm sorry.'

'Why not?'

'Because your mum doesn't want me to.'

'Have you asked her?'

They turned to Nettie who stayed silent, not trusting anything that passed through her mind. If she was to invite him back, this was the moment. Here. Now. The rain thrummed harder as the moment was left behind on the dark street.

At home Catherine stomped around then slammed her bedroom door. Not sure what else to do, Nettie made hot cocoa and brought it to the girl. A mound waited beneath the covers, its small movements timed with sniffs.

'We're all right, aren't we?' Nettie sat on the bed.

'No, you and those stupid pills.'

'My pills? I've always taken them.'

'But why?'

Nettie hadn't realised her daughter even noticed.

'And that stupid piano.'

She kissed the patch of hair at the top of the blanket and went to get ready for bed. Downstairs Harold listened to the shipping forecast and she felt uneasy when she reached into her handbag for the bottle of pills. The inner pocket was empty. She went into the bathroom to check she'd not left them in the cabinet, and saw the pills floating in the toilet bowl, each one a life raft about to sink.

XII

___

It was a muggy summer's afternoon and Waterloo station was relatively empty; the weekend crowds already left for the coast. Nettie waited at a coffee shop and sipped water to ease her headache. Since asking Harold to leave again she'd taken fewer pills, an attempt to pacify her daughter. The last weeks had been hard, with blanks that stretched across her memory. Why she was here to meet Edith, she didn't know. The two of them hadn't spoken since the agricultural fair, Nettie just wanting to lie low. Her sister was supposed to envy her courage, yet Nettie had displayed none of it. Now she felt drained as she sat at the corner table where someone else's cigarette ends curled on a plate. When Edith arrived they briefly hugged.

'You look well,' said Nettie, trying to sound cheerful.

'Oh yes, you too!'

For a moment it seemed things might be all right. They ordered overpriced coffees and chatted about the new musical,

Evita, and other shows. After a minute Nettie cleared her throat.

'I'm sorry it took me a while to return your phone call,' she said. 'It's not that I didn't want to meet.'

'Oh that's all right.'

Their silence was filled with the sound of an announcement, a train was soon to depart and they both absorbed themselves in their coffees. Nettie didn't mean to be closed off but she couldn't bear to talk about last week: dropping Catherine off at Harold's new flat. Having finally left Martha, he was renting a one-bed not far from his office. He'd been excited to see Catherine who walked around inspecting the kitchenette and the window that didn't fully open. No doubt her sister was desperate to ask why she'd not invited Harold back home. Because after all, she should be grateful to have him, shouldn't she? A woman like her being with a man like him.

Edith started to ask, 'And how about—?'

'How are you?' Nettie interrupted.

'I do have news actually.' It turned out Edith had a new secretarial position in west London and liked her manager, who had arranged for her to do more training. And she'd started seeing a man from the RAF who was ten years older. 'He adores me, can you believe it?'

Nettie forced a smile. 'Of course I can.'

'The trouble is, he worries he's too old for me.'

'Well, as long as you're happy together.'

'Do you think?'

At last her sister was confiding in her, only Nettie couldn't assemble the right words. They chatted for another half-hour about mindless topics and parted ways after the final sip of coffee, their breath bitter as they said goodbye. Nettie felt impossibly empty as she waited alone on the platform, wishing she'd suggested they go for dinner or at least spend a little more time together.

A fortnight later she got a phone call. It was past ten o'clock at night and she was surprised to hear her sister's voice, let alone her voice broken by tears. Edith said she was sorry for the awkward coffee. That she was a bad sister. Taken aback, Nettie said *no, of course she wasn't – it was she who'd been in a bad mood* and soon she felt herself gulping back tears. How ridiculous that they could never really say what they felt, like bottles stopped with oversized corks. The next minute the two sisters were laughing, their shrieks becoming higher and higher until they turned into howls.

4

2015

11

August 2015

Nettie wakes early. These days sleep is rarely deep, more a shallow pool into which she dips. It's no bad thing to be awake now, though. Light glows beneath her curtains as the day beckons. Placing both feet on the floor, she calls for Rufus and waits to hear the tinkle of his collar. When no sound comes she rises anyway, putting on her glasses. The dog will be outside with James who has long been up. She sees him sitting on the bottom rung of the ladder. His arms bare. Grubby vest pulled over his chest.

We won't visit with him there, Mum.

Don't worry, she imagines replying. *He'll soon be gone.*

She dresses swiftly – not worrying about her clip-on earrings – and looks for the key to her bedroom door. When she'd returned from the theme park yesterday, James was still wandering about the place. The delivery of tiles was ordered in piles and a few had made it up on to the roof, though you could still see the beams beneath. She'd said she would ask someone else to finish off the job – it was too much for one man. But, despite staring at the smears of dust across his palms, he shook his head. *I can't leave till it's done. Till it's all done.*

Afterwards they'd eaten supper in silence, picking at scraps she'd found in the fridge. Half a slice of ham. A final gherkin. It's a hint, thought Nettie, leaving the empty jar by the sink, its cloudy vinegar scraped of all nub ends. But clearly it wasn't enough. James had merely complained he didn't much fancy gherkins. This morning, however, she is bolstered by a sense of purpose. It doesn't matter if he can't entirely finish the roof – he can cover it over with plastic if need be. Someone in this town will be able to complete the job now that most of the work is done. She makes herself a promise: he'll be gone by the end of the day.

After locking her room, she carries on past the next door and down the stairs. It's tempting to see whether James has written more in his diary but there's no point in looking. And what does it matter anyway? She's become distracted by him, by Tara and that glare of hers.

The yard is littered with scraps of broken tiles, along with tools and a roll of wire she needs to step over. As James descends the ladder his shadow slips over everything. It's a hot morning, the kind of heat that presses down.

'I'd like you to finish today,' she tells him. 'Or at least put a plastic covering across the roof.'

'A plastic cover?' He is affronted by the idea, then wipes his hands on his trousers. 'I'll try my best but I'll need a cup of tea first. I've been up there since the crack of dawn.'

'I'll make it. You carry on.'

She brews tea in the pot that's already on the side – her

wedding china, now covered in stains. She dabs at the pot with a cloth and notices a crack growing down its side. Her pulse quickens. She'd put it away in the cupboard for a reason.

'You've damaged my china,' she tells him the next minute.

He doesn't react. Stood by the barn, he is peering into its darkness where a haze of petrol thickens the air.

'What's going on?' she asks.

In the darkened yard a shape moves. It's Rufus sniffing around.

'Look,' says Nettie, teeth on edge. 'You told me you wanted tea.'

He doesn't turn to her, only stands there – his hair slick – a toy soldier waiting to go into action.

'Come out of there, please, Rufus.'

The sniffing gets louder and a tail flicks in the gloom. James tilts forwards, as if not wanting to move his feet, then goes in after the dog. Various shifting sounds follow as things are moved about. She can hardly remember what's in the back of the barn. She's not let herself go in there for years. It isn't wise, though, why is that?

The warm air is laced with insects that flap their wings and it grows difficult to breathe. She nudges a greenfly from her collar.

'Everything all right?' she manages.

It remains quiet until James eventually walks out with his arms held high, fingers separate, as though he doesn't want them to touch. His mouth gapes too, eyes wide. The dog follows. His fur is smeared with oil and a reddish dust, a strange costume of sorts. From his mouth something clunks between his teeth.

'What are they?' James asks, backing off from where the dog lies on the concrete, gnawing away.

'I don't know.'

'The skull is so small. They look like cat bones, Nettie.'

She frowns. 'We did lose our cat. Years ago. It must've got trapped at the back of the barn.' Shaking her head she wants to rid herself of the memory that's rising through her sub-conscious layers. She doesn't want to think about it.

Feeling James's stare she hurries back indoors. But, like so often, she can't escape her mind and the images that expand: Catherine upset as her dad was packing his car to leave. The girl crying or were those her own tears? She remembers the sobs, quick breaths that shook the farmhouse. And then the cat was missing and Catherine wanted her to help them look. She knew there was no point in searching, though, so played faster and faster as Harold called out, *pussy pussy pussy*. And she carried on violently playing until her fingers were numb and she'd torn, several times, through 'Für Elise'.

Now the kitchen clock jerks its arm around the dial. In the mirror's missing patch of dust she searches the face of the woman who glares back. What is happening? She's supposed to be getting James to finish the roof. Instead he's outside pacing, *scuff scuff scuff*. The sound stops.

'Good morning,' a voice calls.

He says nothing.

Nettie sees Marianne in the yard. She's in the same top and three-quarter-length trousers she wore the other day, her fringe even shorter. 'I dropped by to see Nettie.'

The sun has inched higher and their shadows spill over the yard. Standing beside the barn, James wipes his forehead, showing his muscles, the bulk of him.

Unsure what else to say, Marianne turns towards the

farmhouse. Hoping they'll escape this man's prying eyes, Nettie opens the door to usher in her visitor. Except now he speaks. 'Where's that tea? Maybe Marianne and I could share a pot in the garden, eh?'

'Well I—'

'Why don't you make us tea for two?' he says lightly, his face shifting into a serene mask, then: 'Tea for two. Isn't that a song from a play? *The Sound of Music*?'

'It's from *No No Nanette*,' corrects Marianne, trying for a smile.

'How right you are,' he says and moves towards her. 'So, tea in the garden? I'd love to hear about your community work. And I have some stories of my own.'

When Marianne isn't sure what to say, Nettie clears her throat. 'Actually, James, I'd like you to finish the roof.' She turns to her friend. 'James is leaving soon and the roof needs covering. There might be August rain.'

'I doubt that.' He raises his arms towards the sky that's barren of clouds.

'Even so,' says Nettie.

They lock eyes and without looking away he calls for the dog. 'He found something interesting in the barn, didn't he?'

There's a tinkle of collar and heat swells through Nettie, the yard turning to a streak of faces. Is this all part of James's game? Eyes stinging, she can hardly look at Marianne and must simply wait for her to ask what he's referring to. But the woman's voice is plain, 'Sorry, I don't have much time for tea. I just popped round to talk to my friend here. Nettie – shall we go indoors?'

The kitchen is a retreat of darkness and Nettie breathes the cool air. Objects haven't quite taken shape again, a haze of colours, but she wafts her blouse and momentarily feels better.

'I know, such dry weather.' Marianne does the same. 'Is everything okay here?'

Clattering echoes round the yard and Nettie wants to draw the curtains or even lock the doors. Where has Rufus gone with those bones? Hopefully he's scuttled away with his findings although he could appear at any minute. 'Oh yes, we're fine, thank you.'

'Well, we've potentially got some good news about the fete.'

It turns out Marianne has spoken to someone about having an event and they're meeting with her later today to discuss it. To put a date in the diary, too. Nettie nods along. She doesn't want to seem ungrateful but she's distracted and, feeling unsteady on her feet, merely tries to stay upright. Marianne fetches them both a glass of water and asks again if she is okay. A smell of rot is seeping into the room or is that just the oleanders, turning brown in their jar? She wants to find Rufus and remove the cat bones from his mouth. They shouldn't be chewed, it's disrespectful. Poor Catherine. The girl became vegetarian for a time after that, some sort of sacrifice to the animal world, feeling she'd not properly taken care of her first pet. *Why do some creatures die and others get to carry on?* she'd asked when Nettie complained of this new diet. They lived on a farm after all, she was supposed to be okay with animals meeting their ends. *Why though?* Catherine asked. Nettie had no good answer.

After showing out Marianne she puts away the tea set. Serving him a brew won't make the man work quicker, he'll just loiter around the yard drinking it all morning. At the sink she washes the wedding china, planning to put the whole set in her room. Even if he only stays one more hour she can't have him touching it. Causing more damage. She scrubs harder to get rid of the stains that form rings inside the pot. But a sound makes her stop. In her hands lie two separate pieces which fall apart like cracked bones.

Trying not to be upset, she lowers herself into her armchair. She is exhausted and only wants this to be over. She tries to read the local newspaper, though the pages shake, feel too inky, the news tattooing her. An article on the abbey window is packed with a dictionary's worth of hyperbole. *The worst! Deviant!* The next advertises the primary school's bring and buy sale. There's always something good *and* something bad happening in the world. But society loves focusing on the latter, scratching around for something to get hearts racing. Anger is something definite to feel, to cut through the numb layers.

At some point she falls asleep and dreams of James pacing about the farmhouse. His boots are heavier now and she hears the steady *clack clack*. Footsteps mark the walls, the ceiling, dirt trailing across her bedspread. She knows what he's slowly tracking down and begins to follow. Her hands swish against her skirt and she's light-footed, young enough to keep up. When he reaches the back garden she gets closer until her vision blurs. Where are her glasses? She pats her pockets but they're empty. James moves about again. Without seeing much, she shuffles towards him. Closer and closer. Except the figure by the well isn't James. It's Martha who stands with her pale lips curved as she holds Nettie's glasses.

'Such nice spectacles.'

'What are you doing here?'

'He was my Harold too.'

Nettie steps towards the woman who lets her face be touched. It's smooth and beautiful, though the rest of her is overly frail, a blanket covering her shoulders.

'I'm so very sorry,' Nettie says. She wants to say more but is shoved towards the well.

The woman's laughter is swallowed as she plunges into the wet blackness and everything turns silent.

On waking she gasps for air. Twists uncomfortably in the armchair, damp beneath her thighs. James is stood watching from the kitchen. Once again he's drinking from her wedding china, taking sips and then wiping his mouth. He goes to wash his hands, working soap under each of his nails.

'I never did get that tea,' he tells her. 'So I'm off to visit Tara in the pub. See if she'll make me one or something stronger.'

'What about the roof?'

'Oh, I'll get it done soon enough.' He drops a pile of post on the table and inspects one particular item. 'There's a postcard here.'

12

_____

She waits for James to leave before drifting into the kitchen to look at the postcard. Its picture isn't of a beach or holiday village. It's a photo of a sculpture by Barbara Hepworth – the carving dappled green and shaped into a woman who appears to have two wombs. On the other side the handwriting is instantly familiar:

Dearest Nettie,

How are you? Sorry I've not written in a while. Are you still living in that lovely house in Hampshire? Please write to tell me you're happy and well.

Thinking of you always,
Edith

Not written in a while? It's been almost ten years. She's not even sure where her sister lives any more – perhaps near Leeds where she once mentioned volunteering at an Arts Council-funded organisation. The last time they'd properly seen each other was when their mum passed away and they'd both travelled to her bungalow in Epping Forest. Gerald was organising the funeral but asked the sisters to sort through her personal items – essentially the wardrobe stuffed with dresses, taffeta skirts, mounds of shoes and other paraphernalia that made up their mum. They both sighed at the sight of it all and silently began to sort through, starting at opposite ends.

'How's Harold?' Edith asked as they approached the middle.

It was a year after he'd moved back to the farmhouse. The man had not stopped mentioning how he wanted to return. In fact, he was shameless about it and even Catherine began to roll her eyes when he asked to stay past tea. His London flat wasn't bad and the three of them sometimes spent the day traipsing around the local flower market or walking the canals, although Nettie never stayed the night. Then one Sunday, when she was collecting Catherine, she couldn't stand his sad face as he packed up the girl's things. *You could come home with us*, she'd said, expecting him to say no – he had work the next morning. But he came and slept in their bedroom and then returned day after day. It was strange really, how quickly they slipped back into a routine without quite meaning to. They'd grown used to their own space and were annoyed by each other's habits. By her mess, by his toothpicks at the sink. Even Catherine wasn't sure if the arrangement was working and eyed the two of them warily, looking for signs. At night they slept side by side without touching. They argued about the television. About how he voted Tory. But the heart was a stubborn organ and even though most evenings Nettie resented the noise of the car's engine, she laid a place for him on the table, polishing his cutlery until it shone.

At Christmas Lizzie and Gerald visited for the day and the five of them played songs and danced, the grown-ups drinking too much mulled cider. After Catherine went to bed, they played bridge with couples as teams. On fetching more drinks from the kitchen, her mum told Nettie how proud she was of her for forgiving Harold. Suddenly wondering if the day was a lie, them no happy family, she wanted to confide that she hadn't fully forgiven him. That things were difficult and she wasn't sure what to do. But on seeing her mum so content, she said nothing.

The following spring the sisters packed up the dresses for charity shops in silence. Just when they thought they'd finished, they found further shoe boxes hidden at the back and groaned. How many clothes had the woman had, surely at least half of them too small. But on opening the final box, they found photographs of their dad. His medal too, which she'd wrapped in endless velvet.

On saying goodbye to Edith after the funeral Nettie promised to keep in touch, knowing it was what their mum would have wanted. But as time passed, the thread between them got longer, as it became clear neither would make the trip to see the other. Somehow they couldn't find a way to be close again without knowing exactly why. They knew each other too well perhaps. Knew every flaw.

She now looks again at the postcard. Inspects it for clues as to how it's been handled – a crease or smudge of ink. The lines are neat although the photo has grown gummy as if kept in a bag too long. Perhaps she forgot to send it for a while. Edith is now in her old age too. She doesn't like to think of her that way. Not because it's depressing to age – just that it doesn't seem right for her sister. The wrinkles would outrage her, hooded eyelids like enemy spies.

Now she thinks of it, her sister did ring Catherine a few weeks back, to ask for her address for Grace's birthday. Even if she has got in touch with Nettie as an afterthought it's still something. Not wanting to leave the postcard, she slips it into her handbag and holds it close as she heads for town. Along the main road the thistles release seeds that float for anyone to catch. Although she tries not to get too excited about hearing from Edith she's aware of the postcard the other side of the leather. *I'll write back in a few days,* she tells herself. *No point in being overly keen.* She's always pushed too hard to know the woman, expecting that was normal for sisters. Maybe now they'll finally resume some sort of relationship. Sunlight dapples the pavement and she feels her skin warm.

At last she has heard from Edith.

On Bell Street she checks her watch. Passing the time in the supermarket, she fills a basket with ingredients for one. She'll get rid of James one way or another, no matter what. The decision buoys her steps and she hums to the tinkle of a pop song. Cheddar cheese, crackers, milk and two jars of gherkins. That should do it.

'Need any help packing?' asks the man behind the till.

'No thank you,' she says, laughing as she pulls air into a bag which expands like a parachute.

It's almost eleven when she walks down the street towards

the memorial park. The sun is strong but not offensively so and she sings beneath her breath. Then she catches sight of Tara. Standing on the other side of the pavement, the girl is dressed in a denim skirt and pretty top, and is looking at pictures in an estate agent's window. Nettie grinds to a halt. She wants to go and speak to her but recalls her stony glare. What if she refuses to talk? A minute passes and it's almost as if the girl is waiting for Nettie, though she's not taken her eyes off the houses.

Don't be a coward, Nettie tells herself and crosses the road. 'Hello, Tara.'

The girl turns and presses her lips together, their gloss thick. 'It's you.'

'Is everything okay?'

'Yeah.' She sighs and looks again at the window. 'I'm meant to be back at the pub soon.' Her fingertips press the glass.

'I was worried I did something to offend you.'

'Not really,' she says. Her hair is greasy at the roots and scraped into a bun. A duffel bag by her feet, the same one she had before. 'I just shouldn't have stayed with you. My mum wouldn't like it.'

'Have you spoken to her?'

'She's not picking up. Probably out finding her dealer.'

'Oh dear.' Nettie's flustered for something to say. 'You must miss her.'

'Miss her? The woman's a crackhead.' For a second she's haughty but the expression quickly fades. 'Yeah. A bit.'

Nettie is about to ask more when a man appears at the glass door. Decked out in a suit, he fingers a pink tie that looks expensive. 'Need any help, ladies?' He allows them each a smile.

'Yeah, I need a place,' says Tara, playing the part of customer with hands on her hips. 'What you got for me?'

The man hesitates. 'Perhaps I could give you my card.'

'Nah, I might as well come in.'

Before he can say anything Tara pushes her way into the office and he follows. Nettie grins to see him perturbed as the girl points to various properties, all woefully out of her price range. Beside a barista coffee machine, he tilts his head from side to side, debating how rude he can be within the realms of estate agent etiquette.

Nettie looks at the local properties in the window. Her farmhouse can't be worth much – the whole place ravaged by age – but the land will sell for something, especially as the town expands to meet it. How would she feel about the place being bulldozed? Everything gone. All the memories collapsed to rubble and cleared away.

Inside, Tara is still enjoying some disagreement. It's the wrong place for the girl. She needs to look for the downbeat ones that have properties within most people's budgets. Nettie thinks she could offer to put her up at the farmhouse for a while. But she's still trying to get rid of James. And having Tara around won't help that cause.

Another minute passes and she wonders whether to leave, the shopping bag weighing down her hand. But soon Tara is emerging with a little make-up smeared beneath her eyes.

'I expect all the places in there looked dull, didn't they?' she asks. 'You can do much better.'

'You don't need to cheer me up, all right.'

'Well ...' Glass clinks against her leg. 'I'd better head off. I'm meeting a friend in the memorial park.'

Without asking Tara walks with her in that direction. She seems to have forgotten about returning to her shift at the pub and, instead, babbles about the price of everything in town.

How unfair it is. They pass a sign that advertises *Luxury Houses and Apartments* in front of an immaculate lawn.

'How about non-luxury?' Tara says. 'Just normal flats that families can actually afford, never mind the bloody faux marble worktops and double garages.' In the advert's photograph a white-toothed couple smirks back and Nettie can see why these people are often given sex changes, courtesy of a black marker pen.

'I'm sorry things are hard,' she says when they reach the park gates.

Tara shrugs and falls quiet, wiping her eyes, before she carries on walking. The park is lit up in peaches and yellows, a sway of wild grass flecked with mauve. Tara runs her fingers along the flowers' soft tops as they walk along, letting seeds scatter in the breeze. Nettie knows the park well after various events over the years. Some she remembers well. Others almost completely forgotten. Why does it happen like that? Some memories working themselves in like thorns under the skin, leaving a lovely sting. The path opens up to the lawn where various families and couples lie on blankets. Nettie looks for Marianne by the bandstand but can't yet see her.

'Would you like to join us?' she asks Tara.

The girl is surprised and glances at a group of teenagers who loiter by the cafe. 'No, you're all right, ta.'

'Fair enough.'

As Tara turns to leave, Nettie wants to touch her shoulder. To ask where she'll be sleeping tonight. But it's Tara who speaks. 'By the way, you might want to keep your distance from him.'

'Who? James?'

'Yeah.'

'Has he said something?'

She shrugs. 'He doesn't like you much, does he? He was talking all sorts of shit about you in the pub. They all were.'

Nettie sits on a bench near the bandstand. She's stepped on some thorn seeds and tries to scrape away the remnants. By the time she's finished someone has sat beside her. The girl on the bench must be sixteen or seventeen. Her long tie-dye skirt reaches her ankles, wooden beads tinkling. Opposite stand a much younger boy and girl. Nettie blinks again. The little girl's hair is white-blonde – she's the one who throws stones around the farmhouse. Who she accidentally hit on the arm.

'I don't want to.' Up close she seems nervous.

The older girl drags a sandal across the ground. 'Why not? See – this is why I don't hang out with you more.'

Nettie isn't sure whether to walk away. Have they deliberately sat next to her to perform like this?

Though the boy guffaws he doesn't say anything, looking to the older girl for direction. There's a shifting between them as the little girl fingers a delicate silver crucifix that rests on her T-shirt. 'Fine,' she says.

Pleased by this, the teenager pulls her legs onto the seat, sandals scraping on the rung as she crosses them. Nettie daren't properly look. The boy laughs a hyena call which incenses her. The bag of shopping has fallen open to expose its insides, the jar of gherkins waiting to be smashed. What will Marianne think if she sees them taunting her like this? And her putting up with it. Her mind spinning, Nettie twists around to say something. But as the teenage girl shifts her feet Nettie sees an anklet. It's not unlike Tara's one and she feels a pang of something. This girl is just a teenager finding her place in the world and probably tired of looking after her siblings.

'Yeah?' the girl says. 'Are you all right?'

'Fine, thank you,' Nettie mutters and walks away with her shopping, expecting them to call out but hearing nothing.

She's waiting by the river when Marianne turns up. 'I wasn't sure you were coming. You seemed a little under the weather earlier.'

Nettie glances at the bench. The threesome has gone.

'Are you sure everything is okay?'

Seeing her friend concerned, Nettie begins to tell her about the kids, about James, about everything that's wrong. Except a woman is bustling over with a clipboard. On reaching them she launches into a pre-prepared speech about the events and festivals that take place in the park throughout the year. A real source of town pride, she says as she ushers them around the park's paths. Nettie is familiar with the whole place, of course, having lived here far longer than this woman and feels numb as she listens to the explanations of which stalls can go where.

But as the woman lists cake suppliers Nettie gradually relaxes and, instead, imagines her grandchildren eating ice creams with their mum. Light bouncing from laughing kids to parents to shrubs, the shimmering joy of being alive for one last summer.

'And September would fit nicely,' the woman says. They've reached the iron gates, the tour complete. 'I'll put you down for the 26th.'

'Oh no,' says Nettie. 'It needs to be this month.'

'This month?! Have you ever organised a fete before? It takes weeks and weeks.' The woman is outraged but Nettie holds strong.

'It has to be, yes. Otherwise the kids are back at school.'

'It'll be at the weekend.'

'Kids from out of town.'

The woman opens her mouth without talking, a mime of speechlessness.

'Perhaps you could squeeze us in,' says Marianne with a smile.

'I'll see what I can do. But if it all goes wrong, on your head be it.'

After the woman has walked off down the road, Nettie and Marianne giggle, taking their own tour around the park to talk through plans. Marianne rummages in her pocket and brings out a list of things to organise including several Post-it notes she's attached. The sense of camaraderie is like a balm to everything from earlier that morning and Nettie chatters along about the posters they could make. A pigeon stands in the bandstand, silvery chest puffed as though it's about to burst into song. Everything seems good again, except it isn't. Not really. All this is irrelevant if her daughter won't come with James here.

'Are you sure you're not unwell?' asks Marianne, seeing that she's stopped. The path has come to an end but she doesn't want her friend to walk away.

'Actually there is something wrong,' she says.

They choose a bench that overlooks the river. On the banks, weeds have been tugged onshore like green fingers. As Nettie explains that her guest has outstayed his welcome, the words are quick to flow and she wonders why she didn't confide before.

'I still don't know what he wants.'

'Whatever it is this can't go on,' Marianne says and rises. 'Let's sort it out shall we? I have an idea.'

13

Back at the farmhouse, they stare at James's closed bedroom door. Nettie half expects him to be standing on the other side. Although the place is quiet, she pictures him tricking them, ready to laugh. But when Marianne nudges open the door no one is waiting.

His things are as before – the sheets tightly tucked, the comb left on the bedside table. No diary sits on the chair though. Or among his things.

'I did this once with Pauline's stuff,' Marianne explains as they stand motionless. 'We'd had an awful row so I gathered up all of her clothes and whatnot.'

Marianne steps in first, followed by Nettie whose mouth is overly dry as she picks up the rucksack. The first shirt she folds feels dirty in her hands or maybe she's the dirty one, doing this to someone else's belongings. Soon enough they're both folding and it doesn't take long to pack the clothes. Only the last item – a pair of trousers – refuses to fit as something bulges from a pocket. Marianne pulls out a teddy bear, its tiny striped T-shirt faded, fur worn away.

'This has been well loved,' she says.

But by a boy or a man? wonders Nettie, thinking of the phone conversation she overheard. James begging to see his son.

They're on edge as they walk downstairs with the rucksack, the cup tinkling on its strap, and lean it against the outside wall.

Nettie asks what happened with Pauline. 'Was she furious to find her things outside?'

'Not exactly.'

'No?'

'I tried to leave them outside.' The capped tooth slips over her lip. 'But it started to rain and I worried the water would get through the bag and ruin the jumper on top. So I ended up bringing it all back indoors.'

Nettie wants to laugh but is already thinking of James seeing his bag here. An itch crawls up the sweat on her back.

'It feels wrong, doesn't it?' says Marianne. 'I knew it would, God forgive us.' Her fringe is stuck to her forehead.

Nettie hadn't realised how panicked she was. 'Don't worry. It's my doing. You get off home.'

'No I'll wait.'

'Please, Marianne. I need to do this alone.'

'Well, come see me later if you like.'

The woman takes a final look at the rucksack slumped against the outside wall and leaves. Once alone, Nettie is unsure whether to stay with the rucksack. It seems too much to leave it here unguarded. For all she knows it could contain his worldly possessions. Rufus comes and sits with her while she waits. He plays with the tin cup, though soon loses interest and falls asleep. Shadows pass over the yard as clouds move across the sky, changing the colour of the barn doors from light to dark, and back to light again.

By the time the gate creaks open, she's thick-headed. Spots appear in front of her eyes as if the scene's not yet fully formed. James looks amused as he walks over, then sees his rucksack. 'What's going on, Nettie?'

She clears her throat. 'I need you to leave. I don't mind paying for your train ticket.'

He baulks. 'And the roof?'

'Never mind the roof.'

'That's a real shame. It was starting to take shape and I worry no one will finish the job for you.'

'Perhaps. But my priority is Catherine visiting. And she won't come with you here.'

'Your daughter won't visit, huh?' He cocks an eyebrow, faking a look of surprise though his face is turning deep scarlet. 'Because you've told her I'm some sort of deviant. Why? For wanting to stay here with you. To help you with repairs. Tell me, Nettie ...' He trembles as he steps closer. 'What does that say about your opinion of yourself? Right from the start you've struggled to understand why I'm here.'

'I'm sorry.'

He exhales and rubs his neck. 'Don't apologise, Nettie. Of course I'll leave. And how kind, you've even packed my bags. Catherine and the girls will be here in no time.'

She grimaces but hopefully it's true. 'That's the main reason I'm asking you to leave.'

'Why don't I call her, eh?'

'What?'

'I'll call Catherine to let her know I'm off. So she can be certain.'

For a moment Nettie expects him to walk into the house but he pulls out his mobile phone and dials, walking about the yard. When Rufus gets up to brush against his leg, he nudges him away as if he wants nothing more to do with the place. 'Catherine? Yes, it's James.'

Nettie holds her breath.

'I'm phoning to say that I'm off. Your mother would like me to be on my way.'

Everything swims around her as she calls Rufus over to scratch the soft patch beneath his chin. Why hadn't she done this yesterday? Her grandkids could've already been on the train.

'Yes, so the path is clear,' says James and turns to look at Nettie. 'I have just one last thing to do before I leave.'

She's not sure why she lets him through the door. Perhaps it's the look on his face: the twisted mouth, the pink line where he'd pressed the phone into his cheek. Soon he's pacing the length of the kitchen while she stands at the other side of the table, palms on the chair for support.

'There's something I need to get off my chest,' he says, trying to keep his voice low. 'It's something I don't fully understand. And it's turned in me in a horrible way since I learnt it. Stopped me from sleeping at night, not that I could before. Ever have that?'

'I don't know.'

'Oh I think maybe you do.'

The kitchen air is tinged with the scent of oleanders. The petals have curled and browned, the water murky in the jar. She's kept them too long, she always does, knowing she should throw them away but letting the sweet acridity stain the room.

He pulls his diary from his trouser pocket. 'I was naive at first. When Catherine mentioned your farmhouse I was excited to come and see you, the chickens, the dog, the garden. Although you were reluctant, you did let me stay. I didn't expect that generosity.'

Nettie isn't sure where this is heading. She scoops the dead petals into her hand, feeling them soft, turning to rot.

'And things seemed all right, didn't they? I mean, you were a bit odd. Grumpy. But we had a nice time, didn't we?'

His eyes widen as he stops to wait for her to agree. She manages a nod.

'But then, Nettie ...' He puts down the diary, which falls open, pages filled with scribbles. 'I went to the pub on Wednesday and heard the rumours. It wasn't hard to pick up the meaning. Everyone has something to say about you.'

The agitated look from the other night is back. He shakes his head, smooths his hair over and over again. After this he doesn't know what else to do with his hands.

'What are you talking about?' she whispers.

He lets out a high-pitched chuckle that verges on the hysterical.

'What am I talking about?' He claps his hands, then stuffs his fingers into his mouth as if he might swallow them. After composing himself he glowers across at her. 'I know what you did and would like to know why.'

'I'm baffled by this whole conversation, quite frankly.' It's Nettie's turn to move and she goes to refill the flower jar.

The water shoots noisily through the pipes and he waits until it's quiet before speaking again. 'Funny how we all convince ourselves of the part we've chosen to play in life. The socialist. The good mother. The sweet old lady. Hell is other people, though, isn't it?'

She tries to shrug but feels like she's floating upwards, no longer made of bones but weightless matter.

'You see, I know what you did to your husband.'

The jam jar is filled with water but she has no hands with which to clasp it. Doesn't trust herself not to drop the thing.

'But with flowers?' James continues. 'Oleander? Who'd have thought you'd work out just the right amount because too much and he vomits, doesn't he?'

'No,' she whispers.

'Poor Nettie. It must've been rough – cheating husband, alone with a child? All those years later, both in your fifties, you still resented him because he never changed, did he? But you don't have to deny it. I mean, it's hardly a secret.'

'Why are you saying all this?'

'That's a fair question.' He begins to pace again, touching the diary as though it's some kind of talisman. 'I know you poisoned your husband. What I don't know is why. Why did you do it? Are you glad?'

'Glad?' The word seems abhorrent. She skitters away from him, touches her own damp mouth. For years she's tried to re-member it properly – twenty-five years to be precise. To trace the edges of what really happened, not the images that cloud or else stretch details like a bent mirror. Harold's face was staring back at her, the whites of his eyes enlarged when he realised. Too late. The soup bowl scraped clean with its spiralled white from the spoon's movements.

226

The flowers now fall into the bin, followed by the clunk of jam jar. The spill of water too. Nettie pictures the detached petals spread down the plastic. 'He was in his fifties and getting sick.'

'There weren't any hospital records, though, were there?' James says, frowning as if trying to understand. 'No one else knew of this supposed illness. He was only fifty-eight. In what way was he ill?'

'I don't know.'

'You're getting confused with his dad, perhaps?'

'No, it was Harold.'

'The court documents were clear, I looked them up. He wasn't ill. You invited him back home but still couldn't forgive him.'

'Please stop.'

'You wanted him gone and got your way but paid for it too. Several years in Holloway.'

The words are familiar and bring a nauseous wave that rises, the pungent smell of rotting flowers claiming the room. She wants to say more, to explain and put new words in that notebook. Only the cloud is covering everything: her standing at the hob, a clang of spoon on metal before she crushes the flowers beneath her palms, the spill of their organs on the worktop.

1991

XIII

1991

The first year in Holloway was the hardest. The cells were single with a narrow bed, shelf and chair. On hearing she'd be in a room on her own, she'd been relieved, having pictured large women pushing their weight around, tattooed hands squeezed into fists. In reality, alone, there was far too much of herself. Her grey hairs on the pillow. The knot in her stomach that didn't deserve food. During the night, she imagined disappearing into the darkness, hearing only the other women's voices, her own breath gone.

When morning came the prison was newly stark around her – the scratch of bed sheet, then the corridors that stretched past metal staircases which clattered beneath feet. During meals Nettie both craved a closeness to the women and felt afraid of them. The slang was like a foreign tongue and she realised how insulated her life had become; living in east London she'd considered herself well mixed with neighbours from Bangladesh and India. Whereas later in life she'd become isolated in her ways, her home, her hours of digging in the garden as if contentment lay deep in the earth. Now all the women stood together in the dining hall queues. The curls of hair glistening with wax, the nudge of bodies. One woman called out for her children and rattled the table, telling the guards she couldn't bear it. But most simply got on with the business of being inside and Nettie watched them all sniff at the over-cooked porridge or complain when the fresh milk was replaced by powder.

The first morning she went to sit near a group of black women who chattered away, assuming they'd ignore her. They did. A woman said something about suffragettes having been here for three years. *A white woman in prison for that long?* They refused to believe it and slammed their fists on the table but soon went back to their breakfasts.

Someone sat down opposite, placing her tray so carefully it hardly made a sound. The pale fingers were chewed raw at the ends. Nettie kept her head down. The food was bland and stuck in her throat but she didn't add salt. The woman said nothing and later Nettie saw she was younger than her, in her forties but with a face that seemed wind-beaten, her expression worn away to leave her blank. Over the next days the woman continued to sit opposite. Having seen her talk to friends outside the toilet block, Nettie wondered why she sat with her.

'This food is tasteless,' were the first words the woman said.

'Agreed.' Nettie returned to her lunch. The insides of her mouth were scabbed where she'd begun to chew them and she pressed her tongue against the newest sting. Every time she wanted to ask the woman why she sat opposite, she'd keep quiet. There was no reason to hurry the eventual torment. Or perhaps there was. Not knowing what she planned became a mental attic, which Nettie filled with her worst imaginings.

It happened in the corridor one evening after showering as her hair dripped icy water down her shoulders. The woman approached with a crowd behind. Nettie stopped and raised her arms to shield the blows. But the woman was grinning. 'We reckoned it were you,' said one with a long face.

'Who?' Nettie asked.

'The woman who killed her husband for cheating.'

They slapped her on the shoulder and she jerked back before realising it was friendly. The women laughed. 'Wished I'd had the nerve to kill mine. My bloody hero you are.'

Back in the cell, Nettie's whole body shook. The story was still in the newspapers for anyone to find. She couldn't get used to seeing the articles or the same photograph that circulated – her at some neighbour's party that Harold had insisted they go to. The scowl made her forehead seem large, her face dipped so shadows swallowed her eyes. Although she was wearing a floral dress it was creased from a long church service and blurred where she'd begun to move.

The Romsey Butcher, one newspaper had called her. The name caught on.

That night she couldn't sleep, reliving it all.

The police had arrived not long after she'd rung them. She sat at the kitchen table, having done everything she could to fill the minutes: scrubbed the wood of crumbs, cleaned the soup bowl and pan. Her hands itched where the water had run hot until steaming. The spoon was especially clean but still she'd carried it upstairs to keep in a drawer. Harold was in bed, she told them, before she waited in the hallway while the female police officer went up. The house became quiet for a while and, on returning, the woman rang an ambulance. It was hard to tell what she was thinking. The woman's stiff bun reminded her of Edith, who she'd need to call later. Then the police officer asked Nettie to wait in the kitchen while the ambulance arrived. The blue flash glided across the kitchen walls but the siren wasn't on, a silent scream.

Later at the station she explained:

'It was what he wanted.'

'He asked me to do it.'

'None of it was ideal but that was life.'

The rehearsed lines. She repeated them in case they'd not come out right. The female officer didn't seem to understand. 'That was life?' she echoed. Her male colleague was older, his heavy features set in place. Only when Nettie described the crushing of the petals did his eyes widen, yellowed balls suddenly round.

She explained everything from the beginning. After a separation they were living together again. They had been for the last decade. They had a daughter Catherine who was twenty-four and at nursing college in London. When the female officer asked what her relationship with Harold was like she hesitated. Their relationship was intense. The sort that made you sick when you had too much. But tender as well. Milky tea in the morning, fingers curled against the china. Light through the curtains as they talked. Books and records piled high, their favourites muddled. Arguments about songs. Misremembered words. The boiler he fixed for her baths. The mower she pushed for hours. Feeling complacent, then a kiss that left her raw. It was all these things and a thousand others, so how was she supposed to explain?

The officers waited for a response.

'Had you ever forgiven Harold?' they asked. It was true she hadn't. Long after he'd moved back to the farmhouse, she would still feel a hotness creep around her collar, a tightening of her organs. She wasn't always in control of it, this thing that lived deep inside her and pulsed through her blood when she thought of the past. Even in his fifties the man couldn't be trusted – often lying about money spent on presents she never received.

'You unplugged the phone,' the man said. *They'd searched her house?* Time seemed to have jerked forwards and the female officer's chair was empty.

'Yes.' She should have told them this earlier.

'You hid the phone in a drawer beneath tablecloths.'

'Yes.'

'Why?'

'He wasn't supposed to find it.'

The next morning Catherine came to the police station. For a second after waking in her cell, Nettie was merely glad to see the girl with her dyed blonde hair and denim jacket. Over the years she'd been restless, having failed exams and then got top results on the retakes. She claimed not to care about men but threw everything she had into relationships. Spent every penny on boozy holidays in the sun and ran up debt. At last she'd got her act together with nursing college. Nettie now watched as her daughter stood pale-faced at the door and went to wrap her arms around her.

'What happened, Mum?'

Nettie repeated her lines but they sounded odd. Without having properly slept her mind was like swirling vapours. 'It's all a misunderstanding.'

'I don't get it. How can Dad be ...'

Nettie attempted to explain but Catherine couldn't comprehend why her dad had said nothing about being ill. 'I'm a nurse, I might've been able to help,' she said, cracking her knuckles as she paced. 'He shouldn't have gone without saying goodbye.'

At her initial court hearing she pleaded innocent. It was against her solicitor's advice and yet she couldn't fathom the opposite. What that would mean. There was talk of manslaughter charges, some complicated post-mortem results; then she was back on remand in prison. Over the next few days she became increasingly numb. She pictured everyone at Harold's funeral and wondered what they were saying. Martha. Harold's mum. Whispers among the aisles for her daughter to catch. Catherine promised she understood; that everything would be cleared up soon and she would come and stay a while. But when she later visited, the girl churned with disgust, barely able to look her in the eye across the table. A poisonous cloud of alcohol fumes surrounded her too, each word slurred. She said it was all Nettie's fault. That Nettie had lied to her and let her believe Harold deserted her in this world when he wouldn't do that. *You're a monster*, she'd said. *You killed him to make yourself feel better, how could you do that?* Clearly Catherine wanted an argument but no words went deep enough to explain. Her eyes itched. She said nothing.

When it eventually got to court the hearing lasted just three days. The judge shuffled his notes inside the stuffy room where people turned up to listen. Although Catherine had refused to speak to her for months, Nettie kept hoping to find her face in the crowds. At least her sister came and sat in the same place near the front each day. She nodded at Nettie who stared back,

236

wondering if she was a mirage. Everything seemed unreal. The lines jumbled. *She made a terrible error of judgement,* the man in the wig said, gesturing to where Nettie sat hunched. *Having suffered an awful ordeal due to her husband's bigamy, she struggled to overcome her resentment, as many of us would. She was an otherwise kind mother and wife, though. This act comprised a few minutes of madness that she'll regret for the rest of her waking life.* He'd earlier advised her, again, to plead guilty to the full count of murder, saying it was impossible to argue otherwise. She had clearly planned it out and – contrary to what she'd told him – there was no evidence to suggest Harold was ill, the post-mortem showing no conclusive results. Prior to his death the latest GP report merely noted his complaints of toothache. Even if he was seriously ill the question remained: why hadn't he ended his own life if that was – in fact – what he'd wanted? And there were character reports on her too with friends from the town saying she was angry with Harold. That she went through periods of being completely reclusive. Even her own daughter wouldn't vouch for her character. Nettie couldn't argue with any of it. She understood 'guilty' was the only plea she could make. If in doubt as to her own guilt, she merely recalled the swell of heat as she crushed the flowers against the chopping board over and over. Harold did deserve to die, she remembered that now.

During the first months in prison she refused to sign up for any training. While others went off to study, she stayed in her room where she sat or lay on the stiff bed. In the mirror she observed the grey roots that grew every month and wondered how long her hair would get while she was in here. On the morning of her fifty-ninth birthday she waited until the others were outside, then walked to the library. She felt sick at the sight of Wilbur Smith and other adventure books, their spines soft with love. Instead she found the Bible and flicked through with little interest. It wasn't like she deserved much of a gift.

The only time she looked forward to was Thursday afternoons when the post was delivered and she hoped to hear from Catherine. To know if she was all right and coping without drink. Most weeks, however, the guard walked straight past. When she occasionally did get a letter it was from Edith. They were short, polite notes. The sort you might write to a distant aunt. She mentioned her husband's various accolades but mostly focused on trivial events – the Scouts allowing girls to join and, later in the year, the heavy snow disrupting the railways. But although she never wrote back, finding nothing to write, the letters kept on coming without fail and she kept them beneath her mattress, a thread to her family, to herself.

On seeing a health counsellor the man asked why she had requested the Herbal Health pills.

'They help me.'

'Have you always taken them?'

'Yes, except for a few weeks after my daughter threw them down the toilet.'

'And what happened to you?'

'I can't remember clearly.'

The man was sceptical. 'The pills shouldn't affect your memory. In fact they don't do much at all.'

'You're wrong.'

'I assure you I'm not.'

And then she was off them for the first time since a teenager. She felt dizzy and told the guards she needed meals in

238

her room but no one listened. At night the shadows crept and darkened. Something fluttered in her chest. She didn't know what was happening, what she was capable of. What was this creature that'd always lurked inside her?

In the morning she kept to herself, avoiding the women who called her a hero. At mealtimes she sat at another table and, if tempted to talk to anyone, chewed the skin inside her mouth until she could taste the iron. When one of them passed they might nudge her shoulder but she would remain silent. At some point, however, they began to understand this as her being subversive. As if not responding to other prisoners demonstrated a peculiar kind of strength. Not reacting when guards addressed her, an even greater one. She didn't mean to make a statement. It merely felt as though words were oiled feathers that sat tangled in her stomach. To talk meant pulling one up through her gullet, yanking where it bulged till she coughed up the wet mass. No, words were better kept inside.

After a while she grew used to the way people stepped back when she walked along the corridor. How they passed her toilet roll in the queue for the bathroom. She had never experienced any kind of popularity, if that's what you could call this. It was nothing she deserved, but then, why not profit from it? She was that most peculiar creature, the Romsey Butcher. Maybe even her presence was deadly.

She was surprised, then, when the guards moved her into a shared room. A rise in the number of inmates meant more of them needed to bunk together. Surely not her, though? After more than a year on her own, Nettie felt frustrated by the different space as if entering a whole new country. The sink had no plug and it was overly noisy at night. Her cellmate was a woman in her early twenties named Amber who frequently wrapped herself in a ball on the lower bed. At night the whole bunk trembled with the woman's sobs, while Nettie lay stiffly above. The two women would've had little to do with one another in the outside world. In here they occupied the same space for most of the hours in the day. Even in the showers Nettie was aware of Amber's bare feet a few cubicles down. During the first few weeks she saw the remnants of a bruise across the woman's shoulders. Later heard her talk to someone about her husband's distaste for her modelling career.

Although Nettie knew it was wrong, she couldn't muster any feeling for the woman. Instead she was annoyed by the curls of hairs in the sink. By the volume at which the woman cried or sniffed as though unaware of who Nettie was. It became easier to block out Amber and she spent more and more time memorising passages of the Bible that remained on the top bunk, aware of the beauty infused in each page but unable to absorb any for herself.

It wasn't until one day when she was returning from lunch that she heard the noise from the room: a rhythmic clang. Then saw Amber's hair across her face. Her hands clutched the end of the bed. She was hurting herself over and over and Nettie stood watching. This was the moment to pull her away. Or to call for a guard. But she did nothing as the woman's head was stripped of skin, while the sound of footsteps started down the corridor.

After two women had carried her off, a remaining guard told Nettie *she really was evil*. Why hadn't she called out? After that Nettie tried saying a few words every day, each one a tie to reality. The girl had, at least, been given some sort of psychiatric help. A new cellmate too. When Nettie asked, again, for her herbal pills she was told, again, they did absolutely nothing. A placebo effect, apparently. She wasn't sure whether this was a comfort. Or whether her mind was far too powerful to be controlled, the creature a law unto itself.

XIV

2002

On her release from Holloway she travelled back to the farm-house. For a long time she'd not thought of the place and, once on the bus, considered selling up to move somewhere else. Another town where no one knew her. She could be just another woman approaching seventy, beige with anonymity. But even from the gate she could tell the farmhouse wasn't worth much. Stepping inside she heard the whistling draught, the air frigid despite the mild April weather. The place had been locked up for eleven years.

Her movements around the house were slow. It felt like this was someone else's home or maybe one from a dream. In her bedroom she picked up a comb which felt gummy in her palm. Found her face creams tinged orangey-pink. Something was scuffling in the next room too. Hopefully a mouse and nothing worse. After opening up the windows she sat on her bed and tried to cry but couldn't, only stared at the ceiling's cobwebs that stretched in tiny blankets.

Outside, she walked about the yard and saw the pipework that'd cracked. The fence infested with woodworm.

She then felt a part of herself fall.

The painted message shouldn't have been so gut-wrenching. Even before her court case, she'd found teens smoking outside her gate. But the paint was vivid red, freshly sprayed on the house's back wall.

BUTCHER

It was high up, higher than the grass which had grown so long. Where did they find the ladder? Was it borrowed from a nearby home or had the neighbours written it? Two more houses had been built over the years and she didn't know who now surrounded the place.

She was caught in a daze until a noise distracted her. Someone was on the property. Not at the front door but round the other side. Cowering in the garden she saw a movement through the living room window – a hoodie and streak of face – and waited till the gate clanged shut.

By the back door someone had left a note under a rock. They hadn't even come round the front to push it through the letterbox, as if in too much of a hurry. Were they afraid of her? Or merely disgusted by her home?

FUCK OFF FROM OUR TOWN

Staring at the handwritten letter, she was reluctant to phone the police. It was too soon to have anyone in uniform back here. Instead she placed the paper on the kitchen table, deciding to keep this hate mail as a reminder of what she did. Not that she could forget but her mind had grown murky and unpredictable over the last few years. This letter was something solid.

The night crept in and, when the boiler refused to light, the house grew cold. No tins of food were in the cupboards and she walked about, trying to reacquaint herself with her surroundings. In the wardrobes she had cleared out Harold's things and found only a tie that'd been ravaged by moths, now a sheer ghost of fabric. It seemed there was too much to fix and repair. Time had claimed so much. What was left for her?

The shotgun was on the top of the wardrobe, still in its original box. She felt its weight, which was oddly reassuring, and took it downstairs. Harold had taught her to shoot pheasants but she hated it. The bang was too loud. An injured bird didn't seem a win, even if she did like to eat it afterwards.

You make no sense, he'd said.

Does anyone?

Two bullets sat in the barrel. In the kitchen she wondered what was going through her mind. Nothing much. It was as if this plan had formed long ago in the depths of her consciousness. A simple end. She felt bad for the person who'd find her, though. The kids who might break in and never be quite the same again.

When she picked up the gun, she wasn't even sure it would be possible to kill herself, the barrel was so long.

Footsteps crunched outside. The person was back and a thought took hold: what if they did it for her? Didn't they all want to get rid of her? She went outside but found the yard empty. The garden was the same, just a swaying mass of weeds, so she headed for the field. A shape was moving but it wasn't a person. It was four-legged. A light brown, scraggly dog. Putting down the gun, she went over and saw its barrel of ribs.

The mongrel must be a stray and ravaged by fleas. She stared at the thing until it ran back under a hedge and was gone.

Some logs were in the barn under a tarpaulin. The top ones were damp but underneath they felt rougher. In the sinking light she carried them into the living room and looked around for something to use as tinder. The hateful message would do fine. Maybe she didn't need letters to remember what she did. Even as her mind turned murky, her body remembered. It'd become worn out from the truth of it. The last year she'd begun waking in the night, too, aching all over for no reason. Or perhaps that was just the beginnings of old age. Licks of flames glowed upon the letter, the burning slow to spread but promising warmth.

The next morning Nettie made a list of groceries. She needed a set of pliers too. Paint and brushes. A bottle of turps. The thought of showing her face in town set her teeth on edge, but she could drive to Southampton and be absorbed into the city.

Harold's car still sat in the barn. She wasn't sure why Martha hadn't taken the thing, other than a suspicion she hated it as much as Nettie did. How Harold shot around in it – between them and perhaps other women too. She got inside and tried the ignition which, after several attempts, hummed to life. While waiting for the engine to warm, she looked about. The glovebox was empty except for a map. An old handkerchief was lodged down the side of the passenger seat. Whose was it? Never mind. She pushed it back into place.

In the speckled mirror her face stared back. In prison she'd stopped inspecting herself but now saw the age spots and lines. The hair where grey had orchestrated a full takeover. There was no point in pretending she hadn't changed. She needed to face up to things.

In the end she walked into town. It was another mild day with clouds that drifted in the pale sky. Since she'd left, Romsey had bloated with new estates that brought a grumble of traffic and young families. Outside the newsagent's, the stand announced that the Queen was dining at Downing Street. Schoolkids milled about with their mums. Although various people turned, she passed quickly by and was soon beside the abbey where she was grateful to be alone, standing below its glasswork, which shone in the weak sunlight. In prison she had, at last, felt a connection to God – not so much from reading the Bible but from taking a gardening class. As she'd dug her fingers into the soil she realised He was everywhere. In every bulb and bud. And now across this graveyard. It seemed unlikely Nettie could ask for forgiveness but it was enough to know He'd be listening if she did.

Back at home the dog lay in the field. He looked younger than she'd first thought. His eyes were clear against his ragged fur and, as she stepped closer, he let out a growl that showed he'd stand his ground. 'Fine,' she said, waspish at this intruder. 'Do what you like.'

He skulked around the field for the rest of the afternoon. She put out water by the kitchen door and figured he wouldn't come when she was close but later found a trail of wet concrete. Mostly she went about her work. In the back garden weeds flourished in masses that swayed in the wind. Large green leaves shivered with velvet.

What makes something a weed? Catherine had asked as a girl.

It's something unwanted, I suppose.

Who decides that?

Now she appraised them she thought they were quite majestic. The thorns topped with purple crowns. A crowd of nettles. The oleander had shrunk to a dark leafy apology but remained nonetheless. Should she tear it out right here and now? No – Harold had planted it and, despite everything, she couldn't uproot this trace of him.

Over the next week she mended what she could. Painted the barn doors and replaced some of the fence. But too many things were beyond her, and she knew she'd need to sell the field to pay for the work. The land itself was a bearable loss but the oak tree another story. One windy afternoon she took a rug and laid beneath the branches which cried twisted leaves. What would it mean to lose this tree? What did any of this house and land mean any more?

She was lost in thought on her way back when she noticed the dog had ventured into the yard. He sat on the floor and licked a scrawny paw. 'I should really get rid of you,' she said. 'You'll bring all sorts of disease.' But that night she put out scraps which were gone by morning. Time passed and he became a frequent visitor then a full-blown house guest, curling into a ball on the kitchen floor most nights. She decided not to call him anything in case he left. He became 'the dog' and she thought of herself as 'the woman'. Then, after a while, he was part of the house and she gave him a collar to hear him tinkle when he came close. If nothing else he'd be company. A reason to rise each morning.

XV

Ten months on, it was rare for Nettie to hear from her daughter. If they did speak it was on the phone, conversations stripped of small talk to expose the facts of the situation: Catherine wanted to get on with her life, largely without her mum. Then one winter morning she rang and something felt different.

'Mum? I'm sick.'

'What's wrong?'

'I need to visit for a couple of days. That all right?'

It was February and the boiler was at last working, after Nettie found someone to come to the house. The roof was, however, less than gale-proof and she worried what Catherine would think. Whether she'd regret coming when she saw the state of the place. Nettie had repainted some of the rooms but, mostly, she'd left things unchanged. Instead she spent her days listening to Radio 4 and tending to the garden in all its weed-climbing glory. At least the girl's room was easily prepared for her arrival. Why was she coming after all this time? Perhaps she had an upset stomach and some days to spare. Catherine's nurse training had long been deserted after she claimed it was all too hard work. Nettie imagined she was on benefits but Catherine never said so and Nettie didn't ask.

She fidgeted by the kitchen door. So many years had passed and now Catherine was on her way through town. As the taxi pulled into the yard she held her breath and, sure enough, it was her daughter who got out. Tugging her hair behind her ears, she moved her bulk towards the boot. She'd put on weight but – Nettie realised – she wasn't fat. She was pregnant.

'Hiya,' Catherine said without looking up. The taxi driver went to retrieve her pink roller case from the boot but she waved him away. Beneath a woollen cardigan, a T-shirt stretched over the bulge.

Nettie wanted to wrap her arms around her daughter. An embrace that'd dissolve the years. But Catherine was busy rooting in her handbag for the fare. After the car drove away they hovered in the yard until Nettie remembered herself. 'Would you like to come inside?' she said, overly formal. 'I'll take your bag.'

'Cheers.'

The roller case was reassuringly heavy and, after carrying it upstairs, she gave her daughter time to unpack. In the kitchen she wiped down the sides once again. She had already poured away the bottles of wine and gin at the back of the pantry, not knowing whether her daughter still had a problem but figuring it was better to be cautious. Now doubly so. Addictions didn't end because a woman was pregnant, no matter how much she loved her unborn child.

They drank tea in the living room and for a minute the chink of china was the only conversation, a spoon of sugar its reply. In the back garden frost laced the foliage, the oleander almost hidden in the weeds. The dog trotted into the room but stopped on seeing the guest.

'What a mangy thing,' her daughter said.

Nettie called him closer. Although she'd taken him to the vet for injections, he still had a bedraggled look about him. 'He's my friend.'

She pulled a face. 'What's his name?'

'I don't know.'

'Not much of a friend then.'

After the dog had slunk away, Catherine talked about finding out she was pregnant. 'They told me to stop bleaching my hair. It's only a few streaks,' she said, tugging at the strands.

'And the baby's father?'

'He's a nice bloke. Says he wants to be involved.'

'You'll get married?'

'God no. It's not like that. We were drunk, it's a long story...' She shrugged. 'Actually I guess that's it really. We were drunk.'

For the next two days Catherine lounged around, letting Nettie bring her toast and soup and fetch magazines from the local shop, claiming she didn't read newspapers. It pleased Nettie to learn how many sugars she had in her coffee these days. To know how her daughter disliked television shows that weren't realistic to the letter. They didn't talk about Harold or anything from the last years, as though they were strangers with no idea of the other's past. Nettie didn't mind. How soothing it was to exist day to day, an object without a shadow.

On the Wednesday they walked into town for lunch after Catherine claimed cabin fever. They chose a new restaurant where Nettie ordered them both lemonades. She didn't like to admit she regularly drank gin after dinner. It helped bring sleep closer. The music was loud so they ate without much chatter, tucking into fish finger and tartare sauce sandwiches, with chips from potatoes the chef had forgotten to peel. Things seemed fine until Nettie returned from the toilet to find Catherine had ordered a wine. The waitress set it down between them.

'Is that a good idea?' Nettie asked.

She twisted the glass. 'Oh I'm just getting started.'

Four months later the Royal London Hospital rang to tell her Catherine had gone into labour. The June weather heated the underground and Nettie arrived covered in sweat but thrilled to be told the little girl had arrived safely. It'd been a straight-forward birth, the nurse said as Nettie hurried onto the ward. Catherine was sat up in bed beside a man who held the baby. He was well dressed in a striped shirt and introduced himself before saying he'd go out for a cigarette. Nettie wanted to hold the baby but – her arms suddenly feeling weak – she watched as he returned the girl to Catherine.

'I've enrolled in AA,' she told her.

'We don't need to talk about that now.' The baby's face was all squashed cheeks and a look of disgruntlement.

'I just want you to know, that's all.'

Nettie nodded, thinking her daughter already seemed different, gazing at the baby as if surprised at what she'd created.

She wanted to tell Edith she was a grand-aunt but felt odd about contacting her again. It wasn't that her sister didn't know she'd been released – she'd written, plus later rang the prison in case letters had arrived there. None had. All she could suppose was that things were different now she was back in the real world. An actual person who might one day turn up on her doorstep. Instead Nettie focused on her daughter who visited that summer, bringing a mound of toys, bottles and the other paraphernalia that added up to modern parenting. Nettie didn't mind. It was nice to see the place taken over by a new life. She'd forgotten how demanding it could be to breast-feed a baby and noticed how quickly afterwards her daughter fell asleep on the settee. Days passed with Nettie rising early to sterilise bottles and watch as little Elly discovered the tastes and feels of the house. Meanwhile, her own daughter complained of headaches, so Nettie spent time outside with the child, walking around the garden with the dog keeping a watchful eye on them both. It was nice she was trusted with her. But then, why wouldn't she be? The only time Catherine wrinkled her nose was at the dog.

'He's getting hairs everywhere. Isn't it time he found a new home?'

Nettie stared at the animal who'd stretched out on the rug. Over the months he'd grown more accustomed to the place and claimed particular spots on the floor. Granted, her daughter was only being cautious. She tried to picture herself taking him to a kennel, hearing him whine as she left.

'No, sorry,' she told her daughter. 'He's staying put.'

'Well at least give him a name.'

'Like what?'

'I don't care. Anything.'

In the end it was Elly who named the dog after pointing out a character called Rufus in a picture book. This was the following summer when they'd visited again. 'All right,' said Nettie. 'Rufus he is.'

By the next year Catherine had a second daughter called Grace. Watching the two of them sitting on a rug in the garden, Nettie felt herself tingle at the sight. Who knew what she'd say when they were old enough to ask about their grandfather. Their opinions would shift as they tried to fit her into their drawings of a family, or else she'd drop off the page altogether. For now, though, she'd make every day count.

The years rolled on and for her seventy-eighth birthday she asked that they go away early in June. Elly was eight and an inquisitive child, wanting to explore, while her little sister was desperate to tag along. It seemed fitting they would travel up to Scotland near where they'd been as a family before, and Nettie as a child before that. That it'd make them each think of Harold wasn't the worst thing either. They still hadn't talked about what happened. The single photograph of him in the study prompted no discussion and yet Nettie noticed how her daughter held it sometimes. The photo showed Harold alone on some fishing trip as a teenage boy; his dungarees strained as he loomed large over the lake, sunshine bleaching his face except for the ghost of a smile.

Nettie found a place in a nearby village where there was a garden. The first Saturday of June she changed the oil of Harold's car and drove to the Borough flat where Catherine lived with her girls. It wasn't much but it had a balcony where she stashed Elly's bike and a couple of straggly plants. She seemed to be doing okay in general, with child support coming in from each of the dads, and today the three of them were waiting in matching sunglasses.

Just as they were leaving the M25 Catherine complained of her driving and insisted they swap. 'We'll never get there otherwise,' she said. Soon after, she saw Nettie clutch her seat belt as she changed lanes. Then they were hurtling up the M1 and, on reaching a steady speed, Nettie relaxed. The girls were eating sandwiches in the back and Catherine played a CD of pop music by some robotic woman. It was nice how normal it all felt. The car warmed as sunlight streamed through the windows.

'Do you remember coming here as a girl?' she asked Catherine.

'Not really.' She pushed the huge sunglasses onto her face. Became just a nose and mouth.

'It was lovely.'

'Look, Mum, let's not talk about it.'

'I'm just saying.'

After turning up the music, Catherine sighed and focused on the lane ahead. Nettie twisted round to speak to the girls. Having sucked the life from a carton of squash, Grace announced she needed the toilet.

'Just hold it in,' replied her mum.

'I can't!'

They stopped at a motorway service station where Nettie took both girls to the bathroom. As she walked crookedly to hold their hands, they laughed at her monster-like form and the growls she made. On returning they found the driver's seat empty. Sitting in the car to wait, they watched people pass by with sandwich boxes, one wearing a straw hat. Families out for the day to the seaside or travelling south to the Channel Tunnel. Nettie was glad to be among them.

'Where is your mum?' she said absently.

'She could be gone for ever.'

Nettie twisted in her seat. 'Does she ever leave you?'

'No.' The girl sighed. 'She says she's not allowed.'

The next minute Catherine showed up with newly brushed hair and slid into the driver's seat, igniting the engine without a word. Two hours later they reached the Scottish border and sat quietly as the distance between towns became long stretches of green – fields, farmhouses and cattle grids that bumped beneath them. The girls were playing I-Spy or at least Grace was, Elly declaring herself too old. Her sister didn't care. It meant she won each go.

'Where is this place?' Catherine said when they reached the village. Nettie checked the instructions the owner had given her.

'Don't you have a postcode?'

'She didn't tell me that. But it's fine. It says to pass by the postbox on the left.'

'And where is that exactly?'

They reached the other end of the high street and needed to turn back except a tractor was behind them and soon they were on the main road. Grace finished her game and complained they were both hungry.

'Hold on, girls,' Nettie said, checking the instructions again. 'We'll be there soon.'

They found a spot to turn around just as it was beginning to rain, the tarmac becoming slick. Catherine sped towards the village again. 'Great – it'll be like this all week.'

'Oh cheer up,' said Nettie.

'What?'

'Well, it's not so bad. We're on holiday.'

'A holiday you weren't honest about. You think I would've come if I realised this is near where we went with Dad?'

'Whose dad?' Elly called from the back.

'No one's,' said Catherine as the fields rushed past.

In the next moment the other car appeared as a streak of blue. Later Nettie would realise it came from a side turning, the bush overgrown. As their own vehicle hit its bonnet, the car spun around. A pivot of screaming tyres. Them suddenly at a standstill, straining against their seat belts. And then heavy breaths. Nettie turned to see what'd happened to the other car. In the back seat a little boy was still for a moment before a sickening wail rang out. It came again as a woman jumped from the passenger seat to retrieve him, a gash seeping across his forehead.

'Oh God, oh God.' Catherine gripped the steering wheel.

Nettie got out and asked if he was okay. The boy looked at her blankly, his wound shining with blood. 'I don't know,' said the woman.

The cars were blocking the road so Catherine edged onto the verge. The man in the driver's seat of the other car did nothing, remaining motionless as if stuck in the moment of impact.

'Honey?' the woman called to him. He didn't move.

She turned back. 'We'd better ring an ambulance … and the police!'

Nettie went to where Catherine was pale-faced in the car. It took her a minute to wind down the window.

'She wants to call the police,' Nettie said.

'I'm sorry, I'm sorry.'

'It's okay, Catherine.'

'No it isn't, Mum. I've had a drink.'

'You've what?'

'Several drinks.' She shook in the seat. 'You ... you shouldn't have talked about him. Made me come here. I can't bear to hear his name.'

'I didn't realise ...'

Amidst the damaged cars – the shattered glass – Harold still loomed between them, never quite gone. And she was the one who'd brought them here to confront it. Except it was a little boy who now stood in front of them, a little boy with blood on his fingers.

5

2015

14

August 2015

Nettie stands by the broken window in the landing. It's needed repairing for weeks – the pane soon to buckle – but she doesn't deserve to have it fixed. The kids are right to throw stones. What with Harold. The cat. Then the accident years later when she still hadn't learnt to keep quiet. No wonder Catherine can't bear to visit. She might've been the one drink-driving but it was Nettie who caused it all.

Meanwhile James walks about downstairs. The minutes pass. Or maybe they don't. Maybe the clock has stopped and she remains lodged in time. Is this her own purgatory? The house has always known what she, herself, failed to understand – speaking with its incessant whispers, writing with dust across every surface. For years she's tried to get on with things because sometimes forgetting is all you can do. A form of reprieve. Now she stands until numb, her blood cooling, bones becoming calcified. Her family was right: there's always been something peculiar about her. She married, had children. Took pills, stopped taking pills. Nothing changed. Others will never like her and this is something she's continuously aware of – a valve in her heart letting the word through her bloodstream: *People people people.*

She scuttles down the stairs to where James is followed by Rufus, who hurries between them in a lumbering walk, then slumps on the rug.

'Why don't you want to leave?' she says. It's the most honest question she's asked all week and for a minute he remains quiet, frowning with eyes unfocused.

He pulls himself together. 'I suppose I like it here.' He chuckles. 'Although I've ended things with Tara.'

'I'm not sure I understood what she was doing here in the first place.'

'She's nice enough for a girl from such a screwed-up family.'

'Was she all right?'

'Not really, no. Quit her job at the pub right there and then. God knows what she plans to do now.'

She expects him to be more regretful but he's absorbed in Rufus who rolls onto his side, his milky eyes beginning to close.

'He's not looking great,' James says.

'I'll take him to the vet,' she replies, knowing it's a lie. 'I'm more worried about Tara.'

'Well *I'm* worried about this poor bonnie lad,' he says and ducks down to wrap himself around the dog. A rip gapes across his shirt where he's hurt himself on the roof. It's like he's obsessed with this house to the neglect of everything else. What does he intend to do with her? With them both?

*

The sycamore branches darken to silhouettes as the sun lowers. Stick clacking along the pavement, Nettie isn't sure Marianne will be at home or that she'll have time to speak. After finding a stray Post-it note, however, she decided to return it. Anything to be away from James, who she left beside Rufus on the floor, fawning over the dog. 'Helium machine,' reads the note, an odd notion right now in the dying light.

Seeing the house, Nettie loosens her grasp of the stick. Her friend will know what to do – she pictures the two of them sitting together, exchanging furies before they devise another plan. But as she walks along the front garden path, she slows. The living room is murky with a single lamp on and all she can see are two figures: the pink of Pauline's jumper; Marianne sat on a settee cradling her head. They're talking about something Nettie can't hear.

Perhaps she should turn back. It's hard to know whether she'll help in this situation. As she's wondering what to do, there's a creak.

'Hello?' Pauline keeps the door half-closed, showing a slice of her pink jumper paired with leggings and slippers. 'Can I help?'

'I'm a friend of Marianne's.'

'We're in the middle of something.'

Despite knowing it's her cue to leave, Nettie lingers.

'Let her in,' comes a voice from inside. It's Marianne's although she sounds different – drained of feeling. In the living room she sits with her knees together, her face seems immobile as if moulded from clay.

'I brought your Post-it note,' Nettie says, showing the feeble scrap of paper.

'Thank you.'

Pauline comes in behind, her large feet pressing against woollen slippers whose stitches are beginning to come loose. Rings mark the passage of two mugs across the table.

'I shouldn't have come,' apologises Nettie.

When Marianne doesn't react, it's Pauline who speaks in a light voice, her Norfolk accent rounding the words. 'If you're a friend then you're welcome. I'm the sore thumb here.'

'Well …'

'And I don't mean to be funny but you look like you could do with a drink. Or several.'

'Pauline!' says Marianne, at last breaking her trance.

'She does! I'm only being sympathetic.'

'Is that what you call it?'

Pauline pulls an apologetic face at Nettie. There's something comical about her. Someone who sees the world through a sideways glance while her mind is on greater things. Maybe this is why the women have grown close. Too close perhaps.

'Has James gone?' Marianne asks, gathering herself.

'I'm afraid not.'

'Really? What a pest he is.'

Pauline shoves hands under her armpits. 'Who are you talking about?'

'An unwanted guest,' Marianne says.

'Oh yeah?'

Sinking into a chair, Nettie lets her mind turn. 'He might be someone from a few years ago. He went to see my daughter too. Pretended he was an alcoholic to join her AA meetings.'

'And I thought I was sick,' says Pauline. 'The man puts me to shame.'

As the other women talk, it dawns on Nettie what a bizarre situation she's walked in on. Isn't Pauline an unwanted guest

264

too? She's plonked herself into the middle of their argument and should leave, but is too tired for the walk home. Instead she pushes off the chair to go into the kitchen. 'Excuse me a moment.'

'See?' Pauline says. 'Told you she needed a drink.'

Through the window she sees the dark is setting in, the wings of night unfolding. Maybe she can hide out here. It isn't the worst idea. Or else the three of them can return to the farmhouse and together force James to leave. But no, she couldn't stand the women hearing the awful things he'd say about her. The looks on their faces.

Low voices drift from the living room.

'We could just try it,' says Marianne.

'I told you. It's not going to work.'

A sigh. 'You're the one always turning up. Phoning me.'

'Because I missed you, M, crazy as that now seems.'

'What are we supposed to do then?'

Nettie edges away to where breadcrumbs are spilt across the kitchen table, a quiche crust gnawed of its insides. She wonders how long they've been arguing for. Why Pauline won't take the hint and leave her friend alone. A floorboard shifts and Marianne appears.

'Sorry about this,' she says, her face drained of colour. 'You came here for help and I'm full to the brim with my own problems.'

'Not to worry.'

She attempts a smile and puts dishes in the sink, a rhythmic clatter echoing between them.

'Let me know if I can do anything,' says Nettie.

'What do you mean?'

'You helped me with James. And well ...' She gestures

towards the sitting room where Pauline has put on the TV. A wildlife documentary shows a vulture soaring across a valley.

'You don't understand.' Marianne carries on fiddling with the dishes. 'I've asked Pauline to move in with me.'

'Sorry?'

'We have something. I told you we did. And although she's unsure, I really think—'

'*Pauline* is unsure?' Nettie closes the kitchen door. 'I thought you said she was the one harassing you?'

'I never said harassing,' Marianne replies. 'Yes she's been keen and for a time I felt pressured. But I was lying to myself about what this all means. About what we mean to each other.'

'And now it's you who's wanting to live together?' Nettie can't understand. She's too exhausted to make sense of these women.

'Never mind.' The drawers clink and shudder as she puts away cutlery. 'Don't worry yourself about it.'

Cast adrift from the conversation, Nettie finds herself wandering into the hallway to leave. From her place on the living room settee, Pauline gives a silly wave, the vulture still looking for prey. The television is on silent but it doesn't matter what the woman has heard. It all seems inconsequential as she opens the door and shuffles out.

She's halfway along the street when Marianne catches up with her. 'Hold on, Nettie. I'm not sure what you came here for tonight.' She's out of breath, cardigan flapping in the wind.

'I suppose I shouldn't have come.'

Marianne shakes her head, exasperated. 'I thought you'd understand.'

'Understand what?'

'Relationships aren't easy. Especially not the closest ones.'

'No one should lose a tooth,' Nettie says. 'Such a horrid thing.'

'It's true and she's getting professional help. In the meantime I'll be there for her. It's what love means.'

'I'm not sure I agree.'

Marianne bristles at this and moves closer. Her voice drops so the words tremble between them. 'You of all people should understand this.'

'Me?'

She expects more but the woman is returning to her house, walking up the little path where she is greeted by Pauline. The two go inside together, back into the living room. Nettie stares for another moment. *Her of all people?*

All this time she'd assumed that Marianne didn't know about what happened with Harold. Or – if she did – she'd rise above the gossip. Of course it's not gossip, though. And Marianne is only human.

15

It's the smell she notices first. Smoke scenting the air like on bonfire night. Maybe a farmer is burning wood – but this late? She drifts along the road before realising the burning is coming from her house, where flames stretch hot fingers into the night air. The gate is open and, behind, the barn is engulfed by a fire that crackles and spits, exhaling smoke so the yard is thick with grey. Nettie's throat constricts. What has James done?

She needs to phone the fire brigade and goes to move inside but the man appears and holds his mobile, a haggard look contorting his face.

'You did this?' she asks.

'What?' He's shocked. 'Of course not.'

The two of them stand motionless until they see movement. A teenage girl emerges from the smoke, coughing as she approaches. It's the girl from the park bench. Her little friends wait behind.

'Why?' Nettie calls over.

Keeping her distance, the girl hooks fingers through her belt loops. 'You don't get to live in this big old house. Not after what you did.' They all glare and, ashamed of herself, Nettie looks away.

The smoke continues to billow, rising into different shapes. As the wind changes direction it's pulled towards the kids who splutter. 'You and this mansion, it's not fair,' the girl says again before she motions to leave. They'll have to run past her and James but neither of them will do anything. The man is transfixed beside her.

'I'm going through the field,' says a familiar voice. As Nettie peers she sees a fourth person by the fence.

'Tara?'

The girl hugs herself, clutching her bare hips. 'I'm sorry, all right,' she says, then steps back and knocks something with her feet. A tin of petrol. As the barn roof crumbles, Nettie feels herself caving in. She should've realised the two anklets were homemade, something teenage girls plait for one other. She remembers Tara first in the farmhouse, how reluctant she was to speak to Nettie. How she asked no questions about the kids with the spray can.

After the four of them scatter and disappear, Nettie motions for James to call the fire brigade. He hesitates, gazing at the flames in awe.

'Phone them,' she says. 'Before it spreads to the house.'

For a moment it seems he won't. He'll watch it all burn till there's nothing left – the smile on his lips shows he's tempted by the thought. But then he dials and waits with her outside, the two of them silent before the rising smoke.

*

When the fire brigade arrive they work quickly and soon the barn is a blackened carcass, its insides on display but nothing much to see.

'We'll need you to come down the station,' says a uniformed man.

'Sorry?'

'To press charges.'

She asks if she can do it the following day. Or not at all. The girl's angry voice comes back to her. How she didn't deserve this home.

'We'd definitely like a statement,' he says, a young man with a steady look about him. 'We reckon it's part of this anti-gentrification nonsense that's been going on in town.'

'Maybe tomorrow,' says James. 'It's been a long day.'

After some more formalities, the police and firemen drive away, leaving them to stare at the remains. A blackness has spread across the concrete but the house is at least untouched.

'Why didn't you see them come?' she asks James. 'What were you doing?'

He doesn't reply. He begins pacing around, calling for Rufus. They were told not to inspect the barn until someone had visited, so he edges around it. No dog lies on the ground or over towards the garden and they exchange a relieved glance before he goes to look inside.

The night is newly quiet with only a ripple of wind in the grass. A rattle above. She sees a layer of plastic stretches over most of the roof. James's work. She smiles, feeling odd. There's a sense of finality as she stands, watching the last of the smoke fade, before she goes into the kitchen.

*

The room is slow to collect around her and she pours herself a cup of water to soothe her throat. James's footsteps shuffle above as he continues looking for the dog. It's then she sees it. The shotgun sits on the table, its barrel dull. It doesn't seem real – a brute object but one that can injure or even kill. How did he get into her room? The answer isn't hard. Nothing holds strong in this house any more. As the kids lit the first match, he must've been busy rooting through her belongings.

Her heart works like a clock. A steady ticking in her chest.

Footsteps are on the stairs, getting louder. 'I found the dog,' he says.

'What's this?'

He slowly nods. 'The Purdey? It was stashed beneath your bed. A fair idea to keep it, I suppose, considering.'

'Considering what?'

'Death is part of life, isn't it?' His face is smooth, the lines and angles from before now gone. He whistles to Rufus who lumbers down the stairs towards him. 'Good boy,' he says as he loops fingers beneath his collar. 'He's had a difficult time. Maybe breathed in some smoke.'

'He'll be fine.' She doesn't like how the man grasps Rufus. The dog nudges to get away but quickly gives in. 'Leave him be.'

'You said yourself, he's old. Not much puff left in him.'

'I don't see your point.' Her eyes shift to the shotgun. It seems a trap that's been laid for her, him leaving it there like that. Even after everything she's still not sure what his game is. Whether he's the father from the car crash. And now he's – what? Wanting her to suffer?

'Shoot him,' says James. He motions to Rufus who, now released, slumps to the floor by his feet.

'Don't be horrid.'

'What's the matter? You're no stranger to a mercy killing. In fact, you don't even need the mercy part.'

'I want you to leave or I'll ring the police.'

'Again? They'll be getting sick of you, Nettie.' He moves towards the shotgun and she leans over, picks it up. That the metal is warm against her fingertips makes her recoil but she clutches it anyway and steps back.

'Go on then,' James says, trying to sound casual.

Angling the shotgun at the floor, she calls Rufus over to her. He's slow but makes his way as she opens the back door. A cold gust comes from outside and he hesitates. 'Out you go.' When he refuses, sliding onto his belly, she nudges him with her foot. It's not worth letting him stay. 'I said, out.'

'See? It'd be kinder to be brave. Help the bonnie lad die with some grace, eh?'

'Out.' She nudges the dog harder, her leg pressing against the rough fur of his back, ribs hard with bone.

'Why else did you keep the gun? Someone was always going to end up that way. The eternal sleep?'

James steps closer to them both. Despite his blank face, the rest of him is rigidly straight. Boots polished, the laces pulled into tight knots.

'Please, boy,' Nettie whispers, not knowing what will happen when he reaches them. She angles the shotgun at James but it wavers, there's no way she could shoot straight. Still Rufus refuses to move and she panics, giving him a sharp jab of her foot. The dog cries and lurches out of the door.

It's now just the two of them alone in the kitchen.

James's face pulls into a smile. 'It would be so natural for you.'

'Be quiet,' she says beneath her breath. He edges forwards

before lunging to take the shotgun but she swerves, knocking into a chair which falls to the floor. The hard slap unsettles them both and James remains by the door as she backs away to put two yards between them. She aims the shotgun and this time it doesn't waver as she leans the wooden part on her shoulder, as Harold taught her. She peers down the barrel.

'Okay, all right.' He frantically smooths his hair. Mouth drops open, lower lip shiny.

'I don't want to do this,' she says.

'Don't you?'

The clock ticks as she feels the curve of the trigger. It feels so inevitable to be here like this. It's as though this is where the week has been heading. A cold sweat trickles down her inner thigh.

'Fine,' breathes James. 'If this is what you want then do it.'

'Do what?'

'Get rid of me too. I mean, wouldn't it be easier this way?' His eyes are fixed on the barrel. A blotchiness has crept up his neck, to his cheeks. As he steps forwards she sees a damp patch in the crotch of his trousers. But then he's looking around the kitchen, into the living room. He's forgetting himself and scrutinising her things and she's reminded of all these days he's spent toying with her. Judging her life, her home.

'I've finally figured you out.' He nods in slow motion. 'The night you first pointed your gun at me, I thought you didn't have it in you. Then I learnt about your husband and it was just a matter of time. I should've left but it was sort of fascinating being around you. To see how you loathe yourself. How even when I was awful, you let me be that way because you knew it was what you deserved.'

'Shut up.'

'Even when I brought Tara round, expecting you to throw us out, you did nothing.'

'I said, shut up.' She shivers beneath the cold, bright light.

'So do it, if that's what you want.'

Her finger feels the trigger again. A single tug and that'd be him gone. No more staring at her. No more appraising who she is. The disgusting old woman. First she wants to know who he is, though.

'You called the dog "bonnie". You're Scottish, aren't you?'

'So?'

'You're obsessed with the car too. And you're estranged from your family.'

James raises his eyebrows, waiting for her to go on.

'I know who you are. You're the father of the little boy Catherine hurt that day. You blame her for drink-driving. And me for convincing your wife not to phone the police. You think there's something awful in our family blood. You think we can't help but hurt people.'

A noise drills through the air. The doorbell. James swivels around, touching his trousers. 'Who is that?'

'Catherine.'

Nettie lets the shotgun droop. She can't let her daughter see her this way. The children too. What would they think? But it's night and they're outside. Perhaps the last train has already left. 'Stay here,' she mutters to James as she walks towards the hallway. The doorbell goes again and she leans the shotgun against the wall.

She checks that James is waiting in the kitchen before opening the door. Goodness knows what she'll tell her daughter. But it isn't Catherine she finds on the doorstep.

'I'm sorry for turning up this late,' says Edith. She's a woman in her late seventies, her hair silvery-white and scooped into a low bun. A silk scarf hangs over a trench coat. 'The trains were delayed.'

Nettie can only stare as her sister steps closer. As always her shoes are delicate things – cream with a slight heel – although her ankles are puffy. The same as her own.

'Can I come in?'

'Of course you can.' She shakes herself as Edith steps inside. For a second Nettie almost forgets who's waiting in the living room but then she sees his figure loom.

'I would've come earlier but didn't think,' her sister says.

In the kitchen Edith and James gauge each other. It's hard to know how to introduce them and Nettie is tongue-tied, her gaze flicking from one to the other.

'And, well …' Her sister fidgets with her collar as James stares, ashen-faced. No doubt he's wanting to bypass these two old women. To retrieve the shotgun from the hall or perhaps escape the farmhouse altogether. Edith speaks again, 'It was only when I got the phone call from James's wife that I realised where he was.'

'My *ex*-wife,' corrects James.

'It's hardly the point.' Edith's fingers fly to her lips which tighten into a hard line.

Nettie frowns. 'You know James?'

'He shouldn't have come. I do hope he's not caused any problems. I told him not to intrude and he promised.'

'That was months ago.' James glares, picking up the fallen chair. 'I needed to come here.'

'To Catherine's too?' says Edith.

Heat rising through her, Nettie walks between them. 'Whatever is going on, tell me now.'

Edith asks her to sit down and – despite the flaring in her cheeks – Nettie silently walks into the living room. The armchair is rough beneath her, its fabric cold. She hears her sister tell James to give them a minute and he puts up a fuss, then agrees to go and fetch the dog, closing the door behind him.

'I'm sorry,' her sister says as she sits on the settee. 'That's the most important thing to know.'

'Tell me.'

'The truth is we both missed you and you refused to talk to us. When you and I met in Waterloo all those years ago. For the coffee …' She neatens her scarf. 'Not that I can make excuses. It was a quick, stupid thing. We found comfort in each other. Reminded each other of you.'

'Who is "we"?'

Edith gets up and walks to the mantelpiece where she fidgets with the various photographs, avoiding her eye. 'Harold and I.'

'You slept with Harold?'

'It was wrong, of course it was. And I've stayed away all these years because I felt such a weight of guilt, at times I couldn't breathe for it. Especially when you were later sentenced and …' She touches her throat. 'And there I was with a family.'

Nettie shakes her head as if it'll help the thoughts slot into place. 'All this time, Harold had another child. With you?'

'None of it was ideal and I considered the alternative.' She glances to the window that looks on to the yard. 'Nathan was the one to suggest we say he was James's real father. He was in the RAF at the time and spent long periods away. We wanted the time he did spend with James to be special.'

276

She doesn't want to ask the next question. The landslide of truth into which everything will crumble. The light flickers and the silhouette of a moth creeps around the inner lampshade. For a second Nettie is mesmerised as it slowly stops moving, blinded by the bulb.

'And Harold knew,' says Edith, answering for her. 'I didn't want him to be part of it and he respected that. He sent photos, letters, gifts over the years. But I kept them from James. It seemed simpler that way. No one need find out. But then James did at Christmas. He was rummaging in an old box of decorations and saw a gift tag. I still can't believe I left the damn thing in there.'

'That's why James is here?'

'He seemed all right at first. But over time he got angry, he wanted to know who you were.'

'I'm not surprised. You lied to us both. For years.'

Unable to look at her sister's pleading face, Nettie rises and drifts away. The ground is unsteady beneath her, the landslide on its way, and she expects to fall or faint but stays upright. Focuses on her breathing.

'Where are you going?' Edith calls behind her uncertainly. 'I think we should talk about this some more.'

Nettie doesn't reply. How could her own sister behave that way? Martha was one thing – an outsider, an unknown – she couldn't stomach much anger towards the woman. But Edith? A part of her wants to know the details. She remembers the weepy phone conversation with Edith. How she begged forgiveness and Nettie stupidly thought she had just been talking about their awkward coffee in Waterloo. It was laughable.

In the hallway the shotgun waits. Nettie picks it up and carries it back.

'What's that?'

Everything is trembling around her. The walls radiating heat and moving closer. The pictures staring. Did everyone know but her? Their mum? Their aunts? She can't bear to think of it. How for more than thirty years she's been the only one who didn't know. Once again, Nettie the fool.

'Are you mad?'

Seeing her sister back away makes Nettie pause. The barrel shudders in her arms as she wonders where to aim, wanting to shoot at every wall in the house. At the lie she's lived in for so much of her life. Or does she want to shoot her sister? Or herself?

James reappears and goes to his mum. 'Put it down,' he says, stepping in front of Edith.

It enrages Nettie how he protects her. The woman who deceived them all with a secret she kept like a dirty jewel, showing it to selected people.

'You don't want to hurt her,' he says.

Nettie silently agrees but can't see her way clear. She needs an end point to stop everything charging in her head. To stop them looking at her with their gawping faces.

Edith steps away from her son and Nettie angles the gun. Not at her head, though – her face is still beautiful. Between her shoulders? She can't think what to do. Only feels a hot pulsing through her.

'Your son hates me. He knows I killed Harold,' she says.

'Let's talk about this,' says Edith.

'You never wanted to talk before. All these years you stayed away from me.'

'Out of my own guilt, not because I thought you a bad person.'

278

A tear slips down Nettie's cheek. It's so unexpected she feels a stranger in her own body. Finding the colours of the rug swirl if she looks down, she focuses ahead. On the mother and son. Tight together. She looks for Harold in James's face.

'I have no choice,' says Nettie. 'This is who I am.'

'What do you mean?'

'I've got to face up to things.'

Her sister steps towards her and, as James goes to hold her back, she shrugs him off. 'Mum, don't,' he says, afraid.

'It's fine.' She stands two inches from the barrel of the shotgun. 'This isn't you, Nettie. Because you're not capable of killing out of spite.'

'I am.' The tears choke her throat and she gasps. 'It's why I killed Harold.'

'No.' Her voice is calm. 'I know that's not true.'

'It is.'

'You're wrong.'

James waves an arm. 'Let's go, Mum. We'll get a taxi back home.'

Edith ignores him. 'We might've drifted apart. But I knew you, Nettie. I still do. You might've gone about it the wrong way. But it was an act of love. You know it was. Deep down you do.'

1990

XVI

September 1990

'Odd to think we're in our mid-fifties.'

'Actually I'm fifty-eight,' Harold pointed out. 'But then I've always had a head start.' Another autumn approached and Nettie was considering their ages, something she did now and then, as if to acknowledge the passing of time was to more greatly appreciate life. The last eleven years back with Harold hadn't been easy. She flushed to think of her meetings with a man from the pub whose name she barely remembered; their quick encounters that ended in talk of missing their spouses. Of course Harold was home at the time but she missed how things had been at the start. Beginnings were the easy part. It was everything else layered on top that hurt. The crumpling of a discovered receipt. The watchful eye required at a drinks party. Waiting for him to come home or finding him sat waiting for her. But then there was the laughter that made everything else fall away.

Harold's divorce had been finalised a year after he moved back home and he claimed not to regret selling the family business to pay her share, although on Monday mornings he wandered around looking lost and kept his briefcase in the hall, despite the fact he'd never work again.

In many other ways he carried on as usual. Took care of the telephone bills and other paperwork. He'd begun work on an adventure novel and pieces of paper appeared around the house. 'More lions,' she'd tell him on reading the occasional page.

That morning he was making a chicken and root vegetable pie ahead of their daughter coming to stay. At midday Nettie went to fetch her from the train station, having got her driver's licence three years before at Harold's request. Growing up in London she'd not needed to learn and she was happy enough walking or taking the train but he insisted it made sense. At least she got to wear driving gloves – cream leather ones – and as she held the steering wheel, she felt her ring beneath them. Although they weren't lawfully married she wore the thing anyway. Jewellery could mean what you wanted and it felt right on her finger.

Catherine was waiting in the car park, wearing no coat and a flimsy dress with leggings, a rucksack hitched on one shoulder. She waited until Nettie pulled up before moving an inch, forever testing the limits of what her mum would do for her. Nettie usually obliged. The girl had never stopped being headstrong but that'd serve her well if she put to good use.

'Why didn't Dad come to collect me?' she asked after conceding a peck on the cheek. 'He usually drives.'

'He's busy making lunch.'

'Dad's cooking?' Catherine wrinkled her mouth, not believing this. It *was* unusual for Harold to cook but – more and more – he'd begun to spend time in the kitchen. If he cooked pastry he could sit at the table and ask Nettie to fetch items or turn up the oven.

'How's your course?' she asked her daughter.

'The teacher this term is hot.'

'Oh good. I hear that's what counts.'

They got home and as Nettie walked to the back door she noticed the rose bush was already shedding petals, the weather unusually cold. She'd have to bring the potted plants inside before winter. Catherine went on ahead and – finding her dad sat at the kitchen table – wrapped her arms around him. It was a nice thing to witness. Catherine had always softened around him, never tiring of stories of his business travels or the fishing trips he went on as a kid. When Catherine was younger, the two of them had gone out in his car at weekends, not visiting anywhere in particular, only driving towards the New Forest or along the coastal roads around Southampton.

The pair were now laughing as Nettie entered the kitchen.

'Wine, Mum?' Catherine asked. She'd bought a bottle of red.

'Why not?'

Over lunch Catherine talked about her course. How difficult it was to deal with patients' constant issues and how one problem often led to another, like bed sores or a bug from too much time spent in hospital. It was as if she expected people to turn up in full health and for her to merely congratulate them before sending them home again. One particular old man had lodged a complaint about her smelling of cigarettes and she'd later seen him parked outside in his wheelchair, lighting a cigar. But she liked the course and other students well enough.

Listening to her daughter's stories of drunken nights at the student union, Nettie busied herself fetching extra spoons and serving the wine. When the others had refills she was tempted but stopped at one glass, wanting to return Catherine safely to the station. Harold, stumbling on his way to the toilet, claimed he was drunk but Catherine didn't notice. Or pretended not to anyhow.

It was when they were finishing coffee that Harold touched Nettie's arm.

'Yes?'

He motioned upstairs.

'What is it, Dad?'

'Just something I'd like your mum to fetch.'

Beneath their bed, Nettie – as instructed – found a package which she brought downstairs. It was a jiffy bag that was sealed but with no address written on the front.

'I was going to post it,' Harold explained and passed it to Catherine.

Inside was a record. Their daughter smiled and said, 'You realise I don't have a record player?'

'Maybe you could get one,' Harold said. 'They're a lot of fun. And you get to go round junk shops. Discover all sorts of memories.'

'Other people's memories.' She inspected the cover.

'Still. Everyone's past is fascinating if you use your imagination.'

When Catherine later went to get her rucksack, Nettie picked up the record. It was 'All or Nothing' by Small Faces – the song that was playing the night they met at the dance hall. Him dancing with Edith but later placing his hand upon her shoulder. A price was written in the corner: six shillings.

Harold must have bought it years ago but never played the thing, keeping it for a special afternoon.

After their daughter had gone, Nettie helped Harold upstairs to bed. It was a case of pretending she was also tired and needed a lie-down. Apparently his own father had been treated as a victim by the family. Pawed over and not allowed to drink, especially when he became sullen and angry. He refused to be the same. And – according to him – there was no point in seeing a doctor.

'Of course there is,' Nettie had said the year before. 'If only to help you stay comfortable.'

When his legs began to feel jerky, he'd hoped the sensation was in his mind. Ever since his father was diagnosed he'd been waiting to see if his own body would change. An awful thing to inherit. 'Why not a boat or a country house in the Cotswolds?' he'd joked when first telling her. The jerkiness kept returning, however, until he fell one afternoon while gardening. He reckoned within a few years he wouldn't be able to walk at all. His speech would become difficult too, his motivation would dissolve.

'I think we should at least ask for a medical opinion,' said Nettie. 'What does Martha think?'

The two women were the only people who knew. Nettie telephoned her once and Martha said it was up to him. Although this was an honest enough attitude, it left Nettie uneasy. Martha had never forgiven him really and, over the next months, it pained Nettie not to do more. Seeing him cancel plans with friends and develop a hunch as he spent more time indoors, she was merely a spectator to his decline.

*

Once Harold was in bed she lay beside him, noticing how he fixed his eyes on the ceiling. He was sentimental these days in a way he hadn't been before and, although he never made a sound, he sometimes pressed the heel of his hands into his face. Or kept his eyes locked upwards as if the sadness itself could be contained.

'Do you remember the night you found out about Martha?'

'Of course I do.' She shifted onto her side, facing him.

'After we talked about it, you said you were like a broken toy, all ugly.'

The moment reformed in her mind. The gloom of the kitchen and the doll on the floor. Its flick of plastic eyelids.

Harold's voice was low. 'I was trying to think how to describe you and couldn't. I realised later what I should've said.'

'It doesn't matter now,' she told him. His body was crooked, his trouser leg all crumpled. The man needed to rest and not distress himself. Or her. She didn't want to think about this.

'It needs to be said, Nettie.' He turned to face her. 'I should've said you were a dreamer, full of light and better than anyone I knew. I liked your socialist ideas not because of what they stood for but because they were something you believed in.'

'Really?'

'Really. I'm sorry it took me so long to say. I think you're remarkable.'

She lay on her back. It was like history was being rewritten and she warmed all over as if a different woman. A better one who Harold had loved all this time, though she'd told herself he hadn't.

A smile played on his lips. 'A pity those socialist ideals didn't extend to sharing a husband.'

She refused to laugh but reached for him. 'I always saw things differently, I guess. I didn't feel normal.'

'No one does. Surely the person who feels normal is actually the freakiest of us all.'

As he later fell asleep Nettie lay on her back listening to the starlings pick around on the roof. Even as she grew thirsty and needed to clean up the kitchen she stayed next to Harold, not wanting to leave his warmth and everything they had together.

XVII

It was a clear day in late September when he asked her. They'd gone out into the field and he'd ended up lying beneath the oak tree. She said they should return inside – it couldn't be comfortable on the ground – but he wanted to make the most of the weather. The sky was an expanse of blue, the leaves around them curled into spirals of deep red and orange. Finally Nettie agreed to sit with him for a minute. Their days had begun to pass too quickly, swept along by chores and his time spent writing, and she wanted to make the most of him.

She asked about the night they met. What he'd thought about when he closed his eyes on the dancefloor.

'Nothing really,' he said, stretching out in the leaves.

'You can tell me.'

'I don't know.' He yawned. 'I guess back then I was always dreaming of something, making plans. I wanted to do so much in life, especially when my dad got ill and I knew it was a matter of time for me. But here with you, is where I want to be.'

290

'Okay.'

'And I'd like to be buried here.'

'We don't have to talk about that now.' She picked up a leaf that'd blown onto his shirt, sticking to a button like a corsage. It made her think of dances and weddings, the giddiness of youth. 'It's a little maudlin to talk about your own death.'

'I disagree. You always told Catherine it was a fact of life.'

'I was talking about the chickens.'

'Well ...' He propped himself onto his elbows. 'I don't want a long death, Nettie.'

'Life is one long journey to death.'

'No it isn't, that's just something people say.'

'What? On greetings cards?'

He didn't laugh. 'I'd like you to help me die.'

She studied his face. A smile was playing on his lips as if he were making a joke. That's how she knew he wasn't – it was a difficult truth he'd struggled to share. His eyes shone but he didn't stare up, only straight at her, waiting for a reply.

The thought was like a spinning blade and she strode off, back towards the farmhouse. She couldn't do it. Not now, not ever. And it was wrong of him to even suggest it, and at such a tender moment too. Couldn't they have merely laid a while together on their dancefloor of leaves?

She spent the next few days seething. Sometimes it felt like her love for Harold was no different from an itch that never passed. Forever prickling across her skin, not letting her be. And yet over the last few weeks she'd finally understood she had his love in return and that knowledge meant everything to her. They were finally in the thick of love. What was the point of ruining that now? No, she'd hold on to him for as long as she could.

He didn't mention the subject again and they went about their lives. They travelled to the next town to buy him a walking stick and – despite his intentions to avoid anyone he knew – they saw a couple from Romsey outside the grocer. Harold put on his best act of animated conversation before Nettie helped him, exhausted, back to the car. Catherine rang to say she'd passed some exams and would be home for Christmas. Their daily routine became soothing and she liked how she sometimes caught Harold looking at her and how she returned his gaze. Even when getting out of the bath or dressing for bed, she'd not cover her bare skin. She felt no need to leave him. She had few other friends but he was all she wanted.

Her thoughts kept returning to the question of his wish. Every time she saw him wince as he struggled into his armchair, or glare at his twitching fingers, she became less sure.

And the man was serious about this plan of his. On being asked to prune the oleander she realised that he'd planted it for a reason. Not that any of this meant she needed to help him. Did he even deserve her help? Maybe this illness was the universe's way of showing the man humility. Slowing him down so he'd need to reflect on everything he'd done.

'Why don't you do it alone?' she asked one Sunday night. She'd not meant to speak so abruptly – with Harold sitting in the armchair writing – but the question had been twisting inside her all weekend. He put down his notebook and spoke in a calm voice. 'Because I'm frightened and I can't do it alone. Martha wouldn't understand. Neither would Catherine. But she'd hate to see me this way.'

'The way you actually are.'

'Yes,' he admitted. 'But you're the only one who under-stands. And sometimes it's kinder to say nothing.'

'To lie, you mean.'

'Yes. To lie to the ones you love. To shoulder the burden yourself.'

He asked her to put the oleander in his food without telling him.

Wouldn't that make every meal unbearable? she asked.

He didn't think so.

He wrote down some lines for her to tell people afterwards but she couldn't think about that yet. To do what he asked would be to walk up to a cliff edge, with nothing beyond but dark waters.

Days passed and, on waking every morning, she would as-sure herself everything was all right because today wouldn't be the day. Days turned into weeks and the weather grew colder. Neither of them mentioned it although every now and then he'd ask if she'd done any pruning.

'I'm not sure when I will,' she said.

'There might be early frost,' he said as he lay on the settee.

Everything was in her hands but she wouldn't rush it. He seemed to improve for a time too. The weather carried on granting blue skies and they drank tea out in the garden, him wrapped in a woollen blanket to keep warm. His speech slurred at times but she could still understand him.

Then one morning she was shopping in town when she bumped into one of Harold's friends – a man from the rotary club he'd joined some years ago. He owned several local busi-nesses and was a great fan of her husband.

'How's Harold?' the man asked.

'He's fine. Writing at home.'

'Get him to call me, won't you? A friend and I are planning a trip around Spain on motorbikes. We'd mentioned it to Harold and thought he might like to join us.'

'Okay, I will.'

Nettie had been on her way home but now she drifted back along the high street. Harold wouldn't go on any trips to Spain. Or anywhere else. The realisation weighted her every step. In the good bakery she picked out his favourite pumpernickel bread and then went to buy fresh salted butter. She told herself it wouldn't have to be today – they'd enjoy a little longer together – but on the way back she knew it could not wait.

It was what he wanted, she told herself later, clipping the oleander. The flowers were silky in her hands and she dropped one, then stared at its shiny pink petals in the grass. How could something so lovely end a life? Harold's life. As she broke down on the lawn she pressed her face into the petals as if to share in the suffering, the blotches on her cheeks a proof of her love. This, their final bouquet. Her tears wouldn't help him, though. There was nothing else for it.

After that it was a matter of following the steps. Of heating the leek and potato soup. Laying a chopping board on the kitchen counter and pressing the stems and flower heads with the back of the spoon. It was hard to say what went through her mind. She was doing what he'd asked. Granting him peace. And yet the past lay thick upon her. Their love had worn her out, worn her down. It was a bog without enough air.

Harold was still lying on the settee listening to Radio 4. Soon all she could do was to pour her own bowl, then stir the oleander into his, the plant now smeared into darkish pink and green. She walked over to wake him. A page of writing lay on his chest – the novel only just finished. For a minute longer she stared until he woke up.

'Your story,' she said.

He got himself into sitting position. 'I wanted a more dramatic ending. But the one I have is fine.' He looked at the chopping board. He looked at her. He nodded.

She placed his bowl on the table and sat opposite. Each of his spoonfuls seemed easy enough. It was she who trembled, who wanted to scream for him to stop. Their love was a bog but it was their bog, and light dappled its surface. She wasn't sure what'd be left without him. And yet she fixed herself in the seat as he ate every mouthful until the bowl was scraped clean. Only at the end did his eyes widen and he touched his throat, encircling it with his hands as if measuring the size. 'Nice soup,' he said in a thin voice. Then: 'I'm sorry, old bird. For more than I can tell you.'

After that she took the phone, fearing he'd panic and call an ambulance. He threw up in the sink and she soothed his back, before he lay on the settee and she felt his heartbeat slow. Not sure what else to do, she suggested he go upstairs where he'd be more comfortable. He stood up, groggy, and she struggled with him till they reached the bedroom. But she couldn't stand to watch his crooked form beneath the blankets and returned downstairs. Washing the dishes only took a few minutes, holding the bowls under the steaming water until her fingers were burning. She clutched the spoon's delicate handle and did the same. Although she wanted to keep busy, it seemed wrong to be clearing away like this, as if their house was already the scene of something shameful. She couldn't bear to let go of the spoon and carried it back upstairs. It was a basic silver one but he'd eaten from it over the years. Food she'd grown or he'd made the money to buy. The most simple act of sharing a meal. The labour of a marriage. Not knowing exactly why, she hid it in the top drawer, guessing that no one would find it there. And then she sat on the bed to feel his pulse. His wrist was cool beneath the shirt cuff and for a second she was appalled by how his face was already sunken. But she took off her shoes and lay next to him, telling herself he deserved it. He deserved to be in Heaven.

6
2015

16

August, 2015

Nettie is still pointing the shotgun at her sister. She doesn't know what to do any more. What she thought was true about Harold's death no longer seems right. Outside the darkness is impenetrable.

Edith touches Nettie's arm without getting too close. Shadows pool around her eyes. The woman is tired. Her make-up smudged for once. 'You did it out of love,' she says. How many times has she repeated that? She edges closer. 'You're not capable of anything else.'

There's a thunk as the gun barrel drops to the armchair, though she still clasps the stock.

'Forgive me,' says Edith. 'The way you forgave Harold. They were strange times and none of us are that innocent.'

Through the fog in her mind, a memory forms: the coffee in Waterloo where her sister was making awkward conversation while Nettie remained tight-lipped, barely able to talk. Her sister had tender spots too. She needed her family.

Nettie lets the shotgun drop completely and Edith gently removes it, returning a minute later as she rubs her hands on her coat as if dirtied by its touch. What just happened? Nettie shakes her head and tries to collect herself. The door clicks shut.

'Where's James?' she asks, moving into the kitchen.

The women go outside and see the figure sitting on the bottom of the ladder, the dog next to him curled into a ball.

'You don't have a son, do you?' Nettie says.

He exhales. 'No – just a dog I don't get to see much. But he means more to me than just an animal. It's hard to explain.'

'No it isn't. I know exactly what you mean.' She motions them all back into the warmth.

It's late but no one is ready for sleep. Time seems insubstantial like it'll be forever night. Her sister puts on a pot of coffee and gestures for them to sit down. Still empty of words, Nettie merely nods and pulls up a chair while James refuses. At first it seems his pacing is to warm up but he carries on in this agitated way, moving from living room to kitchen as if sorting something in his mind.

'Which tea set should I use?' Edith asks. 'The Moroccan one or your wedding china?'

Nettie almost laughs. 'It doesn't matter.'

Taking out the Moroccan set, Edith pours them three cups and sniffs the milk bottle Nettie forgot to put away earlier. 'I'll have mine black.'

After the two women have settled at the table, Edith explains, 'It might not be what you want to hear but I feel I should tell you, Harold was very kind. He helped us pay the boarding school fees for James's education. He went to St Peter's School, York, one of the best schools in the country.'

Nettie frowns and says nothing.

'When my husband retired from the RAF the two of us moved up to the west coast of Scotland. It's lovely there. Not far from the caravan park we used to visit as kids. Do you remember?'

The coffee is too hot. Nettie sips it anyway, wanting the drink to wake her from this. Maybe it's a dream and tomorrow things will be back to how they were. Her alone before James turned up. She wasn't entirely happy but at least she knew what to expect.

Her sister continues. 'After a couple of years in the army, James came to live with us until he got himself sorted. We were pleased he then decided to stay in Scotland. Glasgow wasn't far away and it was nice to see him get a flat and a job in finance. A lovely wife too.'

'For God's sake, Mum.' James appears in front of them. 'You still think that was right for me. Don't you get it? All this time I thought someone else was my dad. A man who pushed and pushed me into this life I didn't want.'

'That's unfair, James. He cared for you. He's been worried.'

'I wanted to live in the countryside. I wanted to be a poet. But all that time he pushed for something else and I was oh so intent on pleasing him. This man who wasn't my actual father. All to protect some woman I'd never met.'

He gestures to Nettie, then turns to her with the same deranged look as before. 'I wanted to see who you were. For you to know how it felt to be lied to. And that daughter of yours.'

'I can't believe you visited Catherine,' Edith says.

301

'I wanted to know what this half-sister was like. But not the one she'd show me if she knew the truth. I wanted to see my actual half-sister, know what I mean? So I said I was an alcoholic. People are weirdly loyal to other addicts, like it's this insiders club.'

Nettie grips her cup. 'You came here to punish us?'

'Not exactly. I was curious at first. Then when I heard about Harold dying like that I was even more angry.' He turns to his mum. 'Why didn't you tell me?'

Edith speaks coolly. 'What good would it have done?'

'I would've known!'

The room is hushed for a moment. Nettie thinks of him turning up that first afternoon – polite but lording something over her. Then his days around the house and barn in a loop. 'You've been looking for something too.'

James is embarrassed. 'It doesn't matter.'

'What?'

'I've just had a gun pointed at me,' he says, more agitated. 'Me poking around your barn pales in comparison, no?'

They wait until he speaks again. 'Fine.' He smooths his hair. 'I looked at the letters Harold sent Mum over the years. The photos and things. They weren't addressed to me but they were about me. Asking how I was. In one Harold mentioned a present. Some Small Faces record he wanted Mum to give me.'

'I don't remember that,' says Edith.

'Well we never got it. At least it wasn't in the box of things. For someone who'd told so many lies, you were fastidious about saving the letters and gifts. As if you knew it'd come out one day.'

Edith glances to Nettie. 'No, I never wanted anyone to know.'

Nettie shifts in her chair. She can't help but see how James is grappling with everything he's recently learnt of his family. The man has become fixated on something meant for him – a missing part of his past. But Harold had given the record to their daughter on a whim after a family lunch. It was only a song yet it was a link to his past, without which he was un-tethered.

James mutters, 'It was bought for me.'

'Where is it now?' Edith gets up to serve more coffee.

'Catherine has it, I suppose,' Nettie says.

'No, I looked in her flat.'

'James!' Edith says, surprised at her son.

'She had all these photos of Harold and one night she got drunk and was talking about their car rides together.' He peers out of the window in the direction of the barn where the vehicle is back beneath its tarpaulin. 'I figured since she'd got everything else, she'd have the damn record too.'

They carry on talking but soon run out of energy. James announces he's going to bed and disappears, leaving the sisters alone at the table. Their cups are empty.

'I'll make up Catherine's bed,' says Nettie.

Upstairs, her sister waits on the landing while she puts on new sheets and a blanket. She remembers the day she realised James had been in here and now pictures him upset as he struggled to find the record. Did he even know which one it was? Or merely that it was by Small Faces? It's called 'All or Nothing', Nettie silently tells him as she plumps the pillow.

'Here we are,' she whispers and her sister smiles, timid at the door. It's time for Nettie to leave but she watches Edith's movements as she slides the grip from her hair and runs her fingers through it. How she carefully untwists her silk scarf and places it on the chair. She's travelled for hours and must be exhausted but Nettie can't bear to go to bed just yet.

'I still don't fully understand Harold's death,' Nettie tells her.

Edith looks up, fingers at her buttons. 'It's okay.'

'No, I need to tell you. Why I gave him that oleander, well...' She pats her cheeks with the wedding ring. 'I'm still confused about it. The years haven't helped in that respect but really it isn't a problem of old age. It's just been easier to forget. The mind needs a way to heal itself.'

'And then a young man shows up at your door?'

'Ha, yes.' She shakes her head, then realises the truth as she says it, 'This needed to happen, though. I'm grateful it did and that you're here. All those years spent hating myself...'

'You did it out of love, Nettie.'

'That's it, though. It was *mostly* love.' She looks at her sister, the one who she was always honest with. 'I think it was partly spite too. Just a tiny bit, wanting him to feel pain. I know that makes me wicked.'

'No, Nettie.' She sighs. 'It makes you married.'

They sit on the bed for a moment, their two pairs of shoes in a line. Across the hall there's a pacing which soon stops.

'What about your husband? Do you love him?' Nettie asks.

Her sister half-smiles. 'In my own way. We have to work with the person beside us.' She then kisses her own palm before patting Nettie. 'Time for sleep I think.'

So Nettie stands and wanders out, glancing around once more before her sister closes the door.

The next morning James is back up on the roof. Listening to the steady knock of the hammer, the sisters exchange glances,

Edith still perplexed by her son being at the farmhouse. By the fire-ravaged barn too. In the light of day her old-age habits show: the handkerchief stuffed up her sleeve, the age spots on her cheeks visible beneath the white face powder. She's the same woman, though, and stands up straight in her blouse and skirt while they make eggs for breakfast. Working her way around the table, Edith lays some extra place mats.

'Catherine and the girls are coming,' she explains. 'I phoned them this morning.'

'That's lovely, thank you.'

They put the radio on while they wait and chat about the chalkiness of soil in Hampshire. Light pours through the window and illuminates the wedding china, its golden spots shining. When the doorbell goes Nettie lets her sister get up and – a minute later – Catherine is trailing through with Elly in tow. The girl is as serious as ever. 'Grace is on a play date,' Catherine says, looking from one sister to the other.

The women eat breakfast while the knocking above continues. After Elly goes to look for the dog, Nettie finds the words to tell her daughter what's been happening – about how James is her half-brother. Catherine pushes her chair back but remains seated, unable to leave. She launches into complaints of James's cheek at lying about being an alcoholic. About how he'd spent time in her flat and pretended he had nowhere to stay. How she'd even thought he was good-looking for a while. She's disgusted at the thought.

While listening to her daughter, Nettie takes comfort in hearing her spill the words between them. Many are things she herself had felt but are now being expressed better by Catherine, who's never shied away from saying what she thinks. 'I thought he was a bloody waif or stray. A nobody.'

The conversation becomes tiring and when the back door opens and James steps inside, Nettie leaves to get some fresh air. Voices rise in the kitchen and she wanders into the garden, finding the day cool with clouds darkening above. Over in the field the oak tree beckons and, not caring it isn't her land, she slips beneath the fence. It's something she's never done before in case the farmer sees but her trespassing no longer seems to matter. The grass is silky against her legs and moths flutter in patterns of grey. She reaches the tree where Harold wanted to be buried; Martha wouldn't consider it and soon refused to speak with Nettie altogether. It seems even after they divorced the woman clung to a set notion of Harold. Maybe they all did.

Among the swathes of green, someone is following.

'I'm sorry,' her daughter says on reaching the tree.

'It's fine.'

'No it isn't.' She tugs hair behind her ears. 'Come back inside. It's going to rain.'

'Is it still noisy in there?'

'Not without me.'

They laugh a little but Nettie doesn't move. She wants to tell her daughter more about Harold's death but there aren't the right words. There never have been. Really she should be given her own medical tests, James too. Another day, though. After a rumble above it begins to rain. Motioning to go back inside, Catherine pulls her jacket tighter. 'Come on,' she says. 'You'll catch a cold.'

But first Nettie nudges a tree root with her foot. Notes how each spreads so far across the land in every direction. They wander back to the farmhouse without speaking, only treading through the grass that's darkening, turning glossy. Outside the back door Catherine hesitates. 'I just wish he'd told me he was ill,' she says. 'I thought we were close.'

'You were.'

'And, Mum?'

'Yes?'

'I don't entirely forgive you.' She chews a fingernail before talking again. 'Dad was an addict, he needed love and when you withheld it, he found it elsewhere. Didn't he?'

A smell of wet soil wafts as rain streaks the ground.

'Have you still got the record?' Nettie asks.

'No. I played it too much and it got scratched.'

'So you threw it away?'

'I gave it to a boyfriend. It seemed romantic at the time.'

They laugh and, finding nothing more to say, step out of the rain.

An hour later they've cleared away breakfast and Elly has grown bored of playing with Rufus who's intent on sleeping. The girl asks what else they'll do. 'Maybe town or bowling?' she says hopefully, turning to her grandmother.

'Well maybe,' says Nettie. 'If your mum says yes.'

'Actually,' says Catherine. 'I think we'll get off back to London.'

'Really?' Nettie had expected them to stay at least a day, though in truth she's exhausted herself.

'I don't mean to be rude. It's all just a bit much.'

They collect their things and are soon trailing into the hallway. James keeps his distance but the sisters wait together. Nettie and Catherine promise to see each other again soon, at a family meal. Maybe in London, Catherine suggests. And then the taxi has arrived and they're getting in and driving off again.

Once the sky has cleared, the sisters spend the afternoon weeding while James packs away the broken tiles and equipment. He's not quite finished the roof but finds a number in the phone book which he calls and arranges for someone to visit the following week. 'I'll send you a cheque to cover it,' promises Edith. 'Or maybe deliver it in person so we can spend some proper time together.' As they later stand in the yard, mother and son arguing about whether to walk to the station, Nettie realises she enjoys hearing them bicker. How James is protective of his mum, saying they should take a taxi, but Edith adamant it isn't worth the money.

She wants to say a proper goodbye to him. The man who fixed her gate. And fixed a lot more too. He stands ruddy-faced in the hallway and she hovers behind, expecting him to shake her hand or to say a few parting words. That he was glad to meet her or to at least have figured something out. But he heads silently for the door, leaving Edith to apologise and give her a final kiss.

After the house is quiet again, Nettie goes upstairs to the spare bedroom. James has removed the bed sheets which he's left folded in a pile. The comb is gone and she sits on the mattress, feeling empty in the cold room. What's she supposed to do now? Final droplets of rain cling to the window pane. She sighs and hoists herself up again before noticing a piece of paper on the window sill. It's a leaf torn from his diary, on which he's written a few lines of the lyrics to 'All or Nothing'. Underneath, it reads:

A fine song, isn't it?

Thank you for taking me in.
James

P.S. Look after Rufus, won't you?

17

That afternoon Nettie walks into town. Spots of rain fall and shimmer on the leaves of the horse chestnut. She should have worn her rain mac but, standing by the mirror earlier, felt compelled to put on a colourful dress. To clip on her jade earrings too. As she reaches the high street and sees people collected outside a pub, she strolls on by. Who cares what they might say. None of it matters any more. People are trying to enjoy what they can of the summer. Crossing the park, she sees families with dogs straining on leads; kids with melting choc ices. It's like she's drifting along but really there's only one place she wants to go.

The abbey is open, its cool air sweet with lilies that curl from vases. It seems the place is on show and, sure enough, a young couple is looking about. They inspect the pulpit and altar as if on a shopping trip, next peering at the broken stained glass. Marianne emerges from the vestry and ushers them inside.

Sitting in the back row, Nettie looks again at the damaged window. The hole is luminescent, the daylight announcing a stream of white. As she clasps her hands together, she hopes to see Harold in Heaven. Until now she's fretted she wouldn't but who knows what God has planned for each of them.

As Marianne walks past, pointing out the seating to the couple, she gives her a weak smile. When the visitors have gone, the vicar wanders over.

'How are you?' Nettie asks.

'Not too shabby, thanks.'

'And Pauline?'

'We're going lamp shopping later.' She shrugs. 'I'll see how it goes, you know, take one step at a time.'

'That's all you can do,' says Nettie.

'Well thanks for coming. We should get another lunch sometime.'

'That'd be nice.' She gets up and shuffles to the door, sensing that Marianne is wanting to lock up as she jangles keys in her pocket. 'Sorry,' Nettie says, trying to hurry. 'It's old age, you see. A horrible thing really.'

'Not necessarily,' says Marianne with a wicked smile. 'It's a privilege to age. Don't you agree?'

On reaching the farmhouse she sees a figure waiting by the door. At first she assumes it's James, back to finish the roof. He didn't seem sure of leaving and they still have things to discuss. It'd be worthwhile really, Nettie thinks, opening the gate. He's a decent man, despite everything.

But it's not him waiting. It's Tara. She's dressed in a hot-pink outfit with no straps and, where there should be a skirt, the material divides into trousers. 'He's not here,' she tells her, stopping halfway across the yard. The girl's legs are covered but she pictures the anklet, its orange thread dirtied from age.

The girl nods. 'I know.'

When Nettie doesn't come closer, Tara chews her bottom lip, its gloss rubbing away. 'Thanks for not pressing charges.'

'I haven't decided yet.'

'Maybe you should.' She yanks up her strapless top. 'Press charges, I mean. It was awful what we did. I felt sick afterwards.'

'I'll see how I feel.'

Neither says anything as a breeze works its way through the debris of the barn. The concrete is still dark in patches but mostly the rain has washed away the soot.

'Anyway, I'll be off,' Tara says and lingers another moment before passing by, shoes clomping as she goes.

'Have you got somewhere to stay?' Nettie calls after her.

'What?'

'I mean, you could stay in my spare room if you like. I won't charge you rent.'

The girl chews her lip again, the gloss gone. 'Cheers. I'll think about it.'

And then it's just Nettie stood by the farmhouse. She watches the silhouette of a lone bird on the gate which seems to fix her in its gaze. She gazes back until it pushes off and disappears into the sky.